LIKE GHOSTS IN THE HALLWAY

TAMI BRUMBAUGH

ISBN-13: 978-1945634079
ISBN: 1945634073
.

To those who have secrets
you are afraid to share:
Your happily ever after may be off to a painful start,
but there is hope.
May you find courage, help, and healing.

CONTENTS

CHAPTER 1
BUMPS & BRUISES

There were no police sirens or flashing lights, but the gravel crackling under our tires was enough warning.

Josie grasped my arm, her ragged nails biting into my brown skin. I wanted to reassure her by saying we were safe. It was my duty as her older brother. But I couldn't. My lies were reserved for explaining our bumps and bruises. At least they were until a few days ago.

Two police officers emerged from their black and white car. The younger cop was thin and had blond hair slicked back like a helmet. He chewed on a toothpick as he eased up to the front door. The older cop's belly threatened to pop off his uniform's buttons. His eyes remained focused on the house as he rapped the car window. Our social worker, Mr. Costas, rolled it down.

"It looks like he's still gone, but we're going to check the house to be sure." The cop's hand rested on the gun strapped to his hip. "Stay here."

He joined his partner and knocked on the weathered door. They waited briefly before they twisted the doorknob and stepped inside.

"Can't we just leave?" Josie asked, fidgeting in the back seat. "We ain't got much stuff anyhow. I don't want to go in."

"I do," said Missy. "I want the rag baby Mama made me, and my clothes, and Rat."

7

"Rat?" Mr. Costas turned around in his seat.

"I tamed one of them rats from the kitchen. He comes when I make kissin' sounds and eats right from my fingers. He even lets me hold him sometimes. I cain't just leave him. He'll get lonely."

Mr. Costas shuddered. "I think we need to leave him here for now. His family would miss him and it was hard enough finding *you* a place to stay without you having a...pet."

Missy's gray ghost eyes watered and a tear spilled down her dark cheek. I thought her tears had dried up years ago. The three of us were just shells now, scraped out and empty.

"No one's here," the younger police officer stated from our opened front door. "Come on in."

My stomach churned as I studied the shadows around the dilapidated house. How thoroughly had the police searched? The old shack had hiding places. My sisters and I knew them well.

Josie tightened her grip on my arm. I wanted to support her plea to leave. I wanted to turn my back on this house, this life, forever. My lip curled with disdain as I stared at the door's peeling red paint. Duct tape barely held the cracked front window together, and decaying shingles fought a losing battle to keep foul weather outside. Dysfunction oozed from every rotted piece of wood.

"Are you ready?" asked Mr. Costas. He opened the car door and handed each of us a black garbage sack. "You can put your clothes in these."

No, we weren't ready. I wanted to slam the door shut. Every last hope to function as a family in this house had been pounded out of me, trampled on my bedroom floor. I longed to snatch the car keys and speed away, spraying gravel at the shack and the memories it unleashed. Instead, I eased out through the open car door, careful not to bump the blue sling on my broken left arm.

"Let's get this done," I told my sisters.

Josie bit her lip, her tortured eyes begging me to change my mind. I had to look away, unable to bear her pain with my broken body. I leaned against the car and rubbed my black stubbled hair nervously as I waited. She sighed and scooted across the vinyl seat, her legs sticking to the surface. Missy followed right behind. They shuffled beside me, offering their scrawny shoulders for support as they clung to my t-shirt.

The house loomed before us, ready to swallow us whole. I squinted at each tree and bush, studying shadows, listening for snapped twigs. J.R. was a hunter. Was he stalking us right now?

The younger police officer gave an encouraging smile and opened the door wider. I gritted my teeth and limped through the doorway with my sisters, stumbling into our living room. The mustard yellow and green plaid couch huddled against the back wall. Stuffing seeped through the cushion seams. A thick TV sat across from it and was adorned with two bowls lined with crusted cereal. J.R.'s crossbow, sharpening stone, and a small portion of his hunting knife collection sprawled out on the matted brown carpet. Broken beer bottles covered the remainder of the floor. Mr. Costas opened his notebook and began scribbling observations with a black pen.

My sisters helped me to my small closet of a bedroom. I could feel Josie shaking, which sent shivers up my own spine. I squeezed her arm.

"We're almost done with this place. I've still got one good arm." I waved my trash bag. "I can pack on my own. It'll be quicker if we all get our stuff at the same time."

Josie took a deep breath and nodded. Missy reached for her sister's hand and they drifted towards their own room.

The curling checked linoleum in my room was clean. Too clean. So J.R. had been back to the house after all. He was good at scrubbing when it meant removing evidence. He wasted his time. Josie said the police took pictures before emergency workers wheeled me into the ambulance. My heart beat faster as my eyes adjusted to the dim glow provided by the light bulb dangling from my ceiling. I snatched up a suspiciously large wad of clothing and exhaled once I had stuffed it into my bag.

The only other place where a man could hide was under my bed. I silently struggled onto my bruised knees and lifted the threadbare quilt with shaking hands. Books and cobwebs. I sighed with relief and started to cram my favorite stories into my bag. Fiction was my escape route. I snatched *I Know Why the Caged Bird Sings*, and *Invisible Man* and stuck them with the rest of my books. My journal was tucked under the mattress, hidden from everyone. I pulled it out and flipped through the worn pages. Nearly every inch was filled with my sloppy handwriting. Time to start a second volume. Maybe the next journal wouldn't be as dark or depressing. I stuffed it into the bag.

As I struggled back to my feet, a calloused hand clamped around my mouth. A cold blade pressed on my neck.

"Were you lookin' for me?" J.R. whispered in my ear. "Let me help you up." He yanked me to my feet, crushing my broken arm to his side. "I see you done brought the police. Good thing they's too busy snoopin' around the shed

10

to keep an eye fixed on you." He squeezed my face tighter and shook it. I tasted blood as my teeth bit into my cheek. "Family don't turn on each other."

My head pounded. I had no strength left for fighting. My whole being was battered and raw. I failed to fight him off when I was strong, so what chance did I have now? I was tall for being fifteen, but was no match for J.R.'s 6'4" of hardened muscle. My body tensed as I prepared for the worst.

"Drop the knife and step away," a quavering voice said from behind us.

J.R. spun around, still holding me in his firm grip.

Mr. Costas was holding one of J.R.'s hunting knives between both of his shaking hands. His black-framed glasses were askew and beads of sweat dotted his forehead.

J.R. laughed. His beer-laden breath invaded my nose. "I'll bet you've never used a knife in your life. Your scrawny sissy-boy hands cain't even hold still. Get out of my way."

"I can't do that." Mr. Costas swallowed hard. "Let the boy go and the charges against you won't be as severe."

"What charges? I ain't done nothin' wrong. Now git out of my house or I'll charge *you* for trespassin'."

The two policemen barged into the room with their guns drawn.

"Put your hands in the air," the older cop commanded.

I could almost hear the wheels spin in J.R.'s head as his grip loosened on me. I had a full arsenal of words for my dad, but stupid wasn't one of them. He dropped the knife and raised his arms slowly.

"Now officers, I think we got us here a misunderstandin'. I was just startled by this stranger breakin' into my home. I grabbed the nearest person I could find, not

11

realizin' it was my own kid." He turned to me. A smile was pasted on his face, but his blue eyes sizzled. "Sorry 'bout that, son. You were missin' for a few days, and I didn't know you was back. No harm done."

"This time," Mr. Costas said. His confidence was building now that he had armed back-up. "There isn't an inch of him you didn't pummel a few days ago."

"You think I did all this? To my own flesh and blood?" He started to lower his arms, but the policeman stepped closer until his arms went back up. "JaDon's just a bit reckless. You know how them teenage boys are. He prob'ly got in a fight with another kid, or from the looks of it, a gang. Who was it, JaDon? You need me to go talk to 'em? We've got some rough groups 'round here, officers. We would shore 'preciate some of yer help keepin' them under control."

The younger officer lowered his gun. "We'll keep that in mind."

My jaw dropped. They couldn't possibly be falling for his smooth talk. Not after all the questioning we endured at the hospital. Didn't they read our written statements? Did they believe him over us just because we were kids?

"Thanks, officer. And thank you for gettin' my boy the medical care he seems to have needed." Artificial sweetener coated his words. He dropped his arms. "Now, if you don't mind, I can take over from here."

The heavy-set officer stepped forward and snapped handcuffs around J.R.'s wrists. "We still need to take you in for questioning."

A muscle in J.R.'s jaw twitched. "Handcuffs ain't needed. I don't know what more I could tell you. The gang didn't jump him in my house."

"We can discuss it more at the station," the older officer said, leading him out the front door.

J.R. threw his considerable weight backwards and dug his heels into the weeds. "Wait jest a minute. You cain't haul me out of my home fer no reason. Why am I bein' brought in fer somethin' kids did?"

"We hoped to bring you in peacefully, but you just attacked your son. Again. A criminal complaint is already on file against you. Don't make this any worse." The officer tightened his grip on J.R.'s bicep. His partner grabbed the suspect's other arm.

"What criminal complaint?" J.R.'s eyes shifted to me and his mouth tightened.

I swallowed hard.

"So don't you have to read me my rights and all that nonsense?"

"You have the right to…" the young officer began.

"Nevermind. I know it already. I watch them police shows."

Josie and Missy peeked out of the front door.

"There you girls are. Why you hidin'? I was worried about y'all. Don't you fret. I'll get this heap of nonsense sorted out and be back in no time."

My sisters shriveled and returned to my sides without uttering a word. I put my injured arms around them and pulled them close. The police steered J.R. toward the car.

He turned around to face us. "Behave yerselves while I'm gone. I'm fixin' ta see you soon." His words were a smokescreen to detract from his eyes. His glare was clear. We would pay for our betrayal.

CHAPTER 2
BLACK TRASH BAGS

Mr. Costas waited until the police car was out of sight before he helped us load our bulging bags into the trunk of his car. Black trash bags. It seemed fitting that all of our possessions were now in trash bags. How much were we worth? Who truly cared what happened to us now? I was so worn down by the past that I could not imagine a future.

"Where we goin'?" Missy asked.

"To your Aunt Sophie's house. Looks like that's about an hour away, so if you want to rest in the back seat, you can."

Aunt Sophie. Distant memories bubbled to the surface. Did she still remember us?

"Is that okay, JaDon? Can we sleep?" Josie asked.

I struggled to refocus and turned to Mr. Costas. "Does J.R. know where we'll be stayin'?"

"No. Your aunt clearly said we couldn't tell him."

I took my first deep breath for the day. "Good." I turned to Josie. "Yes. You can rest now."

We climbed into the back seat of the car. Josie and Missy kicked off their worn-out flip flops. The events of the last hour should have kept them wired and uneasy, but in the grand scheme of our lives, knowing J.R. was not around meant it was time to unwind. Soon they nestled together into a tight ball on the seat, resting their heads on my leg. They were used to sleeping in a small space. The sunlight streamed in through the windows, caressing their cheeks. I watched their dark lashes close and the worry lines smooth as their breathing grew steady.

A seatbelt poked the base of my spine, but I shoved it deeper into the seat, hoping Mr. Costas would just assume we were buckled in. I didn't know how I would wrap a seatbelt around my sister's sleeping bodies. It was strange thinking of a belt as protection. All three of us were used to J.R.'s belt leaving scars.

I tilted my head against the sun-warmed glass, longing for sleep as well, but my swollen cheek protested against the pressure. I had to lean back against the padded vinyl seat instead. My eyes felt leaden and shut often, but my mind would not allow me to escape through slumber. I could still picture J.R.'s glare and feel the knife blade on my cheek. Anger coursed through my chest. I hoped they locked J.R. in jail for the rest of his life. My days of defending and protecting him were over.

Mr. Costas looked up at the rear view mirror. "Can't sleep?"

I shook my head.

"Understandable. That was intense in there."

I nodded.

'I'm glad no one was hurt.'

"Yeah. Thanks for comin' in when you did."

"Sure. I did what I could…even though I have scrawny sissy-boy hands." Mr. Costas smiled into the mirror.

I wasn't ready to smile back, but I appreciated his effort. "Don't take anything he says personal. He's been huntin' since he could walk, so knives and bows and guns are almost part of his arms. He only shakes when he's wasted."

"Good to know."

I reclined again, trying to find a position that didn't aggravate my injuries. J.R. had probably been holed up in his hunting blind when the ambulance came for me. Had he been sober enough to hear the sirens? Would he have cared? I brushed Josie's curly black hair off her cheek. She had crawled out of hiding as soon as J.R. stormed out of our shack. I remembered struggling to open my eyes when she called my name. The terror on her face when she saw me was still etched in my mind. Thankfully she pulled herself together enough to call the ambulance and give them directions to our house.

Missy snuggled closer to her sister, a soft snore rolling from her lips. I took another deep breath. She wouldn't look me in the eyes the day after my surgeries. At first I thought it was because I looked all battered and bruised. That might have contributed, but then I discovered she had told the police everything. She thought I would be mad. J.R. demanded that we keep our family life private. He said he would really give us something to cry about if we whined to anyone. Missy spilled it all out. That made investigators question me and Josie until they had our story—or at least as much of the story as I could risk telling. I wasn't mad at Missy. I was scared. No one crossed J.R.

"Did you hear me, JaDon?" Mr. Costas repeated.

"Sir?"

"I asked if you and your aunt were close."

My aunt. More painful memories. "We was when us three were little."

"She's your Mom's sister, right?"

"Yeah. We haven't seen her since Mama…left. J.R. wouldn't allow it."

"I see." Mr. Costas rubbed his chin. "I guess now you'll get a chance to reconnect."

What would I say to Aunt Sophie? We hadn't talked in seven years. The phone rang constantly right after Mama left. We aren't allowed to answer it, but I assumed it was my aunt. She tried stopping by the house a few times, but J.R. chased her off with his shotgun. He even fired the gun at her feet a few times to make his point. I really missed her and Uncle Ron and my cousins, especially our first few years apart. Eventually, their absence sank into the meaningless pit of my life.

Mr. Costas must have thought I needed a distraction. He began some small talk, rambling on about sports, favorite foods, his faithful golden retriever…I eventually tuned him out and closed my eyes. Slumber evaded me, but it was better if he thought I was asleep so he would stop talking. My own thoughts were noisy enough without added chatter. Silence stretched out in the car and I embraced it for almost an hour.

The car turned onto a street that looked vaguely familiar. Houses lined up in a neat little row, and most had green lawns decorated with hickory and sassafras trees. I remembered running barefoot on Aunt Sophie's lawn. I used to love the feel of the cool grass blades on my toes. It was such a nice change from the sharp pine needles and weeds surrounding our own house.

We turned left and parked in front of a light yellow house with white trim.

"We're here," Mr. Costas said.

He didn't need to tell me. I knew this house. A trace of a smile crossed my face as I pictured my cousins and me climbing the big hickory tree that shaded the car. Mama and Aunt Sophie used to stand underneath, so worried one of us would fall.

"Careful, JaDon!" Mama would call. "You know how bad I am at playin' catch. I don't want to have to catch *you*."

I would laugh and start climbing back down because I didn't want her to worry. With her gone, I felt no need to play it safe. Taking risks was a thrill. I loved the adrenaline rush. Now it was one of the few times I felt anything besides pain.

I gently patted Josie and Missy on their backs. "Time to wake up. We're here."

The girls yawned and stretched. Missy wiped drool off her mocha cheek.

"That tree looks familiar," Josie said, craning her head up to get a better view.

"It should," I said. "You used to beg Mama to let you climb it. You were only five and couldn't even reach the lowest branch."

"How 'bout me?" asked Missy. "Could I reach it?"

"Of course not," said Josie. "You're even shorter than me."

"I'm going to go tell your aunt we're here," said Mr. Costas. "Come to the front door when you're ready." He slammed the car door shut behind him.

Josie chewed her lip. "Will Aunt Sophie remember us? I can't even picture her."

"I'm sure she will," I said. "She was crazy about you two. After havin' three boys, she couldn't wait to help Mama put you in dresses and all that girly stuff."

"I remember wearin' dresses!" Missy exclaimed. "They were so much better than your ripped up ol' jeans. I bet we wouldn't get teased so much at school if we still wore dresses."

I opened the car door and the three of us walked up the sidewalk just as Aunt Sophie stepped outside. She had a

18

bright orange tribal print bandana wrapped around her head and wore a flowing turquoise skirt. Her smile lit up her dark face.

"I never stopped prayin' that I'd see you again some day," she said with tears in her eyes. "Look how big you are!" She gathered us into her arms and held us tight. "Oh, you precious kids. Do you remember your ol' Aunt Sophie?" She released us so she could look into our faces.

I nodded. The girls stared at her with blank expressions.

"When Mr. Costas here called me, my heart started thumpin'. Seven years your pa stole from us." Anger flashed across her face, but she shooed it away. "But that don't matter now. You're here. Oh, how you've grown!" She bent down in front of the girls. "Why, you've turned into young ladies. You was just four and five when I last saw you. And look at your thick, curly hair. Just like your Ma's. I used to braid her hair all of the time. Would you like me to braid your hair later?"

Missy and Josie looked at each other uncertainly.

"That's okay. You think about it. We'll have so much fun." She stroked their faces. "I always loved your eyes. Everyone I know has dark brown eyes. You both have such pretty gray ones. I always loved the flecks of blue and hazel in them. I guess that can happen when your pa's white. His eyes are ice blue. And hard. Yours are soft, sweet eyes. And those long lashes. Beautiful."

"J.R. always said our eyes were creepy," said Missy. "He don't like lookin' at them."

"Well *I* do. I could look at them all day." Aunt Sophie stood up. "And JaDon. You're 'bout grown up. I can't believe you're fifteen already. If Grace had been a boy she woulda looked just like you. I don't see a bit of J.R. in that face."

19

"Good," I said.

She nodded. "He done whup you good this time, didn't he?" Her eyes watered. "I begged the police to let me get you three when your ma disappeared. But there weren't no police reports of abuse. They said you had to stay with J.R. I'm glad they finally stepped in."

The girls looked down at their feet. I awkwardly shifted my weight.

"Oh, my. I'm sorry. That's awful heavy talk for just meetin' again." She wiped her eyes and put on a smile. "I'm just grateful you're here now."

Mr. Costas cleared his throat. I had forgotten he was there.

"I'm going to unload their belongings," he said. "Would you like me to take their bags into the house?"

"Oh, yes. Thank you," Aunt Sophie said. "Would you like to join us for dinner? I made pork chops, and collard greens, and the corn bread should be comin' out of the oven soon. I even have a peach cobbler coolin' on the stove."

"Sounds like southern cooking at its finest," Mr. Costas said. "Are you sure I'm not imposing?"

"Not at all. It's the least I can do for you gettin' the kids here." She turned back to us. "Why don't you three go wash up. I'll call in the boys. They're in the back yard and are excited to see you again."

The girls searched my face with nervous eyes.

"Go on, now," I said. "It's okay. I'm right behind you."

They tentatively stepped into the house. Aunt Sophie put her slender arm around my shoulders as we followed them. The weight of it was barely noticeable. Of course, a few pounds didn't amount to much when I already carried the weight of the world on my back.

CHAPTER 3
GNAWING GUILT

I leaned back in my rickety wooden chair and sighed. Every inch of my stomach was packed with pork chops and corn bread. "We ain't had a meal like that in years."

"Yeah. Not since Mama left," said Missy, wiping her mouth.

Aunt Sophie's smile faded for a moment. Was it the mention of Mama? "I'm glad you enjoyed it. We've got to put some meat on your bones."

"What about *our* bones?" asked my cousin, Darnell.

"Your bones got plenty of meat on them. You eat all day long," Aunt Sophie teased.

Mr. Costas stood up. "Thank you for a wonderful meal. I best be going. I've got lots of paperwork to file."

Uncle Ron stood as well and shook his hand. "Thanks for your help."

"Just a minute." Aunt Sophie bustled to the kitchen counter and cut a thick square of peach cobbler. She scooped it onto a paper plate and covered it with plastic wrap. "Here's some dessert for later." She walked him to the door and lowered her voice. "You watch yourself with that J.R. He don't take kindly to people messin' with his affairs."

"I'll keep that in mind." He turned to face us. "I'll call as soon as I know what charges your dad will face. It looks like you're in good hands until then."

We thanked him as he walked out the front door. Aunt Sophie prayed under her breath. "Protect that man, please Father. Protect us all."

Guilt gnawed at my stuffed stomach. We were entangling more people in J.R.'s web, and soon the spider could return. But what choice did we have? Missy had told our secrets and there was no turning back. I could only imagine what would happen if I shared everything *I* knew.

The girls and I helped our cousins carry the dirty dishes to the kitchen sink. Bright yellow curtains fluttered around the opened window. Flour dusted the blue formica countertops. Measuring spoons and mixing bowls filled the sink. Signs of real cooking. They made me miss Mama even more. I grabbed a blue crocheted washcloth and ran it under warm water.

"Thanks, JaDon, but I'll do the dishes today," Aunt Sophie said. "It's probably hard washin' anythin' with your injured arm. All of you kids go to the back yard and hang out like you used to."

She herded us through the door. I inhaled the sweet smell of the lilac bushes that bordered the yard and memories washed over me. Mama and Aunt Sophie used to sit on the white lawn chairs talking while we wrestled and played in the dirt. Sometimes they would grow serious and their conversation would fade to whispers, but often they would smile and laugh. I loved to hear Mama laugh. It sounded like peace and comfort, a sweet melody for my aching ears. She didn't laugh when we were home with J.R. None of us did.

Missy and Josie stood close behind me, timid and uncomfortable. Did they even remember playing here? I pictured them during one of the last times we visited. They were squealing and running while my cousins and I chased

22

them with the garden hose. I remembered their pudgy cheeks and sparkling eyes, their excitement and resilience. Life was hard at home even back then, but they used to be able to shake it off when they left the house.

I turned to look at them now. They huddled together with slumped shoulders, only moving enough to brush away pesky flies. Dark circles surrounded their lifeless gray eyes. Weary souls seemed to weigh down their eleven and twelve-year-old bodies.

Missy caught me staring. "What's wrong? Did we do somethin' bad?"

"No. I was just thinkin' about the last time we was here. Don't you two want to play?"

Josie shrugged.

"What're we allowed to do?" asked Missy.

"I don't know," I said. "Whatever you want. Run around. Look at bugs. Talk to Darnell and them. Somethin'."

They stole glances at their cousins playing basketball, but remained silent and merely dropped into lawn chairs. I sighed in frustration but had to admit, I didn't feel much like talking myself. What do you say to people after being separated seven years?

A black and white shaggy dog poked his head out of a dog house door and sniffed the air. His ears pricked forward. He bounded towards us, barking. The girls jumped back to their feet and hid behind me.

"Stop it, Mop!" yelled DeMarcus.

The dog stopped barking, but continued toward us. He began sniffing my feet.

"It's okay," said Desmond. "He won't bite. He just wants to protect us."

I reached down to pat the dog's furry head. He started to wag his tail, and then pushed through my legs to sniff the girls. Missy and Josie began to thaw behind me. They had a soft spot for animals. It was painful for them to live in a house with a hunter. Whenever J.R. returned to skin his kill, they would run into the woods.

"Can we pet your dog, too?" asked Missy.

"Sure," Darnell answered. "But watch out. You might not be able to get rid of him afterwards."

Missy and Josie bent over to pat Mop's scruffy fur. He licked Josie right on the mouth.

"Ewww," she squealed through a grin.

"He likes you," said Desmond. "'Course he also likes the old stinky possum that lives under the back porch. He ain't exactly picky."

DeMarcus returned to dribbling a weathered basketball on the cement slab. "Do you still know how to shoot a ball?" he asked.

"Yeah."

He tossed it to me. "Go ahead."

I hesitated, recalling the doctor's orders to take it slow while all of my injuries healed. My cast, stitches, and bruises all needed to be protected. But it had been seven years since I made the safe choice on almost anything. I shot at the hoop with my good right arm. It bounced off the rim. DeMarcus took another shot and bounced the ball back to me. This time I managed to sink it in.

"Not bad for having an arm in a sling. How about a game? Do you girls want to play, too?" Darnell asked.

Josie shook her head. I wasn't surprised. At least they were smiling. Mop was on his back, thumping his hind foot while the girls scratched his belly.

Darnell and I played against Desmond and DeMarcus. I could feel tension roll of my shoulders as I dribbled the ball and blocked shots. The trauma from the last few days

24

temporarily faded. My battered body protested against the exertion, but I ignored it. I hadn't played much basketball over the years, and I wasn't going to pass up this opportunity. J.R. thought sports were a waste of time. Once I got home from school I was supposed to do chores or help him hunt. Every shot I took felt like a blast of freedom—even if it was temporary.

Aunt Sophie and Uncle Ron emerged from the house and watched us play.

"You play on a team, JaDon?" asked Uncle Ron.

"Nah."

"You should. You're a natural. I'd like to see what you could do with two arms workin'."

We wound up playing until the sun set behind the roof tops. My doctors would have been alarmed at how hard I pushed myself, but my soul needed the release.

"Everyone inside," Aunt Sophie finally said. "We've got beds made. It'll be like old times when y'all slept over."

The girls gave Mop a few extra squeezes and we drifted inside. We crammed in the bathroom three at a time, to brush our teeth. The girls and I forgot to toss our toothbrushes into our sacks, so we were grateful they had extras. Next we washed our hands with a green bottle of liquid soap that smelled like apples. J.R. would have hated it. I put an extra squirt on my hands and washed them again.

Aunt Sophie stood by the bathroom door. "I was going to put you three in the boys' room, but I'm afraid you'd get lost. It's that messy. They'll work on it tomorrow. In the meantime, I've got you set up out here in the living room. JaDon, you're on the couch. Missy and Josie are on the air mattress on the floor."

I slid under a light plaid quilt and rested my head on a fresh-smelling pillow. Aunt Sophie sat at my feet. She held a small mason jar.

"Do you mind if I put some ointment on your cuts?" she asked. "It looks like the doctor stitched you up good, but my secret recipe will ease the pain and make you heal faster.

"Go ahead."

I braced myself as she scooped a small glob onto her fingers and smeared it gently on a gash above my eye and along my jaw. She even added some to my split lip. It smelled like minty grapefruit but felt like the inside of an aloe leaf.

"Don't lick it," she said.

My skin tingled for a moment, and then the pain started to fade slightly.

"Thanks."

She smiled and squeezed the one part of my arm that was free of bruises. "I should have told you not to push so hard playin' basketball. Shoot, you could barely walk when you arrived. But I could tell you needed to play." She looked deeply into my eyes. "You're a strong young man. Hang in there. We'll get this all sorted out."

She bent down to tuck a light blanket over the girls and kissed each of them on the forehead. "Is there anything else you two need?"

They shook their heads.

"Then I'll see you in the morning." She switched off the overhead light.

Josie stifled a whimper.

"It's okay, Josie," I said.

Aunt Sophie switched on the lamp that rested on the small table by the couch. "Is that better?"

Josie nodded. "Thanks."

"No problem, sweet child. Don't you worry. Me and your Uncle Ron gonna keep you safe."

Once Aunt Sophie left the room, Missy pulled her rag baby out of the blankets. She squeezed it hard.

"Were you hidin' that thing?" I asked.

"Maybe."

"Why? Aunt Josie wouldn't mind you havin' a doll."

"Hard to say. J.R. said I'm too old for such a thing. Even the kids at school teased me when I brought it to class last year, and I was only ten then."

"Aunt Sophie ain't like that," I reassured her.

"She *seems* nice," Missy agreed. "But I don't really know her yet."

Heat flashed in my mind. "That's J.R.'s fault. He chased everyone away after Mama left."

Josie rolled over to face me. "J.R. won't find us here, will he?"

I shook my head. "He's in handcuffs at the sheriff's office, remember? We really are safe here."

"Are you sure?" asked Missy. "He's mighty slippery."

"I'm sure. Now get some sleep."

Josie and Missy snuggled up together with the doll between them, and closed their eyes. Soon I heard soft, steady breathing.

I stared up at the ceiling. An image of J.R.'s cold blue eyes sent a chill down my spine. Missy was right. If anyone could get away from the police, it was J.R. I pulled the quilt under my chin. Warmth and gratitude wrapped around me, deflecting the icy fingers of fear and doubt. Our extended family still loved us after all of these years. I replayed the evening in my mind and felt my eyes slip closed.

CHAPTER 4

ORANGE BANDANA

"Should we wake him?"

"No, not yet."

"But he never sleeps *this* late."

"He needs the rest. His poor body is tore up somethin' awful."

"I hope he's still alive."

"I'm sure he is."

"But this isn't like him. He's always the first one up."

"That's just 'cuz he usually wakes up from a nightmare. If he actually slept late, J.R.'d smack him for not doin' chores."

"But he's already slept through breakfast and lunch. He's probably starvin'."

"He can eat when he wakes up. Leave him be."

Something felt like a bug on my cheek. Then my forehead. My eyes eased open. Missy's face was inches from my own. Her curly hair dangled into my face.

"He's alive!" Missy patted my cheek.

I pushed her away. "Of course I'm alive."

"Are you hungry?" asked Josie. "Do you want breakfast or lunch?"

"Or both?" asked Missy.

I rubbed my eyes and stretched. My muscles ached even more than yesterday. "I really slept that late?"

Josie nodded. "We slept in too. Just not as late as you."

Aunt Sophie walked into the living room. She wore a different orange tribal scarf around her head. "JaDon. Awake at last. Are you hungry?"

"Yeah. Sorry I slept so late."

"No problem at all. I knew you needed the rest. We had BLTs and fried potatoes for lunch. Would that do? I set some aside for you just in case."

My stomach started rumbling. "That sounds great." I pulled my aching body to the edge of the couch and stood up. My vision blackened and I had to sit right back down.

"Head rush?" asked my aunt.

"I guess so." I stood up slowly this time, and waited until my head cleared before I stumbled to the table.

Aunt Sophie placed a white plate with two BLTs and a heap of fried potatoes in front of me. She poured a tall glass of sweet tea.

Missy sat right beside me and watched me take a bite of the sandwich. She grinned as I chewed.

"What?" I asked with a full mouth.

"Can you taste it? She put *four* pieces of bacon on your sandwich. Four!"

I swallowed. "It tastes great."

"Yeah it does." Missy watched me take another bite. "And the tomatoes are plucked right from her garden. Mama used to grow tomatoes too. I remember 'em. Don't they taste amazin'?"

"Give him some space, Missy," Josie said.

Aunt Sophie smiled as she gathered our blankets. "I'm glad you're excited about the food, Missy. My boys barely taste it. Seems like they just about swallow it whole in their rush to fill their stomach."

She began folding the girl's quilt, and the rag baby toppled to the floor. Missy blushed and held real still beside me as Aunt Sophie picked it up. She stroked the yarn hair. "I remember this doll," she said in a hushed voice.

"I know I'm too old for a doll…"Missy began.

"Nonsense. Follow me." She dropped the quilt and led the way down the hall to her bedroom.

The girls drifted behind her. I stuffed in another bite of fried potatoes and joined them. A queen-sized bed with a bright, multi-colored quilt lined one wall and an oak dresser with an attached wall mirror lined the other. Perched on the dresser was a vase of dried flowers, a stack of books, and a faded, threadbare rag doll.

Aunt Sophie carefully picked up the doll and held her to her chest. "My mama made this for me when I was little. She don't look like much now, but I used to sleep with her every night."

The girls stroked the doll's flowered dress. Aunt Sophie smiled. "My mama, your grandma, is in heaven now, but every time I look at this here doll, I remember how much she loved me." She looked Missy in the eye. "Your mama made that rag baby special for you and poured her love into it. There's no shame in sleeping with something like that."

Missy smiled back at her, a little sparkle returning to her eyes.

Josie kept her eyes low. "I still have my doll, too. She's in my bag of stuff."

Aunt Sophie stroked Josie's hair. "I'm glad. Your mama would be, too."

The air was thick and tender. I wasn't used to it. "Yeah, well, I guess I should find my rag doll," I teased.

"You laugh, but your mama made you a stuffed dog that you drug around everywhere when you was little. She talked about makin' you a doll and J.R. would have none of it. He told her that no son of his would be a sissy boy. The dog was her compromise."

Memories seeped into my head of a black and white stuffed dog. It wasn't long before it turned black and gray from all the times I snuck it into the woods with me while J.R. hunted or had me working in the back. It was a good memory gone bad. Maybe that was why I blocked it out of my mind.

"I remember your stuffed dog," said Missy.

"So do I." Josie's eyes watered. "I didn't know Mama made it for you. No wonder you were so upset when J.R. threw it out."

I winced. Funny how forgotten pieces of the past can still come back to sting. I remembered J.R. yelling about how I was too old for a stuffed toy and throwing it into the dump. I snuck back and rescued it, stuffing it under my shirt. It was covered in rotted food and mud, but Mama helped me wash it. I kept it hidden during the day and only brought it out at night. It was our secret for several months, until one morning I was careless and left one of its floppy ears poking out of my blanket. J.R. saw it and was furious. He smacked me across the face. Mama grabbed me and the dog and stood in front of us, telling him to leave us be. He started beating on her instead and threw the dog into the fireplace.

"JaDon? Are you okay?" asked Aunt Sophie.

I looked down. I was clenching my fists and breathing hard. "Yeah," I mumbled.

"How about you finish your lunch and then we all go for a walk? I think we could use some fresh air."

DeMarcus, Darnell, and Desmond joined us on the walk with the condition that they could bring their skateboard. They took turns rolling along beside us. We walked on cement sidewalks through rows of houses with green lawns

31

and thick-trunked trees. Everything seemed neat and orderly, so different from the random collection of houses and shacks near our own.

"Have you ever ridden a skateboard?" Desmond asked me.

"A few times. My friends at school sometimes let me try," I said.

"Do you want to ride ours?" he continued.

"No, he would not," my aunt answered for me. "You do see the cast on his arm and the stitches all over his body, right?"

"That didn't stop him from playin' basketball last night," said DeMarcus.

"That was probably pushin' too hard," she agreed, "but at least he didn't have much risk of fallin'. Your skateboard is far more dangerous."

"Not if you've done it before," said Desmond. "Do you want to ride it, JaDon?"

I did, but I didn't want to offend Aunt Sophie. "I probably shouldn't."

"See? The boy has common sense," said Aunt Sophie.

"He's only sayin' that because you guilted him into it," Darnell said. He turned to me. "Can you honestly say you don't want to ride it?"

I was trapped. "Well, no but…"

"See Mama?" said Darnell. "Let him live a little if he wants to."

"But his arm…"

"We'll run along beside him and catch him if he starts to fall," said DeMarcus. He placed the skateboard in front of me.

"I can't watch," said Aunt Sophie, covering her eyes.

"I'll be careful," I assured her. I pushed off slowly with my cousins on either side. The rush of air was welcome on my face. I closed my eyes and soaked it in.

"There's a hill coming. You might want to stop for now," Desmond advised.

I opened my eyes. "That's okay. I've got this." I pushed off toward the hill.

"Lord, have mercy," my aunt said.

The wheels spun faster as I raced down the steep hill. My cousins ran faster trying to keep up, but soon fell behind. I extended my arms trying to keep balanced. My arm in the sling couldn't help. I wobbled and swerved. I tensed my body in case I had to jump off. Finally, the skateboard slowed as the hill leveled into a flat surface. I managed to stop and step of the board. My cousins finally caught up to me, yelling in triumph.

"Way to go!" Darnell exclaimed.

We walked back to Aunt Sophie and the girls.

"Oh, my, child. You 'bout gave me a heart attack. Are you okay?" My aunt fanned her face.

"I'm fine. That was great!"

"Do you want to go again?" asked Desmond.

"No," my sisters answered for me.

"That was quite enough," added my aunt.

I resisted the urge, and merely walked beside my cousins as they took turns riding the rest of the way home.

After dinner, the entire family stepped outside. The girls immediately began playing with Mop, and my cousins and I began a game of basketball. I was sore and tired, so eventually joined my aunt and uncle on the lawn chairs. Uncle Ron was reading a thick hard-back book.

He looked up at me. "Are you still a big reader?"

I nodded.

"Have you ever read *The Testament* by John Grisham?" he asked.

"No. Is it good?"

"It's one of my favorites. Care to hear some of it?"

"Sure."

He returned to the beginning of the book and began to read out loud. His deep voice was expressive and soothing. I soaked in the words. Soon my sisters and cousins sat around us on the cement slab. We were drawn into the story. The only movement was when someone sought a more comfortable position. I studied Uncle Ron's face as he read, and couldn't help but wish he was my pa instead of J.R.

Three chapters later, Aunt Sophie announced that we needed to head to bed. We stretched and went inside, brushed our teeth, and crawled under the covers.

Aunt Sophie bent over the air mattress and prayed, "Thank you, Lord, for sending these precious young ones to our home. We love you. Amen."

Missy reached up and squeezed her tight.

"You remind me of Mama," she whispered.

Aunt Sophie choked up. "Thanks, sweet girl."

"Can I hug you, too?" asked Josie.

"Of course."

Josie hesitantly squeezed her around the shoulders. Aunt Sophie's bright bandana slipped, exposing her bare head.

Missy sucked in her breath. "Where's your hair?"

"Missy, hush!" hissed Josie.

"No. It's okay," said Aunt Sophie, as she readjusted her bandana. "I started losin' my hair during my last round of chemo. I decided it looked better to just shave the rest off." She fingered Missy's messy curls. "Don't worry. It'll grow

34

back. Soon my hair will look more like yours. In the mean time, I save time stylin' my hair and get to wear all sorts of bandanas."

"What's wrong with you?" asked Missy.

"Missy!" I reprimanded, even though I wanted to know, too.

Aunt Sophie looked at me. "It's no secret. I would have told you sooner or later. I have cancer. But I beat it four years ago, and I'll beat it again. I'm one tough lady. Bein' strong runs in our family."

"Good," said Missy. She nestled down under the covers with her rag doll. "I hope you beat it forever."

"Me, too. Sleep tight, sweet ones." She switched on the lamp and turned out the overhead light.

After Aunt Sophie left, Josie sat up. "Do you think Aunt Sophie will really be okay?"

"She said she beat it before. I'll bet she's fine after the chemo is over," I said.

"Good. I really like her."

"Me, too," said Missy. "And Uncle Ron. And Mop. And DeMarcus. And Desmond. And I think Darnell. They make it so I don't miss Rat."

"I'm glad," I said.

"I like staying in their house," Missy added. "It smells like peaches and hugs."

I raised my eyebrows. "Is that so?"

"Yes, doesn't it, Grace?" she squeezed her doll.

"I thought your rag baby was named Tanya," Josie said.

"She was, but now I can name her after Mama without J.R. getting mad."

CHAPTER 5

NEEDING GRACE

Murmured voices and the sound of silverware scraping on plates woke me up. After rubbing my eyes, I tried to focus on my surroundings. Flowered curtains. Clean white walls. The smell of coffee brewing and sausage frying. I sighed in relief. My nightmare had placed me back in our shack, fighting off J.R.'s blows. It was good to be awake.

"Good mornin', JaDon." A smiling black turbaned face peered down at me. "You're awake much earlier than yesterday. We're just starting breakfast. Would you like some pancakes?"

"Yes, ma'am," I said, stretching my sore muscles.

"Come on, JaDon," said Missy. "They have syrup, or boysenberry jam, or marmalade and butter…I'm in pancake heaven."

I grinned and joined the family at the table.

"Ron already had to leave for work, but the rest of you can take your time," said Aunt Sophie. She placed a full glass of apple juice and a stack of four large pancakes and two sausage links in front of me. "Dig in."

I slathered orange marmalade all over the top pancake and took a huge bite. "This is so good. Thanks."

"Glad to do it." She finished her final bite of pancake. "I thought you boys could hang out at the creek if you want. Me and the girls are goin' to Charlotte's house."

"Who's Charlotte?" asked Josie.

"A friend who lives at the end of the street. She has a daughter a few years older than you. I told her you was comin' and she said she needed to clean out some closets. There should be some clothes that you might like a bit more than JaDon's old jeans and t-shirts. No offense, JaDon."

"None taken."

The girls beamed at each other. My heavy heart lightened.

"Can we go right now?" asked Missy. "We're done eatin'."

Aunt Sophie laughed. "How's about I play with your hair first. They might not all be awake yet over there."

Darnell rolled his eyes. "You'd think they was dolls, the way Mama acts."

"Don't feel left out, JaDon," said Desmond. "I can do your hair, too. Would you like braids or curls?"

Aunt Sophie swatted him with a dish towel.

"Have you seen our go cart?" asked DeMarcus.

"No," I said through a mouth full of sausage.

"You'll love it. You could even drive it with one arm," said Desmond.

"We built it from scraps at the junk yard. Pa had to help with the engine, but most of it we did ourselves."

"Be careful, now," Aunt Sophie instructed. "JaDon's got enough injuries without you addin' to the list."

"Come on, JaDon. Let's go," said Darnell.

I crammed the last pancake into my mouth and grabbed my shoes. The day was off to a great start. I left my worries on the couch as we headed out the garage door.

Desmond flipped on the light. "Check it out. Pa got the motor from a guy who wrecked his motorcycle. The seat was from the junkyard. It used to be on an old tractor. We welded the frame together from old car frame parts."

I ran my hand over the seat. "This is incredible."

"We can take turns drivin' it to the back roads. There's even a jump we can go over," said Darnell.

It didn't take long for them to show me how to use the gas pedal and the brakes. I already knew how to drive our truck from watching J.R. There were times when he would start weaving from lane to lane on the road after one drink too many. Sometimes I managed to get him to pull over so I could drive us the rest of the way home.

We kept the speed down on the go cart until we got to the dirt roads behind the subdivision. Darnell pulled onto a back trail and floored it. He only slowed down when he barreled toward an impressive dirt mound. Desmond, DeMarcus and I whooped and hollered until he circled back around to meet us.

"I know. I know. I'm amazing." He tossed me the helmet. "Try it!"

I strapped it on, adjusted the improvised seat belt and pressed on the gas. I let it gradually get faster. A bug plastered against my grinning teeth. I spat it out but kept going. This was freedom. I pressed the gas pedal to the floor as I approached the jump. Faster and faster I drove until I hit the top of the jump and flew through the air. Adrenaline surged through my veins. I landed with a bounce, barely managing to right myself, and stepped on the break. Dust swirled around me as my cousins ran to my side.

"Are you okay?" Desmond asked.

DeMarcus helped me remove the helmet and seatbelt. "Do you have a death wish? That was too fast even for someone with two working arms."

"Sorry, guys. I guess I got carried away."

"Yeah, you did," said Darnell. "But that was so cool!"

We continued taking turns on the go kart until well past lunch. We finally pushed the dirt-covered machine back into the garage.

"It's about time you boys came home," said Aunt Sophie. "I left turkey sandwiches and chips on the table."

We all stormed the kitchen, suddenly starving.

"Wash your hands, first!"

I was clean and had inhaled a sandwich before I noticed Josie and Missy standing beside the table expectantly. Their hair was braided in corn rows with white plastic beads on the ends. They each wore floral sundresses and sandals.

"Wow," I said. "You actually look like girls now."

They spun around, letting their skirts twirl at their knobby knees. Their faces glowed with excitement as they showed me more outfits. The corners of my mouth turned up. It had been a long time since I saw them so happy. The cowering girls from a few days ago were gone. They chased Mop out the back door. I turned to follow, but Aunt Sophie called me back.

"Can I talk to you a moment?" she asked.

"Sure."

She folded up the quilt I used the night before and sat on the couch. I sat beside her.

"Please forgive me for bringin' this up, but I just cain't help it. I've been waitin' for seven years to find out what happened to your ma. I know it has to be a painful subject, but can you tell me anythin'?"

My throat tightened and I looked at my grimy legs. "I'm not sure what happened."

She nodded and looked at a picture of the two of them hanging on the wall. "We was so close. She told me she and J.R. had problems. She wished she had known how he really was before he sweet-talked her into marryin' him. But she loved you kids with all her heart. I know that if she couldn't handle it anymore she would have told me. She would have asked for help. J.R. said she run off with another man, but she never mentioned anyone else. And she wouldn't do that to you kids. I know she wouldn't leave you. Especially not with that…with J.R."

My eyes were still glued to the picture of Mama on the wall. It was several minutes before I could speak. "He told us she left because of all our whining. He said we drove her over the edge, and she couldn't take it no more. She left for another state and didn't want to ever come back."

"You don't believe that, do you? That doesn't sound like her at all."

I chewed the inside of my cheek out of habit and winced in pain. The cuts from my last confrontation with J.R. had turned into canker sores. I refused to let a single tear fall. "I did complain the day before she left. I was hungry. J.R. usually brought home enough meat from huntin' to keep us fed, but it was winter and he was having trouble findin' much to shoot. He was drinkin' more than usual too, so he couldn't fire straight. Mama made soup out of what little food was left. I ate my bowl of soup, but complained because it didn't fill me up. She gave me the rest of her soup. I shouldn't have done that."

Aunt Sophie squeezed my shoulders. "There was nothing wrong with sayin' you was hungry. And *that* sounds more like her—puttin' the needs of you three before her own."

I nodded. "But that night, she told J.R. she needed to get a job so we could have more food. They got in a huge fight. She said it was his fault that she didn't finish her nursing degree. He had promised her she could still go to school

40

when they got married." I could still hear the yelling in my head, and had to stop for a moment to clear it out.

"I remember how sad she was when he moved her out to that old house." Aunt Sophie grabbed a tissue and blew her nose. "She was too far from the college and he wouldn't let her drive the truck. He said it was only temporary, but it didn't take long for Grace to figure out that was just more of his manipulation."

That sounded about right. I closed my eyes, trying to recall details I had stuffed away. "They kept fightin'. And he kept drinkin'. She told him she was tired of him beatin' us kids and that if he didn't stop she was finally goin' to leave him." My head was pounding. I rubbed the temples trying to relieve the pressure. "He yanked her to their room by her hair. She yelled at us to go feed the cat."

"You had a cat? I didn't know you had any pets."

"We didn't. That was her way of tellin' us to go to our hidin' spot. She sent us there whenever J.R. was drunk and was goin' crazy."

Aunt Sophie's eyes watered. "Go on."

"We couldn't hear very well while we were hidin', so I don't know what else they said. We hid all night."

"All night! You poor things."

"That wasn't unusual. We did that several times before. What was different was we finally heard J.R. drive away in the mornin', and she didn't come to get us, to tell us it was finally safe. She would always let us out and hug us and make us hot chocolate with colored marshmallows. Even if it was hot out. And she'd tell us he was sobered up now and everythin' would be okay."

Aunt Sophie scooted to the edge of the couch. "Did you see her again after that?"

I shook my head. "J.R. said he drove her to the train station that mornin' and that she told him to tell us good-bye and that maybe when she wasn't so mad she would write us a letter."

"Did you ever get a letter?"

"No. J.R. said she sent a couple, but that he threw them into the fire since she deserted us."

Aunt Sophie shook her head. Tears poured down her cheeks. She tried stopping them with her tissue so she could talk. "She loved you kids more than life itself. Do you really think she would have left you out of her own free will?"

"I don't know what to believe any more."

"I tried callin' your house when I didn't hear from Grace for a few weeks."

"J.R. wouldn't let us answer the phone."

"I figured that, so I came by your house over and over. Your pa always chased me away with that blasted rifle of his. I finally sent the police, but J.R. must've concocted some really convincin' story because they dropped the case. He threatened me after that, sayin' if I didn't leave things alone that you kids would pay for it. I didn't know what else to do. I should'a found another way to get you away from him." She stroked my swollen cheek. "Now look what happened."

"It's not your fault," I said.

She patted my hand. "That's debatable, but at least you're here now. Let's just hope that man stays in jail."

I clenched the fist that poked out of my sling. "Where he belongs."

CHAPTER 6
FROG GIGGIN'

The sun wandered behind the hills, eventually disappearing from view. I leaned back against the porch steps, savoring the peace that pulsated from the house. The tall glass of sweetened iced tea rested on my leg. The condensation soaked into my jeans, but I didn't mind. I took a long sip, enjoying the cold sensation that trickled down my throat.

Josie and Missy sat on either side of Mop, feeding him his dry dog food one piece at a time. His hairy tail flopped from side to side.

"They're spoilin' him," said DeMarcus. "He'd better not expect *us* to do that."

"He'd go into shock if you even dumped food into his bowl," said Darnell. "Mama usually feeds him."

"I've fed him before," protested DeMarcus.

"What…Once or twice?" Darnell asked.

DeMarcus shrugged. "Twice. I think."

"Like I said. Mama usually feeds him."

"Do you guys got pets back at your place?" asked DeMarcus.

"Just Rat," said Missy, scratching behind Mop's ear.

"Rat? What's Rat?" Desmond asked.

"Rat's a rat of course." Missy shook her head and gave Mop another piece of food.

"Wow," said Darnell. "Mama would freak out if we bought a rat."

"J.R. didn't know about Rat," Missy said. "Rat was smart. He'd go hide with his family under the floor boards whenever J.R. came stompin' in."

Darnell's eyes widened. "Oh."

Josie blushed. I took another sip of tea as an uncomfortable silence settled over us. This was why I never talked about my home-life at school. It was too easy to reveal our dysfunction.

Suddenly, Damon burst out, "You ever been frog giggin'?"

"A few times. Why?" I asked.

"This would be a good night for it. And I'm cravin' some fried frog legs."

"That does sound good," said DeMarcus. "You want in on it?"

I shrugged. "Why not." Anything to change topics.

Darnell opened the screen door. "Mama! Are you okay if us guys go frog giggin'?"

"Go ahead. I'll batter 'em up tomorrow."

Missy put her hands on her hips. "What about us? We want to go, too. Don't we, Josie?"

"I guess."

"You look too girly for catchin' frogs. You might get mud on them dresses," I teased.

Missy looked down at her sundress and sandals. She smoothed the floral skirt and looked up. "We still got yer ugly clothes. We'll go change into 'em. Don't leave without us!"

She marched into the house. Josie followed reluctantly.

Desmond rolled his eyes. "They's just gonna slow us down, ain't they."

"I heard that," Missy yelled from inside. "We won't neither!"

Within minutes, my sisters were dressed in jean shorts, old t-shirts and flip-flops. Our cousins yanked on their mud boots and grabbed a couple flashlights, nets, and buckets with lids. We walked until the house light no longer illuminated our way. The moon wasn't full, so Desmond and Darnell both flipped on their lights.

The heat of the day melted into a cool night. We climbed down the creek bank and trudged through the shallow water. Mud and sludge oozed into my shoes, cooling me down even further.

"Ew!" Missy said, announcing our presence.

Darnell turned and shook his head.

She scowled, made a zipping motion over her mouth and kept walking.

Desmond stopped suddenly and pointed to the mud at his right. I squinted in the dim light. Before I could even decipher the shape of a bull frog, his hand shot out and grabbed the creature firmly around the belly. Darnell yanked the lid off the bucket and immediately slammed it shut once the frog was inside.

I grinned. I preferred frog gigging with my cousins. It seemed like a fair game. When I went out with J.R. he blasted the frogs with a twenty-two rifle.

Desmond spotted and caught two more frogs before Darnell and DeMarcus caught their first. I was still empty-handed. I knew I could blame my bad luck on only having one working arm, but I really wanted to catch some frogs.

"There's one," Josie whispered, pointing by a stump.

"Grab it," I said.

"I don't wanna hurt a frog." She backed away.

"I'll get it." Missy crept toward the frog and grabbed it by the leg. It squirmed out of her hand and hopped toward the other bank. "Slimy little things," she muttered.

We sloshed through the creek as quietly as possible for several minutes before I spotted a still shape in the dim flashlight glow. Without a word, I inched forward. I reached for it, but it jumped right at Darnell. He snatched it and threw it into the bucket.

"Good job. You scared it right toward me," he said.

I nodded and then scowled as he turned and sloshed through the water. I was determined to catch a frog on my own before we headed back. My cousins each caught another frog before I had a second chance. Finally, I heard a frog talking to my left. Its head peeked out of a shallow pool of water. My hand shot out, this time grasping the frog and holding tight.

"I got one!" I yelled.

Darnell sloshed over and peeled back the bucket lid long enough for me to toss it in. A feeling of satisfaction washed over me. Success at last.

"Our buckets are almost full," said Darnell. "A couple more and we can head back."

Desmond and I each caught another frog at the same time and crammed them into the bucket. I grinned. This was just the distraction from life that I needed. We trudged through the brush hanging along the creek's edge.

"Snake!" DeMarcus yelled.

Missy and Josie screamed. I searched the eerie darkness, unsure of which way to go.

"Where is it?" I asked.

"I'm not sure now," he said. "It was headed right toward you."

My heart started pounding. One of my classmates got bit by a water snake and actually died. Josie and Missy splashed up the banks and began to run. Where was that snake?

"Shine the light over here!" I said, my voice cracking.

Darnell whipped his light back and forth in my direction. I squinted at every stick, hoping the snake wasn't poisonous. Where did it go? The idea of it slithering up to me sent a shiver up my spine.

"There it is!" Darnell yelled, pointing next to me. He and his brothers ran up the bank toward the girls.

"Where?" I spun around. "Where?"

Snickering erupted on the bank. I looked up just as Darnell dropped to the ground laughing.

I glared at them. "Let me guess. None of you saw a snake."

"Oh, I've seen a snake," Darnell said. "Just not tonight."

"We scared all of you good," DeMarcus said through his laughter.

The girls stood stone-faced.

"I want to go home," Josie stated.

"Fine," said Desmond. "We have plenty of frogs anyhow."

Darnell reached out his hand to help pull me up the bank. I ignored it and climbed up myself, careful to keep my sling out of the water.

"Don't be mad," Darnell said. "We couldn't resist. It might make you feel better to know we did the same thing to Desmond and he started cryin' like a baby."

"Did not!"

"Yes you did," Darnell continued. "And you told on us so we had to clean all of the frog legs by ourselves."

"Good idea," said Josie. "I can't stand cuttin' and pealin' frogs. So all we need to do is tell your ma…"

"Don't tell Mama," said DeMarcus. "Her lecture would be 'bout as bad as the skinnin'. Maybe worse. We'll take care of the frogs if you don't give us away."

"Deal," said Missy.

The rest of the evening we chatted while our cousins struggled with the frogs, removing their legs and pealing their skin. They stuck the legs in a bowl of cold water with a little salt.

Aunt Sophie and Uncle Ron walked in just as the boys finished the last frog. "The six of you make a good team," Aunt Sophie said. "Thanks for catchin' and cleanin' so many frogs. I usually have to beg to get any help with the skinnin'. I'll fry 'em up tomorrow."

"We were glad to help," said Josie, grinning at her cousins.

"It's a good thing you're here," said Uncle Ron. "Now we might actually get some work out of these three. I'll have to think of some good projects for you to do."

My cousins scowled, but I smiled. Working would make me feel like I was part of the family, and this was a family I actually wanted to claim, even with the fake snake scare. No abusive dad. No missing mama. No crumbling, rat-infested house.

CHAPTER 7
PRISON CELL

The next morning, my sisters stood side by side at the sink. Josie scrubbed the last traces of cheesy eggs and bread crumbs off each plate while Missy dried and stacked them on the counter. I chased away the last ghostly image from my recurring nightmare, and stood to stretch while my cousins sprawled out on the couch and floor.

"Don't get too comfortable," said Aunt Sophie. "Your pa set out some stain and paintbrushes. He wants you to work on the fence."

"How much of the fence does he want us to stain?" asked DeMarcus.

"He didn't say. I would assume that means the whole thing."

"What? That'll take us all day," Darnell complained.

"Not with all three of you workin' hard," said Aunt Sophie. "Now get to it. I'll have the frog legs ready for your lunch break." She turned to face me. "How are you feelin'?"

"Better."

"You're welcome to rest on the couch or in the back yard. You seem to be movin' around better, but my heart still hurts just lookin' at you." She studied my face. "Your bruises aren't black and blue anymore, but it looks like you'll be colorful for a while yet."

"Yeah. He looks green now. What planet are you from?" Darnell teased.

Aunt Sophia placed a paintbrush in his hand. "Get to work."

"Actually, if you don't mind, I'd like to help with the fence," I said.

"Really?" Aunt Sophie squinted at me.

"Really?" My cousins raised their eyebrows and elbowed each other in the ribs.

"I'm not much good at just sittin'. I still have one good arm."

The phone rang.

"Hold that thought," said Aunt Sophie. She reached for the phone. "Hello? Oh, hi, Mr. Costas. Yes. They're great kids. Of course. They're welcome to stay here as long as they want." She turned her back to the rest of us. A long silence followed. "How much was it set for? I hope so. I will. Bye." She turned to face us and found everyone staring at her intently. "Mr. Costas said J.R. was taken before a judge yesterday. The judge decided to keep him in jail and a bond was set at $50,000. There's no way he's got that kind of money, right?"

The girls and I each shook our head.

Aunt Sophie smiled. "Good. Then we're okay for now. His hearing is scheduled for July 28th, so we'll just hope the judge decides to do whatever is necessary to keep all y'all safe."

Relief percolated in my chest, but I was afraid to acknowledge it. J.R. was good at talking his way out of tough situations. I could enjoy the next few weeks, but after July 28th my peaceful world could disappear.

Josie and Missy huddled close to my side, feeding off my insecurities. My cousins sat back down on the couch.

"Well, that's great news," said Darnell. "We should do something to celebrate, like three-wheelin', or…"

Aunt Sophie pulled him back to his feet. "I'm not distracted that easily. Get started on that fence. All three of you."

They grumbled as they stood and trudged to the back door. I held out my hand for a brush.

"You sure you still want to work?" she asked.

"It'll be a good distraction."

And it was—at first. My cousins summarized all that had happened in the seven years we were separated. They asked questions about my school and sports, but avoided mentioning Mama and her disappearance. Aunt Sophie must have told them to leave it alone.

By the time we finished one side of the fence, sweat was running down each face and soaking our shirts. Darnell repeatedly flicked stain at his brothers, but it blended in with their dark skin. Finally, DeMarcus had enough and wrestled him to the ground.

Midway through the second length of fence, my mind began to wander. I pictured J.R. pacing in his prison cell. Was he by himself, or did he have to share a cell? He was probably in a foul mood, knowing his kids had finally reported his abuse. How was he releasing his anger? He had to be craving a beer. I could almost smell the decaying odor of whiskey. Had the police unlocked the shed? Had they found the equipment? J.R. was smart enough to get his buddies to move everything. Had he done it before getting whiskey-brewing and selling added to his criminal record?

The girls and I weren't allowed in the shed. J.R. kept his business quiet because he didn't want to have to pay the high taxes on brewing beer. Late at night, he and his buddies would haul gallon milk jugs filled with his corn whiskey or "white dog" out of the shed and into the truck. He might actually make decent money off it, if he could resist drinking so much of it himself.

The smell of the whiskey on his breath made my stomach clench. Partly because it smelled like the guys at my school when Mexican food was served in the lunchroom. Partly because I associated pain with the odor. Most of my beatings came when he was drunk.

I propped my paintbrush on the bucket of stain and stretched my arm. It would help if I could switch painting arms occasionally. How long would I have to keep my arm in a sling?

Aunt Sophie glided across the grass on bare feet. She was holding a large blue plastic bowl. "Watermelon break." She handed each of us a thick slice of watermelon.

I bit into it gratefully, letting the red juice run down my fingers. "Thanks." More juice dripped on my shorts and bare legs. I didn't mind. It felt hot and sticky like summer.

"You boys are half-way there. I'm impressed. It looks so much better. I'll call you in when the frog legs are ready."

"You're sure Papa wanted us to stain the *entire* fence?" asked Desmond. He tossed his watermelon rind into the empty bowl and spit out two seeds.

"If he didn't, this will be a great surprise. Keep goin'." She gathered the rest of the rinds and headed back inside.

"We ain't had to work this hard in a long time," DeMarcus complained. "Does J.R. make you work this hard?"

I nodded. "But he doesn't give watermelon or frog leg breaks. And he doesn't hand out compliments if we do a good job."

By the time we came in for lunch, I was sore, speckled with stain, and my head ached from breathing in all of the fumes. The fence, however, was finished and looked new again. We took turns washing our hands with paint thinner and soap in the bathroom sink and finally sank into chairs at the kitchen table.

Aunt Sophie placed bowls full of sizzling hot frog legs, homemade French fries, and creamy coleslaw on the center of the table. "You boys wash up and then we can eat."

"We already washed," said Desmond.

"You did? Well, you all still look dirty to me."

"It's stain, Mama. Us kids are stained," said Darnell. "We might look like this forever. All because Papa wanted a good-lookin' fence."

"I'll bet I could scrub it off of you. Want me to try?" she asked.

"No. We'll work on it later. We're sore and starvin' and just want to eat," said DeMarcus.

"I guess scrubbin' can wait."

We heaped the food on our plates, prayed, and dug in. I savored each mouthful, enjoying my aunt's skills in the kitchen. Mama was a good cook, too, but it had been seven years since I tasted her cooking. My chewing slowed. I let my mind wander to the previous day's discussion. Aunt Sophie was right. Mama loved us too much to just leave. Either J.R. kept her away with his shotgun and threats like he had with our extended family, or she really was dead. I chewed a bite of fries. I'd always had my suspicions, but had tried desperately to stuff them to the back of my mind. It was the only way I could continue living with J.R. all these years.

It wasn't the only time I had to file away his actions and refuse to examine them in the light. J.R.'s conscience had snuffed out years ago. My sisters and I had to close our eyes and focus on survival. We were trapped in his snare. Our only hope for release was if he was locked in jail…or dead.

"Are you okay there, JaDon?" asked Desmond. "You're not eatin' much."

"Did I make the frog legs too spicy?" Aunt Sophie questioned. "The boys like me to kick everythin' up a notch. I should have toned it down for all of you."

"No. The frog legs are great." I corralled my thoughts and crammed them back down deep. "I was just thinkin' about how much I loved your cookin'."

Missy waved a pair of frog legs in the air. "Yeah. These are so good I don't feel that bad for all the frogs who died for us."

Josie pushed her frog legs to the other side of her plate. "Thanks, Missy." She nibbled on her coleslaw while the rest of us finished eating.

"You boys deserve a dip in the pond, if you want it." Aunt Sophie said as she gathered the dishes. She turned to the girls. "Do you want to go swimmin', too?"

They nodded eagerly.

"Well, it's settled then. We'll let our food settle and then take a dip in the water. Who knows, I might even get in."

An hour later we were splashing in the pond. Josie and Missy's swimming suits were faded and stretched out, but it was probably a good thing, as the suits would have been the wrong size otherwise. The girls were too happy to care. I pulled my sling off my arm and wrapped the blue cast in a plastic sack before easing into the water. My stain spots remained, but I felt some of my surface worries float away in the water ripples. Aunt Sophie dipped her toes into the pond, smiling as she watched us unwind.

"I thought you said you might get in this time," teased Darnell. "You're wearing a swimmin' suit."

"I'm workin' up to it," she said. "The water is still a might chilly to me."

I took a deep breath and plunged down deeper. When I opened my eyes I found minnows nibbling at plants and a tiny turtle scuttling past. I came back up for air. Aunt Sophie unwound her bright turban, and placed it carefully by her towel. I tried not to stare at her bald head. Even without hair she seemed confident and strong, and...safe. She dropped into the water, inhaling sharply from the cold.

We alternated swimming and sprawling out on the bank until the sun began to drop in the sky. Reluctantly, we wrapped our prune-like bodies in thick towels and walked home.

By the time we all showered, Aunt Sophie had dinner on the table and Uncle Ron was home. My stomach growled as I scooped some of the chicken and dumplings into my bowl.

"You boys sure look pretty," Uncle Ron said.

"What?" Desmond arched his brows in confusion.

"It's like God tried something new and gave you dark skin with light freckles. I like it."

"Very funny," said DeMarcus.

"You did a great job on the fence. I didn't expect you to get the whole thing done in one day."

Darnell glared at Aunt Sophie. She smiled and shrugged.

The doorbell rang. Mop barked and jumped at Aunt Sophie's feet as she shuffled to open the front door.

A familiar voice slipped in. "Remember me, Sophie? It's been years. I just came by to see if you happened to have some things that belong to me."

CHAPTER 8
MORE SECRETS

I dropped my spoon. It sank into the thick stew until it was smothered by dumplings and vegetables. My growing hope in a life worth living sank right along with that spoon. I swallowed my mouthful of chicken, but it stuck in my throat. With shaking hands, I reached for my glass of water to wash it down.

"Hello, J.R." Aunt Sophie's voice exuded loathing.

My sisters' gray eyes widened in horror at the mention of his name. They huddled together at the table. We all held still, barely breathing, hoping he would not barge inside and see us.

Uncle Ron pushed back his chair and rushed to his wife's side at the door. "I thought you were in jail."

"Good to see you too, Ron. Now, how did you know I was in jail? Are them cops keepin' you informed 'cuz you've got my kids?"

"How did you get out of jail?" asked Aunt Sophie.

"I posted bail. My buddies came to my aid. That's what good friends do. Unlike family. I didn't even bother callin' y'all."

"That's good, 'cuz you would've wasted your time. I'm guessing your *friends* are more loyal to your whiskey-makin' than to you," said Uncle Ron. "Enjoy your time out of jail, 'cuz you'll be back soon."

56

"You'd like that, wouldn't ya? Well, in the meantime you can hand over my kids. I figured you was the only family they got left, so that girly-man who took 'em would drop 'em here. I'll just collect 'em and go." J.R. took a step toward the door, but Uncle Ron blocked his way.

"I didn't invite you in, J.R. You best be goin' home."

J.R. pushed his way around them and his cold blue eyes settled on me. "Hey, there, JaDon. Just like I thought. Pack up yer stuff and let's go."

A wave of queasiness washed over me. The pain from my cuts and bruises seemed to intensify with every step he took. Part of me wanted to grab the girls and run. Another part wanted to fight. His hands were empty. Did he have any weapons hidden?

Missy and Josie cowered in their chairs, quickly fading into their former nervous selves.

J.R. smirked, feeding off their fright. "You girls get yer things, too. We need ta leave."

"Now wait just a minute," said Aunt Sophie. She placed her hands protectively on the girls' shoulders. "We didn't get a call from the court sayin' you could have yer kids back. Until then, they're stayin' here."

He turned his head slowly and twisted his face into a sneer. "I warned ya once not ta meddle with these three. They belong to *me*. Not you. Do I have ta have a gun in my hands to make ya listen? Are ya deaf *and* dim-witted?"

Uncle Ron's chest swelled. He couldn't match J.R.'s 6' 4" height, but he couldn't be intimidated that easily. His thick arms could still slow J.R. down if needed. "Looks like you're unarmed now. You can't insult my wife. Get out of our house."

"Gladly. Once I have my kids."

Aunt Sophie grabbed the phone and dialed 911.

"Hang up the phone, Sophie," J.R. commanded, taking a step forward.

Uncle Ron blocked his brother-in-law's path.

"I need police to come to our home right away," Aunt Sophie said, looking straight at J.R and talking quickly. "We have J.R. Chambers out on bail, threatening us in our home. He's tryin' to take the children he abused. Our address is 16923 West Haven Street."

J.R.'s nostrils flared. "That was a mistake, woman."

Aunt Sophie slammed down the phone. "Oh, I've made plenty of mistakes, all right. I made a mistake lettin' my sister marry a no 'count loser like you. I made a mistake not going to the police when she'd come to my house beat up and claimin' she just fell. I made a mistake not fightin' harder for these here kids when Grace disappeared." Her black skin flushed a deep red and her voice climbed. "What did you do to her? Did you chase her away *or did you kill her*?"

Josie whimpered and grabbed her sister's hand.

Aunt Sophie looked down, and her anger seeped into regret. "I'm sorry, girls. I didn't mean to…"

"I don't have to answer to you," J.R. spit out, oblivious to their distress. "What goes on in my home is none of yer business."

"It *is* my business when it involves *my* sister and *my* nephew and nieces. You beat JaDon so bad you put him in the hospital. Oh. Wait. *You* were too wasted to even get him to the hospital. If Josie hadn't called the ambulance, he probably would've died on the floor in that rat's nest you call a cabin."

"You don't have all yer facts straight, but I ain't got time ta set ya right. Come on, JaDon. We got ta leave *now*. Girls, grab yer stuff."

I studied his empty hands clenched into fists, and then I looked at Uncle Ron and my three cousins. Images of my last beating burned in my mind. I didn't budge. He would have to hold a gun to my head before I would walk out that door with him. My survival odds were much higher where I was. The girls shuffled to stand behind me.

J.R.'s eyes narrowed into slits. "You best come with me now or there'll be a price ta pay later. Let's go."

Uncle Ron held his ground. "You're the only one who should be leavin'."

Desmond, DeMarcus, and Darnell slowly stood up and joined their dad, creating a formidable wall in front of me and my sisters.

Sirens blared in the distance. J.R. swore and knocked over a side table. Several framed pictures slid to the floor, cracking the glass. He picked up a large shard in his calloused hands and stepped toward Uncle Ron with a disturbed smile distorting his lips.

Josie started crying.

The sirens blared louder. J.R. scowled and threw the shard at my feet.

"Don't think this is over," he snarled as he stormed to the back door. "You know I'll be back. And next time I won't be empty handed." He yanked the door open and ran off into the night.

Aunt Sophie rushed to the door and locked it behind him. "Thank you, Jesus." She gathered Uncle Ron and her children into a big embrace and then squeezed my sisters and me tight.

When she released us, my shoulders sagged. We had only delayed the inevitable. Safety in numbers only worked if weapons weren't involved. If the police didn't put J.R. back in jail, none of us would ever be safe again.

The sirens came to an abrupt stop, followed by pounding on the front door. "It's the police."

Uncle Ron hustled to let them in.

"We received a call about a disturbance. Is everyone okay?"

"J.R. Chambers just slipped out the back. He was threatenin' my family, tryin' to take the kids," Uncle Ron explained.

The policeman nodded. "I'll place an officer at the door and call for backup. What was he driving?"

"I'm not sure. He ran out the back door, but he had to have a way of gettin' here," said Uncle Ron.

"He drives a beat up dark green Ford 150 truck," I said. "But I don't know if that was how he got here. He didn't have any guns with him, and his truck usually has his huntin' rifles in the back."

"I'll call it in. You folks sit tight. We'll find him."

"Thanks, officer," said Aunt Sophie.

I sank into the couch. Josie and Missy sat on either side of me, pressed up close. Their scrawny legs were shaking, so I wrapped an arm around each of them and held them tight. We could feel the security of the last few days dissipate. I stubbornly fought to hang on.

"J.R.'s only been out this way a few times," I told them. "He don't know it like he does our woods back home. There's a chance the police might catch him."

"That's right," agreed Aunt Sophie. She sat at our feet. "Don't worry. J.R. may be slippery, but he's only one man. They have lots of police out searchin'. Once they catch him, they'll lock him up tight."

Darnell peeked out the back window. "There's a police man   standin'   beside   the   door."

60

DeMarcus ran to the front door. "There's one by this door, too."

"See?" Aunt Sophie squeezed the girl's hands. "We're protected, and soon they'll catch J.R. No need to worry."

Missy looked up at me, her gray eyes lined with tears. "I should've kept my mouth shut, huh, JaDon? I shouldn't have spilled our secrets to the doctors and police. J.R. warned us to keep quiet. He wouldn't be so mad at us if I had done what he said."

Would that have been better? I didn't know. There was no going back now. "He would've found something else to be mad about. It'll be okay."

I heard myself say the words, but did I believe them? J.R. wasn't the forgiving type. If he beat us over leaving the milk out of the refrigerator, what would he do for us refusing to follow him out the door? He could always count on us following his commands and covering for him when he beat us. How many times had I lied about the cause of my black eyes and split lips? I'd even lied about the bruises on my sisters, and what horrible kind of person could do that? He knew I'd keep his secrets.

Until now. Now all he knew was we'd started talking. He had secrets bigger than our beatings. I knew things he couldn't let the police hear. He couldn't afford to let me keep talking. If he wasn't caught soon, we were in a heap of trouble.

CHAPTER 9
MOVIE MARATHON

The night crept by at an agonizingly slow pace. My sisters huddled close to my side. Their smiles from mere hours ago were stomped out. I desperately hoped J.R. would be caught quickly, before they fully retreated back into their empty shells. They begged for the lights to be left on. The rest of us were eager to oblige. None of us wanted additional shadows. It was hours before they could unwind enough for their eyelids to grow heavy, but they finally curled into a ball together on the couch, resting their heads on my lap. Memories paraded through my mind of the many times we had slept like this hidden in the hallway behind the movable slab of drywall.

Aunt Sophie tucked her patchwork quilt around all of us and prayed: "Please protect these children, Father. Wrap this whole house in your safe arms." She grabbed an extra blanket and settled into the boy's room.

Uncle Ron leaned back in the recliner with a baseball bat rested across his lap. The cops had assured us they would keep surveillance over our house all night, but I still couldn't find sleep. Every gust of wind seemed to make the house creek, sounding like footprints across squeaky floors. In my mind, shadows transformed from swaying trees to a man hiding outside.

The minutes felt like hours as I waited for news of J.R.'s capture. Every time my eyes closed and I began to drift to sleep, I saw his cold blue eyes glaring at me. I'd feel his fists and hear the moaning from the hallway. I'd wake up with a start and struggle to stay awake. My mind fought to remain positive. Maybe the police caught him, but just didn't want to wake us up until morning to let us know. I was afraid to let my guard down. Not knowing we were safe meant not sleeping.

I was grateful when soft light filtered through the windows and birds began to chirp. The girls snuggled deeper onto the couch, releasing my leg. I stretched my aching calf muscles, being careful not to wake them.

Uncle Ron was still sprawled out on the recliner, his legs elevated on the foot rest. I studied his dark face. His mouth sagged open while he snored, revealing a capped silver tooth nestled among the white ones. His nose was wide and flat and two wrinkles creased his forehead. He wasn't a particularly handsome man, but I could see why my aunt loved him. He was steady and calm, even when he was angry. His hands were used to work and protect instead of to inflict pain. While staining the fence, I could not help but feel jealous as my cousins talked about playing basketball and fishing with their father. What would our lives have been like if Mama had married a man like Uncle Ron instead of J.R.?

The side table was upright once more. I picked up one of the photos that now had cracked glass due to J.R.'s tirade the night before. It was our family picture, taken several years before Mama left. Josie clung to Mama's skirt. The crack divided Mama's image in half, but I could still see her holding Missy as a toddler in her arms. A younger version of myself stood in front of J.R. His hands were planted firmly on my shoulders. My hair was cut close to my scalp even then.

"No boy of mine is goin' to have an afro," J.R. used to say.

Aunt Sophie was right. I *did* look like Mama, except with lighter skin. Her eyes were a warm, dark brown fringed with long black lashes. She had high cheek bones like me, with a small nose and full lips. Her teeth were exposed in a wide smile that seemed forced. None of our smiles were convincing, even back then.

J.R. looked tall and handsome. He had broad shoulders and muscular arms, a strong chin and those ice blue eyes. These days he had developed a bit of a beer belly, but he still made ladies turn to stare when he walked into a room. If only his insides weren't so repulsive.

Aunt Sophie shuffled into the living room rubbing her eyes and adjusting her turquoise floral turban. I quickly returned the photo to the table.

"Did you get any sleep?" she asked.

"Not much."

"I was afraid of that. I tossed and turned all night, too. Of course, some of it could have been that I was restin' on somebody's size fourteen shoe." She rubbed my shoulder. "Can I fix you some eggs and grits for breakfast?"

"Yes, please."

She continued on to the kitchen and began scooping coffee grounds into a filter and cracking eggs. A knock on the door made us both jump. Uncle Ron woke suddenly and grabbed the bat. My heart started pounding, though my mind doubted J.R. would knock at this stage of his game.

Aunt Sophie peeked through the curtains. "It's okay. It's an officer." She opened the door.

"I'm sorry to bother you, Ma'am. I just wanted to let you know I received a call from the station."

Uncle Ron immediately walked to the door. "Did they catch him?"

"No, sir. I'm afraid they didn't. They wanted you to know they're still searching. If at all possible, we'd like for your family to remain indoors for a little longer. Several officers and I will alternate shifts to watch your house."

My heart sank. Daylight hadn't ended our nightmare.

Aunt Sophie's shoulders sagged. "Thanks, officer." She studied his wrinkled uniform. "Have you been on duty long?"

"Yes, Ma'am."

"Can I give you some breakfast?"

"I would appreciate that, but I have to keep an eye on your house."

"Then I'll give you a plate of food and cup of coffee to take to your car."

"Thank you. That's mighty kind of you."

Aunt Sophie disappeared into the kitchen and returned moments later with a plate full of eggs and grits and a steaming cup of coffee.

"I appreciate this," the officer said.

"We appreciate you keeping an eye out for J.R." said Uncle Ron. "Let us know when he's found." He closed and bolted the door behind the officer.

Aunt Sophie slipped into her husband's arms. "That man...How much more pain does he have to heap on his kids?"

Uncle Ron held her close. "It'll all work out. He can't stay hidden forever."

Josie looked up at me, her lips quivering. "Did they say J.R.'s still out there?"

I hadn't realized she was awake. "Yes. He still hasn't been caught. But I'm guessin' he'll eventually go home and they'll grab him."

Missy held her sister's hand. "And this time they'll lock him up. Right?"

"Right." I tried to smile for her.

"And throw away the key."

"And throw away the key." I hoped.

We were all very quiet at breakfast.

Finally Darnell said, "So...we can't go fishing?"

"Not today," said Uncle Ron.

"No go karts?"

"No."

"Basketball?"

"No."

"What else is there to do?" asked Desmond.

"You could watch movies, or play video games, or text your friends," Uncle Ron suggested. "Just don't tell them details about *why* you're stuck inside."

"I can't believe you just said that," DeMarcus turned to me. "I don't think I've ever heard them words from my parents."

"Movie marathon, here we come," said Darnell.

Aunt Sophie shrugged. "Might as well. It'll be a good distraction. I know we just ate breakfast, but is anybody up for popcorn?"

We camped in front of the TV for most of the day. Everyone took turns choosing a movie. That was a new concept. J.R. ruled the remote whenever he was home. My cousins had a whole collection of horror movies, but we all avoided those. No need to add to our fears.

Missy and Josie snuggled up to Aunt Sophie, soaking in her obvious adoration for them. She braided and twisted

66

and rebraided their hair. I was glad. I tried brushing their hair right after Mama disappeared. Evidently I was too rough, because it got so they would hide whenever I grabbed a brush or comb. Eventually they learned to do each other's hair, but there were lots of days where they went to school looking like they had been electrified. Too bad girls didn't just shave their heads, too.

By evening, I was actually tired of watching movies. I could see why adults typically didn't allow extended periods of vegetating in front of the TV. I felt sluggish and had a crick in my neck. We settled in to our original sleeping places, with the exception of Uncle Ron, who resumed his post on the recliner holding the baseball bat.

The phone rang. Uncle Ron struggled to his feet and grabbed the phone. "Yes? You're kiddin' me. Okay. We'll be waitin'. Thanks."

Aunt Sophie poked her head out of the bedroom door. "Anythin'?"

He shook his head. "Not yet. They're still searchin'."

Missy clutched her rag baby to her chest. I noticed Josie even held her doll now. They huddled under their blanket on the air mattress. I was much more comfortable with the couch to myself, but now that my thoughts weren't distracted with movie story lines, my brain allowed thoughts of our predicament to seep back in. There was still no sign of J.R. Was I really that surprised? Sometimes he would stay out in the woods for days while he hunted. I needed a paper signed once while he was gone, and walked right past him three times before he hissed at me to stop stomping around scaring the animals away.

Maybe J.R. would decide to never come back. I tossed that thought around for a while, seeing how it would play out. No. I didn't want to have to look over my shoulder every day, wondering if he was in the shadows ready to pounce. The police needed to find him or we would never truly be free.

Why had J.R.'s buddies given him money to post bail? Was it just so he could keep making whiskey? Was it a gift or a loan? I knew his drinking buddies, and I didn't consider them the generous type.

Was it my fault that bail was even an option? If I had told the police everything I knew, would the judge have kept him locked up? If they found him again, it might be time to tell everything. I had blocked out the details, but my journal would explain it all. My journal even had directions to the evidence. J.R. couldn't maneuver his way out if *I* started talking. I knew much more than the girls. Unfortunately, J.R. knew my silence was vital. He had to convince me to be quiet—by any means necessary.

CHAPTER 10

SOAKED THROUGH

The next morning I woke up to a ringing telephone. After failing to decipher the fragments of Aunt Sophie's phone conversation, I stretched and ran a tongue over my teeth. I brushed them last night, but there were still bits of popcorn kernels stuck in the back.

Uncle Ron and the girls were already sitting at the table. They motioned for me to join them. A cast iron skillet sat on two checkered hot pads in the center of the table. It was filled with sausage gravy. Golden biscuits were piled in a basket next to it and a bowl of sliced apples dusted in cinnamon sugar sat on the opposite end of the table.

"Help yourself," Uncle Ron whispered.

Darnell stumbled out his bedroom door. "What's for breakfast?" he blurted.

"Shhhh." Uncle Ron pointed to Aunt Sophie talking on the phone.

Desmond and DeMarcus joined us at the table and quickly filled their plates. I broke apart a biscuit and scooped gravy over it until none of the plate remained visible.

Aunt Sophie hung up the phone and dropped to her chair. We all looked at her expectantly.

"Mr. Costas was callin' to give us an update. They still haven't found J.R. They think he left town, so they've sent his photo to police stations all over…"

"Good," said Uncle Ron.

"…and called off the search."

I looked up in alarm. "What?"

"They'll still keep an officer here and at his house, but they don't feel like they can justify so many officers searchin' at this point. He hasn't been back to his place yet. They confiscated all of his guns and knives, so at least he shouldn't be armed. They think he's long gone. The police said we could go outside now, but they would like us to stay in the backyard for one more day, just to be safe." She turned to Uncle Ron. "They said you could go to work if you need to."

"Maybe tomorrow. I'd like to be here just in case."

She nodded.

"So…how about a game of basketball?" Desmond suggested.

"Yeah. Guys against girls," said Darnell.

"I don't know if we feel much like playin' right now," I said.

"Oh, come on," said Desmond. "We've been cooped up for too long. If we stay inside and sit around we're just goin' ta think about the hard times we're in. I'd rather think about a basketball than Uncle J.R."

I sat for a moment thinking it over. He was probably right. I looked at my sisters, afraid that the comfort they felt in this home had dissipated with J.R.'s arrival. Were we back to where we had started? I turned to the girls. "What do you think? Are you up to it?"

My sisters looked at each other hesitantly, and then nodded.

Aunt Sophie hugged them. "Good. I'm ready to get out of the house, too. I don't know about these teams though. Five boys against three of us girls? That don't seem fair."

"Pa can be on your team, too. That evens it up," said Desmond.

"That still won't make things even," I said. "My sisters never play."

Missy put her hands on her hips. "We play at school during gym and recess. We can beat you any day."

I smirked, glad her spunk hadn't been stamped out. "Maybe if *both* of my arms were in slings."

"How about we all finish breakfast and then we'll find out," said Aunt Sophie.

Darnell stabbed half a biscuit on his fork, swirled it in gravy, and jammed it into his mouth. "It's so on," he said while chewing.

Minutes later, dishes were stacked in the sink and everyone was in the backyard battling over the ball in their pajamas. My cousins and I quickly took the lead.

"This is too easy," Darnell jeered.

Uncle Ron threw the ball over his head. The ball swished into the basket. "Oh, really? We're just warming up."

"Lucky shot," Darnell retorted.

Missy stole the ball from DeMarcus and threw it to Aunt Sophie. She started dribbling the ball towards me. I awkwardly stepped out of the way. She sailed past me and shot the ball. Two more points.

My jaw dropped.

"Why'd you let her through?" Desmond demanded.

"I…"

"You didn't think I could make a basket, did you?" Aunt Sophie smiled.

"Well, I…"

"You didn't feel comfortable blocking an old lady?" she continued.

71

"I don't think of you as old it's just that you're…"

"I'm sick so you didn't want to risk hurting me?" she finished.

Heat rushed to my face. "I guess."

She gave me a hug. "That's sweet, but don't worry. I can take it."

Darnell grinned. "Yeah. She fouls us all of the time. Don't let that turban throw you off. She's actually really good at basketball—even with cancer."

We continued playing until the boys won two out of three games. By that time the sun was climbing and we were sweating.

"How about some iced tea?" asked Aunt Sophie. She slipped inside while the rest of us sprawled out on lawn chairs.

A few minutes later, she poked her head out the sliding glass door. "Girls, can you help me carry the tea?"

Missy and Josie hauled themselves up and joined her inside. I closed my eyes and relaxed. I was sore and tired from our game, but it felt good to play with family. I soaked in my rare feeling of contentment. So J.R. hadn't ruined our time here after all. Maybe the cops had scared him enough that he was gone for good. I dared to imagine what it would be like to stay. It would be a small taste of heaven to be part of a family that enjoyed being together and didn't have to constantly be on guard.

A cold, wet blast on my neck sent a shiver down my back. I spun around. Missy grinned at me, holding a squirt gun in her hands. Josie and Aunt Sophie were armed as well, and began shooting Uncle Ron and my cousins. I flipped my lawn chair over for protection from the icy shots.

My sisters whispered to each other, pointing and devising a plan. Darnell took advantage of their lack of focus

72

and grabbed Josie's gun. Desmond grabbed Missy's gun and soon they were chasing the girls around the lawn. Aunt Sophie kept shooting Uncle Ron until he started to come after her. Laughing, she ducked inside and closed the door.

By the time she reappeared, the remaining squirt guns were empty and everyone had wet splotches on their pajamas. She innocently began handing out glasses of iced tea as if nothing had happened.

"Thanks, *dear*," said Uncle Ron.

"You're quite welcome."

She winked as she handed me my iced tea. "Feel cooler now?"

"Much."

"Good." She sat down. "Do you guys remember runnin' through the sprinklers when you were little?"

The girls shook their heads. I replayed fuzzy memories of us jumping up and down in the spraying water while Mama and Aunt Sophie laughed.

"Whenever it would get too hot, you boys would beg for the sprinklers. The girls would sometimes join in. Even Missy, until her diaper got soaked."

"Could we do that again?" asked Missy.

"You bet," said Aunt Sophie. She got up and dug through a large plastic bin by the house. Victorious, she pulled out a faded yellow sprinkler and attached it to a green hose that was already snaking around the yard. She cranked on the water. "Whenever you're ready."

Missy held her breath and dashed through the spraying water. Josie watched her for a few minutes, a smile growing on her face.

Her sister ran back and grabbed her hand. "Come on, Josie. It's fun!" She pulled her close to the sprinkler.

Soon they were both drenched and giggling.

"Do you boys want to join in?" asked Uncle Ron.

"Nah. We're too old for that kind of thing," said DeMarcus.

"Speak for yourself." Darnell dashed into the water.

Desmond shrugged and joined him. I looked expectantly at DeMarcus.

"Oh, all right," he said.

Aunt Sophie hustled inside and tossed me a plastic bag. I pulled off my sling, stuck my arm in the bag, and joined them in the sprinkler. The water was freezing at first, but soon felt good as we took turns dashing through the spray. The grass grew water-logged and slippery, only making running on it more entertaining. We cheered for the craziest tumbles through the water. My cousins sputtered and shook their soaked hair as they laughed.

We finally wore out and flopped on the grass. Uncle Ron turned off the sprinkler and Aunt Sophie handed each of us a soft blue towel. I pressed my face into it, inhaling the scent of citrus laundry detergent and wiping my face dry.

Aunt Sophie began walking through the garden, pushing aside the zucchini plants that crawled over the stepping stones. She plucked five ripe tomatoes off the vines that emerged from wire tomato cages and headed to the back door. "Now that you're soppin' wet, all of you might as well change out of your pajamas. I'll open the washer door and you can throw them inside."

By the time we were all in dry clothes and the washing machine was sloshing its contents in soapy water, Aunt Sophie had pasta tossed with tomatoes and cheese on each of our plates at the table.

Once we were all seated, Uncle Ron prayed, "Thank you, Lord, for your protection and for the chance to enjoy time as a family. Bless this food to our bodies. Amen."

I stabbed the tomatoes and pasta on my fork. Tomato juice trickled down my arms. I debated between licking it off and dabbing it with my napkin. I looked around the table. Darnell was licking juice off his arm so I followed his lead. Our plates were soon empty.

We all helped clear the table while Aunt Sophie quickly filled the dishwasher. Josie washed the table with a green cloth, smiling as she worked. Relief washed over me. She seemed to have recovered from our scare.

"How about a game of spoons?" suggested Uncle Ron.

We gathered back around the table as he quickly explained the rules of the card game. After the second round, he leaned back in his chair. "I may never go back to work again. Stayin' home with all of you is much better than hammerin' nails."

Aunt Sophie patted his arm. "We love havin' you home, but we also love bein' able to buy food."

He shuffled the cards again. "I guess earnin' money does help."

We played three more rounds before hearing a knock at the door. Aunt Sophie inhaled quickly. "It's probably just one of the cops, right?"

The hair prickled at the back of my neck. I tried to control my racing thoughts. J.R. wouldn't come in broad daylight. If he tried, the police would grab him before he even reached the front steps.

Uncle Ron got up slowly and walked to the door. He looked out the window and his shoulders visibly relaxed. "It's Mr. Costas." He opened the door.

"I'm sorry to barge in without calling," Mr. Costas said. "I just got a call from the police station. I'm afraid I have bad news."

CHAPTER 11
READ THE NOTE

"What is it?" asked Uncle Ron. "What's the bad news?"

Aunt Sophie rushed to his side. "Come in, Mr. Costas. Have a seat. Can I get you some iced tea?"

"Don't go to any trouble for me."

"It isn't trouble at all. Now sit."

Mr. Costas sat in a chair at the kitchen table and adjusted his glasses. "We may be short on time, so I'm going to have to get right to the point."

"Good," said Uncle Ron.

The rest of us gathered around the table.

"I told you earlier that the police confiscated all of J.R.'s guns and knives. It turns out they may have missed a few. We found the truck you described, JaDon. It was deserted on the side of the road about five miles away. But you said it was loaded with most of J.R.'s hunting rifles and handguns, correct?"

"Yes." My stomach began to churn. "Let me guess. It was empty."

"Almost." Mr. Costas sighed. "The guns were gone, but a note was left on the driver's seat."

"Can we see it?" asked Uncle Ron.

"The police had to keep the original for evidence, but I took a picture of it."

"Read it." I started rubbing my head in nervous anticipation.

"I'm not sure you want everyone to hear it." The social worker nodded at Missy and Josie.

"We need to know, too," said Josie.

Mr. Costas looked at Aunt Sophie. She closed her eyes and nodded. He read, "Cops, I know you got my kids at Sophie's place. I seen the cop there, but know the cop ain't seen me. If I don't want to be seen, I won't be seen. Ask my boy. Return my kids to this truck by Tuesday and I won't bother nobody. Otherwise, I'll take them my way, and I don't care none who gets hurt. Don't try nothing stupid, cuz I'll be watching."

"That low down…" Uncle Ron began.

Aunt Sophie nudged him. "So what do we do now?"

"You're going to have to split up. And quickly, I'm afraid."

"What?" Uncle Ron's fists tightened. "What do you mean, split up?"

"The police will be here any minute to offer more protection while you pack. We have two vans from social services coming soon. Sophie and Ron, you'll go with your boys in one vehicle. I'll go with JaDon, Missy, and Josie in another vehicle. Both vans will be identical and will have shaded windows. We'll drive in opposite directions. If J.R.'s watching, he won't be able to follow both groups."

"But he'll see who's getting in each van, and know to follow ours," I said.

"Not if we load up in your garage with the garage door closed." He turned to Uncle Ron. "I'll need you to pull out your car so the garage is empty."

"And then what?" asked Aunt Sophie. "We drive around for a while and then meet up some place?"

"I'm afraid not. At least not for now."

Josie and Missy began whimpering.

"Why not? When will we be with them again?" Aunt Sophie pulled the girls and me closer.

"We need you in separate locations until we catch J.R. It sounds like he's quite the hunter, so we want to slow him down as much as possible. He needs more than one trail to follow. The police are probably just being extra careful. I can't imagine it taking long to catch him if he follows in his truck. We already have cops watching it."

"Then he won't use the truck," I said. "He's too smart."

"But you don't have any other vehicle, right?" asked Mr. Costas.

My voice dragged with dread. "No. But it doesn't matter. J.R. will figure out something else."

"Well, then the plan really *is* necessary. You should start packing."

"Pack for how long?" asked Darnell.

"A few weeks. You'll be able to wash clothes if it takes longer than that." Mr. Costas turned to me. "You and the girls should pack everything. Do you still have your bags?"

"Yeah." I looked at him for reassurance, but he was looking at the girls, and then my cousins, then my aunt. Why was he avoiding eye contact? Was he telling us everything? I didn't voice my concern, because Josie and Missy were already shaking.

Some of our clothes and shoes were sprawled out around the living room, but we quickly stuffed them back into our bags. Josie handed each of us our new toothbrushes and checked the bathroom for straggling brushes and combs. Missy and I started folding blankets while we waited for our cousins to finish packing.

Mr. Costas looked out the front window. "The extra police and vans are here. I know this was sudden, but we need to get going."

Uncle Ron backed his car out of the garage, and the two vans pulled in. The police closed the garage door and opened the van doors. My cousins started loading their suitcases.

Aunt Sophie hugged Missy. "You got your rag baby?

Missy nodded. A tear trickled down her cheek.

"Now, now." Aunt Sophie wiped the tear away with her thumb. "We'll get through this, sweet child. You just hang on to your doll and your big brother and sister. It sounds like we'll be back together soon."

She turned to Josie and drew her into the hug. "They'll catch him and then this will all be over. You can do this, beautiful girl." Josie clung to her side, her eyes clenched tight.

Mr. Costas picked up their trash bags, and guided the two frightened girls into the van. I followed behind, hauling my own bag.

Aunt Sophie squeezed my arm, stopping me. "Be strong, JaDon. Those little girls are blessed to have you supportin' them. I don't know what's down the road, but I know God's watchin' over us and will see us through. I love all of you like you was my own."

My eyes filled with tears, but I refused to let them fall. I wanted to tell her I loved her too, but all I could choke out was, "Thanks."

Mr. Costas and a police officer sat in the front seats of the van. Josie and Missy strapped themselves into the middle seats and I settled into the back.

The officer called his partner in the other van. "Are we good to go?"

"Yes. Move on out."

The officer hit the garage remote control, and started backing our van into the driveway. I craned my neck, searching for J.R. He was nowhere to be found. I wasn't surprised. The old hickory tree waved its branches in the wind. The girls and I hadn't even climbed it yet. I pictured Mama at the tree's trunk, watching us leave. We drove to the end of the street and turned left. The other van turned right. Missy waved at them over and over, but I knew they couldn't see us through the shaded windows.

"Can you tell us where we're going now that we're out of the house?" I asked.

Mr. Costas and the police officer looked at each other.

Mr. Costas turned slightly. "We'll stop for dinner when we're close to the border."

"The border? The border of what?"

"The state border. We need to get out of Arkansas for now."

"So what state are we goin' to?" I asked, trying to keep my voice steady.

"Missouri."

"We don't know anyone in Missouri," I stated. "Where are we going to stay?"

Mr. Costas sighed. "That's all I can tell you for now. But don't worry. We've got it all worked out, and it shouldn't be for very long."

We sat in silence, each of us staring out a window. I figured I should say something to comfort the girls, but I couldn't think of anything. My mind was still trying to absorb the idea that Aunt Sophie's home was no longer safe. What would happen if J.R. wasn't caught soon? How long would we all be forced to stay away? Guilt began to nibble on me. Our aunt, uncle, and cousins were kicked out of their own home, thanks to us. If we hadn't shown up on their door step, they would probably still be sitting at their table playing another round of spoons. Now none of us knew where we were headed or for how long.

Missy suddenly turned around in her seat. "What about Mop? He's still in the back yard! What if J.R. hurts him?"

"I'm sure Mop's fine. Why would J.R. want to hurt the dog?" I asked. "He just wants us back."

"But he might hold him ransom, or threaten to hurt him so we give up." Missy said.

"I think he knows that no one would give in for that trade," I said.

"What if we're gone more than a day?" asked Josie. "Who will feed him and make sure he has water?"

Mr. Costas turned around. "Do you know where they keep the dog food?"

"Yes." Josie answered. "There's a big bag just inside the garage door. Mop's food and water dish is right beside his dog house in the back yard."

The officer looked in the rearview mirror and smiled. "I'll call the officer watching the house and make sure the dog gets fed each day."

Josie exhaled.

Missy leaned back in her seat. "Thanks, officer."

"No problem."

She popped back up. "And if he finds a ransom note for Mop, he'll let us know, right?"

"Right."

"And protect Mop if J.R. gets any crazy ideas. Right?"

"Yes."

Missy slumped back in her seat. "Good."

Silence returned. I leaned my head on the back seat and closed my eyes. I hoped J.R. would lose patience and follow us with his old truck. Then the police could catch him and we could stop the van and return to Uncle Ron and Aunt Sophie's house. I shook my head. The odds of that happening were slim. J.R. could wait for the perfect shot on a buck for hours. This could be a very long night.

"Are you guys getting hungry?" Mr. Costas asked at last.

"Yes," each of us answered.

"There's a McDonald's sign. Does that sound okay? We can't exactly stop at a sit down restaurant."

"That works," I said.

"What would you like to order?"

I couldn't remember the last time we had been to McDonald's. I had to rack my brain to remember the menu. "A hamburger and fries?"

"How about you girls?"

"The same," said Josie.

Missy nodded. "Me too."

The officer flipped his turn signal and we took the exit off the interstate. He pulled into the parking lot, and turned around to face us. "Here's the deal. Our goal is not to be noticed. We'll head straight to the bathrooms while Mr. Costas orders the food. I'll stand right outside the bathroom doors. Then we walk calmly back to the van. Don't talk to anyone or give eye contact. Got it?"

We nodded.

We were in and out of the restaurant within minutes and back on the road. I took a bite of my sandwich. It failed to compare to Aunt Sophie's food, but it was still much better than what I was used to eating. The fries were slightly crisp and greasy, just the way I liked them. I licked my fingers after the last fry was gone.

The girls and I dozed on and off over the next few hours. I was ready to be out of the van and into a bed. "Are we almost there?" I finally asked.

"We're getting close," Mr. Costas answered.

"Are we staying in a hotel or at someone's house or what?" I asked.

"At someone's house."

"Is it someone you know?"

"Not personally, no." Mr. Costas began drumming his fingers on his leg. "It's a family approved by the state. They do foster care."

I sat up. "Foster care? I thought we were just going somewhere for a few days."

"You are," our social worker quickly answered. "We just thought this route might be best since we don't know an exact length of time until we get this whole situation settled."

"Aren't you staying with us?" asked Josie. "You're not just dropping us off, are you?"

"We'll stay until you're settled in. Then we're driving back to Arkansas. We don't want the vans to give away your location in case J.R. figures out the route we took."

"So where are Aunt Sophie, Uncle Ron, Desmond, Darnell, and DeMarcus staying?" I asked. "They're not staying with a foster family. Right?"

"Right."

"Are they in Missouri, too?"

"No."

"Where are they?"

"It's better if you don't have all of the information. We won't be telling them where you are either. It's safer this way." Mr. Costas sighed. "I'm sorry, JaDon. I know this is hard. We're just trying to keep all of you safe."

"I know." I looked out the window, trying to appear calm for my sisters. We were powerless once again. It felt like we were tossed back in the middle of a big lake, in so deep our feet couldn't touch the bottom. There were promises of a shore we could eventually swim to, but nothing was in sight.

The sun began to sink down the sky. I was able to watch it directly, due to the shaded windows. We finally turned into a gravel driveway and pulled up to a small tan house. Large trees swayed in the breeze. The nearest house was a considerable distance down the street.

"Here we are," said Mr. Costas.

"Stay in the van until I make sure the couple is home and that it's safe," said the officer.

Missy unbuckled and crawled into the back seat with me. "We'll be okay, right, JaDon?"

I patted her bony knee. "Of course. The cop will check it out, and then we'll stick together."

"Even while we sleep? They won't put us all in separate rooms, will they?" Missy started chewing her fingernails. She had stopped doing that a few days ago.

"If they do, I'll come in to your room and sleep on the floor."

"Me, too," said Josie.

The officer walked around the van and opened the back. He grabbed a garbage bag in each arm. "It's clear. You can come out."

Mr. Costas opened the side door. We all slid out and began stretching. The officer started walking up the cement steps. Missy grabbed my right hand and Josie held onto my sling as we followed.

Mr. Costas put his hand on my shoulder. "Actually, JaDon, can you go back into the van?"

"Why?"

He rubbed the back of his neck. "I'm afraid *you* won't be staying here."

CHAPTER 12
JUST TEMPORARY

I turned slowly and stared at his face in disbelief. "What?!"

Mr. Costas sighed. "We thought it would be safer if the girls stayed here and we took you a little further down the road. If we…"

"No."

"Wait. Just hear me out…"

"We're not splitting up."

Missy wrapped her arms around my waist. "We won't leave him."

"Not ever," Josie added as she twisted her fingers tighter on my sling.

"Now hang on," said Mr. Costas. "I know this is hard, but it's just temporary. It'll be harder for J.R. to trace you if you split up."

We climbed back into the van, stubbornly clinging to each other.

Mr. Costas continued. "You always say what a good hunter he is. He's proven you right. We hoped he'd reveal himself on the drive, but he didn't. Don't you think he would have a better chance of tracking two girls and a boy who were all placed into the same home? From what we've seen, he's particularly intent on finding you, JaDon. We need to get you away from your sisters. You can blend in easier on your own."

86

"Blend in? How long are we talking? Does it matter how much we blend in if we're only going to be hiding a few days?" My heart was beating fast.

"I *hope* it's only for a few days. That's what we're all hoping. But we honestly don't know. We need to be prepared...for the worst."

"But it's my job to protect my sisters. How can I do that if you split us up?"

"You can protect them more by being in a separate house. For now, at least." Mr. Costas finally looked me in the eye. "I'll check in on them and make sure they're okay. You have my word."

I looked down at my sisters. Tears were streaming from their ghost eyes down their haunted faces. I couldn't lose them. I racked my brain for a solution. Mr. Costas and the cops were the only ones with a plan. I swallowed my sadness. "Maybe he's right," I finally said.

"No, he's not," cried Missy. "He's wrong. We stick together. Always!"

Josie shook her head, sobbing. "Don't let them split us up."

"It's just for now," Mr. Costas repeated.

The officer returned to our side. "The family is waiting for you girls, and we need to get going. The longer the van stays here, the more likely J.R. can figure out where you are."

My brain was whirling. I knew J.R. wouldn't stop looking until he found me. I knew far more about him than his abuse and whiskey brewing. The girls didn't know everything. Maybe he would leave them alone if they weren't with me. Maybe they really were safer on their own until J.R. was caught. My heart was aching. I'd never lived anywhere without them.

"I'll go," I said at last.

"What? You can't leave us!" Missy exclaimed.

"Can I talk to my sisters alone?" I asked.

Mr. Costas nodded. He and the officer walked closer to the house. We huddled in the van.

"Listen. I know this feels all wrong, but they have a point. J.R. is more intent on finding me. There's stuff that J.R. doesn't want me to tell. Things you don't even know…"

"Like what?" whispered Josie. "You can tell us."

"Not without putting you in more danger. If I'm away from you he might leave you alone. We can be back together as soon as he's caught."

"But what if they don't catch him right away?" Josie squeezed my arm. Her hands were clammy and shaking.

"Then I'll find a way to come back to you."

"You promise?" asked Missy. Her bottom lip quivered.

"Yes. One way or another we'll be back together soon."

Mr. Costas walked back to the van. "I'm sorry, kids, but we have to get you inside."

I walked the girls to the steps, biting the inside of my cheek so I wouldn't cry. The girls wrapped their arms around me and squeezed tight. They were both sobbing. I finally untangled their arms. "I'll see you soon," I promised again.

Josie looked me into the eye. "No matter what."

I nodded. "No matter what."

The officer led me back into the van while Mr. Costas knocked on the door and escorted the girls inside. My eyes clung to them until the door closed. I took a shuddering breath as my heart shrank in my chest.

As soon as Mr. Costas climbed back into the van, we backed out of the gravel driveway and resumed our journey. I looked at the empty seats and closed my eyes.

"I'm sorry, JaDon," Mr. Costas said.

I didn't reply. We were silent for over two hours before finally stopping in front of another house. Mr. Costas opened the van door. I stepped out into blackness. We gathered my trash bag of belongings and walked to the front door, while the officer searched the front yard. A porch light switched on, revealing a red and brown brick exterior.

"Are you ready?" asked Mr. Costas.

I shrugged. I had no words left in me.

He knocked on the glass storm door. A minute later, a thin woman with short brown hair and wire-rimmed glasses poked her head through. "Hello. Is this JaDon?"

Mr. Costas extended his hand. "Yes, it is. I'm Mr. Costas, his social worker."

She shook his hand. "Michelle Winters. Please come in." She stepped inside. "Everyone else is asleep, so I'd appreciate it if we could talk quietly. And remove your shoes, if you don't mind."

"Of course. We're sorry it's a little later than we anticipated," Mr. Costas said as he slipped off his shoes. "If you will show JaDon where to sleep, I'll let you get back to bed."

"Right this way." She turned and walked up a half flight of narrow stairs. "You'll be staying in the guest room, which is this first door on the left."

I walked inside the room and dropped my trash bag on the clean cream carpet. A full-sized bed covered in a light blue quilt lined one wall. A small dresser and mirror of light ash wood pressed against the other wall, next to a closet with sliding doors.

"Do you want to take a shower now?" she asked.

"It can wait until morning," I said. "I don't want to keep you up."

She pursed her lips. "Actually, I can barely hear the shower, so it's fine. You probably feel dirty from your drive."

I looked at Mr. Costas and raised one eyebrow. He gave a slight nod.

"Oh. Well, that would be great. Thank you."

She pointed to the bathroom across the hall. "There are towels on the counter, and shampoo and soap in the shower stall in case you don't have your own."

"Thanks, ma'am."

"All right then. Can I see you to the door?" she asked Mr. Costas.

"Yes. Thank you." He turned to me and patted my good arm. "I'll keep you posted, JaDon."

As soon as they left the room, I sank onto the wrinkle-free bed. The white walls were bare except for a round clock and an 8 X 10 framed photo of a clear mountain stream. I sniffed the floral room deodorizer. It was so strong, I had to rub my nose to keep from sneezing. My eyes were heavy and I just wanted to crawl under the covers and forget this evening had ever happened. It was hard to believe that just this morning, I was enjoying life with my extended family, playing basketball and spoons. Now I didn't even have my sisters.

Mrs. Winters poked her head through the doorway. "Oh. Well, hello. I thought maybe you would already be in the shower. Feel free to head to the bathroom. Is there anything else you need?"

"No, thanks."

"Okay then. I'll see you in the morning."

Convinced a shower was required, I dug through my plastic bag until I found a t-shirt and pajama pants, and trudged to the bathroom. A spotless mirror covered one wall above the white sink and countertop. I grabbed a white washcloth and pulled aside the floral shower curtain. I was almost afraid to step in the tub. It was a gleaming white, without a stray hair or smudge. How could anyone keep a house this clean?

After a quick shower, I dressed and slipped under the blue covers. The pillow was starched and stiff, and smelled like more wildflowers. I punched the pillow a few times to soften it up and let my eyes sink shut.

In my dreams, I found myself shaking in the passenger's seat of a strange car, covered in blood. J.R. was behind the steering wheel tearing down a gravel road.

"This is what happens when you open yer big mouth," he said. "Now get out."

I stumbled from the car and sat on a pile of rocks by the lake. A sticker bush poked my back, but I didn't care. I deserved pain. The car rolled into the water and began to sink. I wiped a tear quickly, hoping he wouldn't notice.

"You're crying?" J.R. spat on the ground in disgust. "How'd I ever get me such a baby? Need me to wipe away those girly tears?" He raised his hand to strike me.

I jolted awake. When I realized where I was, I let tears soak my pillow until I fell back asleep.

The next morning I woke up to whispers. I wasn't ready to be friendly, so I rolled over and pretended I was still asleep.

"Mother didn't tell us he was black."

"But he's not *really* black. He's more a milk chocolate color, or like one of those fancy frappacino drinks mother likes."

"Do you suppose he's nice?"

"It's hard to tell when he's sleeping. It looks like he was in a fight."

"What? Because of the sling on his arm?"

"That and look closer. He has greenish spots like bruises. And stitches."

"So you think he gets mad easy? Do you think he'll get mad at us?"

"I don't know."

"Maybe he was in a car accident instead."

"Or had a brush with death. Oh, I wish Mother would tell us *something* about him."

I couldn't stand hearing any more of their speculating, so I yawned and stretched to give them warning before I opened my eyes.

"Hello," said a freckled, red-haired boy around twelve. "I'm Michael."

"And I'm McKenna," said an orange-haired girl about nine. "Would you like to eat breakfast? Mother sent us to get you."

I rubbed my eyes. "Yes. Thanks. I'll be right there."

They stared for another awkward minute before leaving. I shut the door, got dressed, and joined the family at the table. Michael and his father wore buttoned long-sleeved shirts. McKenna and her mother were in skirts and pressed blouses. I looked down at my wrinkled t-shirt and shorts, grateful that at least I had chosen a shirt without stains.

"What kind of cereal do you like?" asked Mrs. Winters. She pointed to a row of cold cereal choices lined up perfectly straight on the kitchen counter.

I looked at the boxes. "Cheerios would be great," I said.

Mrs. Winters grabbed the box and placed it beside my bowl. "Would you like milk?"

"Yes, please."

She handed me a china pitcher with milk inside it. I poured cereal into my bowl and added milk, very aware that four sets of eyes were watching my every move. I returned the pitcher to the center of the table. A drop of milk rolled down the spout and landed on the white table cloth.

I cringed. "Sorry."

Mrs. Winters quickly dabbed up the milk with a flowered napkin. "It's okay. I can wash the tablecloth after breakfast."

Mr. Winters smiled at me. "What would you like to do this fine summer day?"

"I hadn't really thought about that," I answered. Now I saw where his children got their orange hair. "It looks like you all are dressed for church or something. Is it Sunday?"

"Oh, no. It's Thursday," Mr. Winters clarified. "I have to skoot off to work here in a minute. But the kids have the day free to play."

"Do you want to play chess?" asked Michael. "I'm the school champion."

"I haven't played much chess," I admitted.

"How about checkers?" Michael asked.

"Oh, not checkers," said McKenna. "Then all three of us can't play at the same time. "How about Chinese Checkers? Then I can play too."

"I guess that would be good. You might just have to review the rules." I took a bite of cereal, careful to eat over the bowl. The family watched me chew.

"Do they have Cheerios where you're from?" asked Michael.

"Michael! Really!" exclaimed Mrs. Winters.

"Sorry, Mother. I was just curious. You said not to ask where he's from, or about his family, or how he got hurt. It's all a mystery really. You didn't say anything was wrong with indirect questions."

"It's all right," I said. "Yes. We have Cheerios where I'm from."

"I see. What's the state bird?" Michael asked.

"Michael!" Mr. Winters exclaimed.

"What? Too obvious? Okay. What's your favorite baseball team?"

"Finish your breakfast, Michael," said Mrs. Winters.

"His home team might not be his favorite," said Michael. "That's a safe question."

"I like the Royals," I answered.

"Hey. Me, too. See, Mother? So does that mean you are from Kansas or Missouri?"

"Michael!"

"Okay. Okay. I just had to sneak it in."

I fished out the last Cheerio and was about to slurp the remaining milk like usual. I looked around the table and decided against it. Everyone dabbed their faces with a napkin. Mrs. Winters collected the cereal bowls, washed them in the sink, and then organized them in the dishwasher. She gathered our juice glasses and washed them as well. After clearing the rest of the table, she folded the table cloth and carried it to the laundry room.

"I'm off," said Mr. Winters. "JaDon, welcome. I'll see all of you tonight."

The rest of the morning was spent with round after round of Chinese checkers. My mind drifted. What were Missy and Josie doing?

CHAPTER 13
DRESSER DRAWERS

I soon discovered that although they occasionally played board games, the Winters family spent most of their time on electronics. Michael and McKenna watched movies or played games on their smart phones. Mrs. Winters was usually at the computer catching up with friends or gathering cleaning tips on the computer. When Mr. Winters was home, he was usually watching sports. Michael loaned me one of his old iPods, so I wouldn't be left out. Several days passed with us only talking at meals. The isolation made me miss Josie and Missy even more.

On a particularly cloudy morning, Mrs. Winters walked into my temporary room. She handed me her phone.

"It's okay. Michael let me borrow his iPod," I said.

"I'm not letting you use my phone to play games. You have a phone call. It's Mr. Costas."

I instantly sat up in bed. Hope began brewing in my chest. "Thanks."

She left the room, closing the door behind her.

"JaDon. How are you?" Mr. Costas asked.

"I'm okay. Any news?"

"Is there anyone around you listening?"

"No."

"Good. Are they treating you well? Are you getting enough to eat? Do you need anything?"

"They're treating me fine and I don't need anything except my sisters. Is there news? Have they caught J.R?"

Mr. Costas sighed over the phone. "No. He never went back to his truck or the house. Two people in the area have reported stolen cars, so he's probably using one of those. One car is a silver Honda Accord. The other is a black Toyota Corolla. Neither cars stand out on the highway, so we're disappointed he isn't using your big green truck."

"Yeah. I'm not surprised he switched. How are Josie and Missy?"

"They're still trying to adjust. Their foster mom said Josie isn't talking. Missy will answer yes and no questions, but that's all. At least they're eating and sleeping some, though I guess they huddle in the same bed. They have two twin beds, but they can't sleep unless they're together."

I was silent for a moment, picturing them in a strange house without me. I reflected on his words.

"JaDon? Are you there?"

"Why did you call the lady they're staying with their *foster mom*?"

It was Mr. Costas' turn to be quiet. At last he said, "We didn't know how long it would take to capture J.R. Just in case, we needed to place you all with families in the foster care system who were willing to house you for an extended time, if necessary. I thought it would be even more traumatic if I placed you in a home and then had to place you in a long term home later."

"So you think this is going to be long term?" Panic was creeping into my voice.

"Hopefully not. But it's better that you and your sisters are somewhere safe, just in case."

"Can I at least see them?"

"We'll talk about that soon. For now, let's just see what the next few days hold."

I didn't respond.

"Hang in there, JaDon. I'll talk to you again soon, okay?"

"Yeah."

"I've got to make another call. It will all work out. Bye."

"Bye."

I felt the urge to throw the phone at the wall, but reconsidered since it wasn't mine. And the wall wasn't mine. And this house wasn't mine. And the family wasn't mine. I just wanted my sisters back.

A few minutes later, Mrs. Winters knocked on my door. "Are you done with your phone call?"

"Yes. Sorry. Come on in." I handed her the phone.

She studied my face. I tried to mask my frustration, but I knew it wasn't working.

"Not the news you wanted?"

I shook my head and looked at the floor.

"I'm sorry to hear that. Mr. Costas said your case is confidential—for your protection and ours, so I'll try not to pry, but if there's something we can do to make things easier on you, let us know."

"Thanks."

She stood up and straightened the quilt. I was glad I had at least remembered to make the bed. I watched her eye my pile of clothing in the corner.

"I do laundry at 10:00 every day. Would you like me to wash your clothes? I'll go get the laundry basket."

She returned seconds later with a white plastic basket. I helped her shovel my clothes inside.

"When they're washed, you're welcome to actually put them in the dresser drawers. Every drawer is empty. Would you like me to throw away your plastic bag?"

"No."

She cocked her head to the side and raised a brow.

Could I tell her I hoped I would need it soon to be reunited with my sisters? Was I allowed to mention my sisters? Probably not. "I may need it. I can fold it up and put it in one of the drawers."

"Oh. All right, then." She straightened my stack of books perched on the dresser, and ran her hand along the *Invisible Man* cover. "Do you like to read?"

"Yes."

She smiled. "Then I have something to show you. Come with me."

I forced myself to my feet and followed her down the stairs to the main floor. She opened the door to a small office. A mahogany desk sat in the middle of the room, but I barely noticed it. I sucked in my breath. Every wall was lined with bookshelves packed with books.

"All of us were big readers until recently. For some reason, we don't seem to find the time anymore." She adjusted her laundry basket. "You're welcome to read any of the books while you're here."

A small smile tugged at my lips. "I'd like that. Thanks."

"Sure. I'm going to start laundry. You can look through the books now if you want. They're in alphabetical order. When you return a book, try to put it back in the right place."

"I will. Thanks again."

Looking at the wall-to-wall books cheered me up in the most unusual way. I ran my fingers along the spines of some of my favorites. There was a wide assortment of fiction and non-fiction, hard backs and paper backs, classics and new releases. I read the back of *The Book Thief* by Markus Zusak and was hooked. I also grabbed the entire *The Hobbit* and *Lord of the Rings* collection. I had read the series many times, but I wanted something familiar to read again.

I returned to the room I was using and propped up pillows on the bed. I stroked the cloth cover of *The Hobbit* and felt comfort as if I was visiting an old friend. Soon I was lost in the pages with dwarves and a fretting Bilbo. I escaped from my personal nightmare into a fantasy world—and was grateful.

Hours later, Michael entered and sat at the foot of the bed. "What are you doing?"

"Reading."

He looked closer at the cover. "I think I read that one. Do you like it?"

"Yes. I've read it before, too."

"I don't read much anymore."

"Why not?"

"I'd rather watch stuff."He scratched his freckled nose.

"Oh."

He left, and returned moments later with a book. "Can I join you?"

"Sure."

He sprawled out on the floor and was soon silent. I didn't mind having him in the room. He was no substitute for my sisters, but having him there was better than being alone.

Mrs. Winters walked by the room. "It's 12:00. Time for lunch." Her eyes strayed to the floor. "Oh, there you are Michael. What are you doing?"

"Reading."

"Really? Well, good for you. You're welcome to return to it right after lunch."

We followed her to the dining room. McKenna was already seated and nibbling on her sandwich.

"What kind of jelly would you like today?" asked Mrs. Winters.

"Blackberry," said Michael.

"Grape," I answered.

Mrs. Winters spread the requested jelly on a piece of bread for each of us, and then paired it with another piece of bread slathered in peanut butter. She cut each sandwich into four triangles and placed a sandwich in front of us both. I grabbed an apple to go with it. I had learned quickly that Mrs. Winters did not care for cooking. Each breakfast consisted of cold cereal, pop tarts, or toast. Each lunch was a sandwich and fruit. Dinner varied slightly, but was usually very simple. Of course, she did not have much time to cook because she was always cleaning or on the computer.

Mrs. Winters sat down with her own sandwich. "So…is anyone excited about tomorrow?"

"What's tomorrow?" asked McKenna.

I cocked my head to the side, curious. Michael kept eating.

"It's school enrollment day. Can you believe it? The summer is going by so fast." Mrs. Winters beamed. "Soon you'll get to see all of your friends and be in school all day. Won't that be fun?"

"No," said Michael.

I stopped chewing. The peanut butter stuck to the roof of my mouth. "You just mean for Michael and McKenna, right?"

"No. For all three of you."

"But I have to go to school back in…back home," I said.

"I wondered about that, too. But I talked to Mr. Costas on the phone before he asked to speak to you. He said that all of your paperwork is being faxed to the school here. You don't have to worry about a thing."

Whose life was I living? Certainly not my own. Were my sisters about to enroll in school also? Without me?

"We'll all be in different schools," said McKenna. "My elementary school is the closest. It's near Michael's middle school. Your high school is on the other side of town. I've heard it's nice though. Does he get to ride the bus, Mother?"

"Yes, he does."

"You are so lucky." McKenna took a sip of milk. "I've always wanted to ride the bus. Mother drives us. When I'm in high school, I want to ride the bus, too."

I picked at my sandwich. "Lucky" was not how I would describe myself. If I was lucky, I would have had a different father. Even if my luck would only extend back a few weeks, the police would have caught J.R. right away, so we could have stayed with Aunt Sophie. If I was lucky, I wouldn't be forced to adjust to a new school. It was enough that I had to adjust to being without my sisters and staying in a different home with strangers. No. I did not feel lucky.

"May I be excused?" I asked.

"Yes. Back to your book? I'll take your plate and wash it for you."

I drifted back to the bedroom and sank to the floor. Images of a fist repeatedly pounding my face flashed through my mind. A steel-toed hunting boot kicking my stomach. Drunken words hissed in my ear. Through it all I had clung to life, willing to live for my sisters hiding in the hallway. They depended on me. Now they were far away. Who was protecting them? What use was I to anyone here?

CHAPTER 14
SCHOOL SUPPLIES

Enrollment lasted for several hours. I stood in the back at the elementary school and then later at the middle school, watching while McKenna and Michael stood in long lines with their mom, gathering school supply lists, calendars, information sheets, meal payment plans, and other assorted papers. Once school fees had been paid, and shot records and information sheets were updated, we finally drove to the high school.

I paused for a moment before getting out of the car. The school was massive with huge windows covering most of the front, and steel letters that spelled Lincoln High School. The rest of the building was tan brick. The bushes and trees were large and trimmed. Such a contrast to my school back home. We had twelve different double wide trailers scattered around campus connected with sidewalks, with a large gym, lunchroom, and library in the middle. Our lockers were outside along brick walls, which I didn't mind as long as it was warm and sunny. On rainy, cold days it was miserable.

"Big, right?" McKenna smiled at me. "I can't wait until *I* get to go to school here."

"I can," said Michael.

We followed the sidewalks to the main door and walked inside. Signs led us to the gym, where there were numerous tables. Staff members and teachers helped us sign the correct papers. I hadn't pre-enrolled, so the school counselor helped me select my classes. I would have to wait to receive my actual schedule. Other students shuffled from table to table, many looking bored and more interested in their phones than the people around them. I was glad to see a whole variety of races and skin colors. At least I wouldn't stick out too much with how I looked. I was assigned a locker and practiced opening the combination several times before we left.

"What did you think?" asked Mrs. Winters. "Will you mind going to school here?"

"It's not home, but it looks good," I said.

"I'm glad to hear it." She pulled peach antibacterial gel out of her purse and squirted some on her hands. She passed it to her kids, who then passed it to me. I squeezed some on my hands, returned it, and then awkwardly rubbed it in. I wasn't sure I really wanted to smell like peaches, but it wasn't worth causing trouble.

We drove to Walmart and got out of the car. "Everybody have their supply lists?"

McKenna pulled hers out of the stack of school papers and waved it in the air. "Got it!"

Michael held his up.

"How about you, JaDon?" Mrs. Winters asked.

My stomach sank and blood rushed to my face. "Me? Oh. I don't have money for school supplies," I mumbled.

"You don't have to pay."

I looked down and wished I could disappear. "But I don't want you to have to pay, I…"

"I'm not paying. It's all been arranged. Now find your list."

I looked up in surprise and did as I was told. Maybe this wouldn't be as painful as I thought. I scanned the list. It was so long. Who was actually paying for all of this stuff?

We walked aisle by aisle in the school supply section, filling our cart with the long list of pencils, pens, paper, and random school items. McKenna was very particular about each notebook and folder she chose. I just threw in whatever was cheapest.

"Come on, JaDon," McKenna said. "Have fun with it. The folders share your style with the whole class. Look." She shoved her stack of notebooks and folders in front of my face. "What can you tell about me from these?"

I flipped through the stack. "You like cats and things that sparkle?"

"Exactly." She grabbed my stack of folders out of the cart. "And what do these say about you?"

"That I like black?"

"No. That you don't care. At least choose some of the sports folders. Aren't there any you like?"

"I guess."

"He can choose whatever he wants," said Michael. "Don't let her boss you around."

The folders with pictures and designs were twice as much as the plain folders, so I didn't feel right replacing all of them. I traded one black folder for a basketball folder and left the rest the same. I put the basketball folder on top of the stack, so McKenna would see it.

"Are you guys going to decorate your locker?" McKenna asked.

"Of course not," said Michael. "Only girls do that."

"Oh, come on," said McKenna. "How about you, JaDon."

"Probably not."

She sighed. "You guys are missing a huge opportunity. When I have a locker, I'm going to cover every inch of the inside with fancy paper and pictures. Then I'm going to put a pink shag rug on the bottom and one of those locker chandeliers on the top."

"Then where are you going to put your books?" asked Michael.

"I'll make room."

"No one even sees the inside of your locker," he argued.

"Yes, they do."

"Well, then no one cares."

"They do, too."

"That's enough, you two," Mrs. Winters said. She handed each of us a pen. "Go through your lists, and check off everything you already have in the cart."

We did as instructed.

"What do we still need to find?"

We added more highlighters, glue sticks and graph paper to the cart. I reached for a scientific calculator, but pulled my hand back when I saw the price.

"It's okay. Really, JaDon," Mrs. Winters said. "You'll need it."

"I've never bought a calculator before."

"Then what did you do for class?" asked Michael. "I have to use mine all the time, and I'm not even in high school yet."

"I borrowed one."

"What a pain." Michael grabbed the calculator and stuck it in the cart. "Moving on."

I chewed the inside of my cheek. It was so easy for them to spend money.

Kleenex boxes and antibacterial wipes were on each of our lists, so McKenna tossed them in the cart.

"What about backpacks?" asked McKenna. "My backpack from last year is worn out."

"Mine, too," said Michael.

We made a detour to the backpack aisle. Michael quickly stuck in a camouflaged pack. McKenna took her time opening and closing each back pack and began weighing her options.

Michael turned to me. "Which one do you want?"

"But…"

"Choose a backpack, JaDon. Really," said Mrs. Winters.

I stuck a black pack in the cart. Ten minutes later, McKenna added her sparkled blue pack to the mix.

"Is that it?" asked Mrs. Winters. "Did we get everything checked?"

"Yes," McKenna stated.

Michael and I nodded.

"Excellent. Let's go."

As we crammed our items on the conveyer belt at the checkout, I rubbed my head. I'd never had all of the supplies on my list. J.R. would let us buy a pencil and one package of paper each, and then he'd tell us to fend for ourselves and borrow the rest. It was humiliating asking people for a pen or more paper. I tried to spread out my requests, but sometimes I forgot and asked the same person. If I got an eye-roll in response, it was like a beating. What would it be like to start the school year with everything I needed? I didn't have to leech off classmates. Maybe the beginning of school wouldn't be that bad.

We loaded the bags of supplies into the trunk of the car and drove home. I watched the houses and trees pass by my window. If my school supplies were paid for, did that mean that Josie and Missy's were as well? Would they get to pick out a backpack and fun folders and notebooks? What kinds would they chose? Would their taste be similar to

McKenna's? I tried to imagine their school building. Did they get enrolled today? If only they were here with me.

When we arrived at the house, McKenna emptied her bags onto the center of the living room floor. She grabbed a black permanent marker and sat down.

"What're you doin'?" I asked.

"I'm labeling my stuff. Teachers want our names on everything. Last year, I even had to put my initials on every single crayon. That would have been fine if I had only bought the twenty-four crayon box like was on the list. I bought the ninety-six pack. It took me forever to label them all. This year I grabbed a sixty-four crayon box. It should be much easier, but this could still take a while."

"Do *we* have to do that?" I asked Michael.

He shook his head. "No. Just the little kids."

"I'm not little," McKenna protested.

"Compared to us you are," Michael said. "In middle school and high school they figure you'll keep your stuff in your locker."

"Good," I said. "Labeling sounds like a lot of work."

McKenna wrote her name on one of her cat folders. "I wish we had a cat. I'd get a white one and name her Princess."

"Do you have *any* pets?" I asked.

"No." McKenna wrinkled her nose. "Mother says they're too messy. She says she doesn't want dog or cat hair everywhere and doesn't want them to have accidents on the carpet."

"What about a fish or something that stays in a cage?"

"She says they'd stink," said Michael. "We've tried asking many times. It's hopeless. Do you have any pets...or did you...I mean..."

"No. I didn't have any pets. One of my sisters had a pet rat…sort of. The other one had a stray cat that followed her home and stayed for weeks…but that's not a good story." I cleared my throat to clear my mind. "My cousins had a dog named Mop."

"Do you miss them?" asked McKenna.

"The pets? Not really."

"No. I mean your sisters?"

"McKenna! Mother said not to ask about his past," said Michael.

"Sorry," she said. Then she turned to glare at her brother. "You do it all the time."

"Do not."

"Do too."

"It's okay," I said, wanting to avoid a fight. "And yes, I do miss them. All the time."

"That must be hard. I wish they could have come here with you."

"Me too."

Dinner that night was spaghetti and meatballs. Mrs. Winters boiled water in a huge dark blue pot and dumped in the noodles. She poured a can of spaghetti sauce into a smaller blue pot. The sauce soon grew hot and began to bubble and pop. One pop was particularly powerful and splashed sauce onto her long white apron.

"Oh, my." She tried wiping it off with a wet washcloth, but it was a stubborn stain.

I was reading on the couch at the time. McKenna and Michael were back in their rooms using their smart phones.

"JaDon? Would you mind stirring this sauce, while I change aprons and stick this one in the wash? I don't want it to stain permanently."

"Sure." I stirred the sauce with a wooden spoon and inhaled the smell of oregano and tomatoes. Soon I was transported back to several nights ago, when Aunt Sophie was stirring homemade chili at the stove. What was she, Uncle Ron, and my cousins doing now? Were they able to go back home yet?

"Thanks, JaDon," Mrs. Winters said as she returned in a different apron. "I've got it now. I should have asked earlier. Do you like spaghetti?"

"I like just about anything. I've never been picky." It was true. My tastebuds were never very discerning. I knew the food Aunt Sophie made was extra good, but I could eat anything. One time I even ate something I sorely regretted.

I should have known better than to trust J.R. when he said he was cooking dinner. He told Josie to get rid of the stray cat, but she quickly became attached to it. She used to smuggle it in to her bed at night. J.R. found it in the house. He said he chased it off but later I discovered he had skinned it. I only learned the truth after we had all eaten J.R.'s stew. I didn't want Josie to find out, so I buried the skin.

I left for the bedroom. Suddenly spaghetti and meatballs did not look very appealing.

CHAPTER 15

NEW NAMES

The next day, the doorbell rang. A minute later it rang again. I looked at the clock in my room. It was 10:00. Mrs. Winters was probably doing laundry and couldn't hear the doorbell.

"Do you want me to answer the door?" I called out.

No one answered.

I stuck my head through Michael's doorway. "Should I answer the door?" I asked again.

He was on his phone with his earbuds in, watching a video. A quick check on McKenna revealed the same.

The doorbell rang again.

I walked down the stairs and shouted around the corner. "I can get the door if you want."

Still no response. I shrugged, unlocked the front door and opened it, revealing Mr. Costas.

He frowned. "JaDon. What are you doing answering the door?"

"Mrs. Winters was busy doin' laundry and her kids were on their phones."

"Then you should have gone to get Mrs. Winters and told her about the doorbell." Disapproval leaked into his tone. "Never answer it yourself, even if she isn't here."

"Nice to see you, too."

"Sorry, JaDon. But this is important. It could have been J.R. at the door. If Mrs. Winters had answered, he still

110

wouldn't necessarily know you were here, and you would have a chance at safety. If you overheard him and could tell he knew you were staying in this house, you could have escaped out the back. You should be safe here, but we still need to be careful."

My shoulders sagged. "You're right. I didn't think it through."

Mr. Costas' features softened. "Understandable. I didn't mean to jump on you, I just want to keep you safe."

Mrs. Winters walked past the door, carrying a basket of laundry. "Oh. Mr. Costas. I didn't realize we had a visitor."

"I'm sorry to disturb you. I was just checking on JaDon, and reminding him that he should never answer the door."

"Oh. My. I didn't hear the door bell. It won't happen again. We'll be more careful." She shifted the basket to her other hip. "Would you like to come in?"

"Yes, please."

"Can I get you anything to drink?"

"No, ma'am. I'm fine. I need to update JaDon, if that's all right."

"Certainly. I'll go put clothes away upstairs so you can talk."

"I appreciate it." Mr. Costas turned to me after she left. "Can we go sit down?"

I nodded and led him to a couch in the living room. "How much does she know?" I whispered. "Have you told her the risk she's taking having me here?"

"We don't feel she *is* at risk as long as we're careful. She does know that we are taking precautions hiding you and your identity."

"And she's okay with that?"

"Yes. Obviously she said that if there was ever any risk to her family she would be done. We don't think that will be an issue, but I still want you to be extra careful."

"I'll try," I promised. "How are Josie and Missy?"

"Better. I think Missy is starting to adjust. She was excited to show me all of her school supplies."

"I wondered about that. So they have everything they need for school?"

"Looks that way."

"And Josie? How is she?"

"She's still shaky and a bit withdrawn, but I see improvement. They both asked about you, of course."

"When can I see them?"

"I wish I knew. Soon, I hope. The cops thought they had a lead on J.R., but it came up empty. We'll keep trying."

"But can't I at least visit them while we wait?"

"We might be able to arrange that eventually. Let's just give it a little more time." He pulled several folded papers out of his briefcase. "For now, I do have a letter from each of the girls. I know that's not the same thing, but hopefully it will help."

I grabbed the letters eagerly. "Can I write them back?"

"I was hoping you would." He pulled out more paper and a pen and placed them beside me on the couch. "I'll have a short talk with Mrs. Winters and then stop by your school. That will give you time to write something before I come back to say good-bye."

"Thanks."

"Of course. Did you already get supplies for school?"

"Yes. Thanks. That was a first."

"That's what the girls said. I'm sorry that was another thing you had to endure over the years. Do you need anything else? Do you have enough clothes?"

112

I felt heat rise to my cheeks and looked away. I wasn't about to start begging. I already felt like a charity project. "I'm good."

Mr. Costas opened his mouth to say something, but closed it quickly when he saw my discomfort. "Okay. One more thing before I go. I hate to ask this of you, because I know you've been through too many changes already, but the police and courts thought it was necessary."

Dread washed over me. "What?"

Now it was his turn to look uncomfortable. "The police thought, well the protective services recommended that…" He closed his eyes and rubbed his temples. "They think you need to go by a different name…for safety reasons."

"Seriously?"

"I know it will be hard to get used to, but if J.R. were to somehow get close and check school records or snoop around…We just need to make you and the girls harder to find."

"The girls have to change their names, too?"

He nodded. "I'm so sorry."

"So what's my new name?"

"Jason."

I rolled my eyes. "It could at least be a cool name."

"We tried to keep it similar to your own in case you slip up and say the wrong name. It will almost sound the same, but it's not as unique and easy to spot. If someone calls Jason, you may still turn instinctively, so it wouldn't be a huge change."

"Do I need a new last name, too?"

"Yes. Williams. We needed a common last name. We figured you wouldn't get called by your last name much, so it didn't matter that it was a big change."

"Jason Williams. What about all my school enrollment papers? Don't they have my real name on them? Do we have to go back and make changes?"

"No. The papers I faxed to your school already have your temporary name on them."

"But we filled out some papers at enrollment."

"Did *you* actually sign anything? Because I had already told Mrs. Winters about your name change, and she was supposed to make sure your real name wasn't on anything additional."

I paused to think a moment. She had actually filled out the few papers that were left. "Oh. I guess we're good."

"Like I mentioned earlier, I'll go back and make sure everything is set at school."

"Will the teachers know any of the truth about me?"

"Only that you're in the foster system, and are living with the Winters. It's best if you don't tell them more than that."

I took a deep breath. "What about my sisters? What're their names for now?"

"Jody and Hillary Jones."

My left eyebrow shot up. "Hillary? That sounds nothin' like Missy. Jody I get for Josie. But why Hillary?"

Mr. Costas smiled. "That was your sister's idea. She said that's her favorite name, and it's what she goes by in her fantasy world. We figured maybe it would actually be the easiest thing for her to remember. Plus I don't think she would have agreed to anything else."

"Probably not." I sighed in resignation. "Jody and Hillary Jones it is."

"I'm going to go talk to Mrs. Winters so you can read the girls' letters and get started on your own."

He left the room and I headed upstairs, eager to see what my sisters had to say. I flopped on the bed, and unfolded their papers. Missy's was on top.

Dear JASON,

That name looks so strange. Did you hear I'm going to be Hillary? I've always wanted to be called that. Are you okay? We miss you. The people we're staying with are nice, well Mr. XXXXXXX is very nice. Mrs. XXXXXXX is sort of nice. She gets grumpy easy, but she's older, like a grandma's age so maybe that's the way old ladies are. I don't know cuz I don't think I ever met our grandmas or grandpas. Did I? She does dress us nice and cooks good food. Though not many desserts. She says sugar is bad for us. I seen the school we're going to. It's so nice! And we got all the pens and pencils and stuff we need. They have a pet cat here. Sometimes it will play with me and sometimes it goes and hides. Still, it makes me not miss Rat so much. I don't miss J.R. at all and hope they catch him soon so we can be together again.

Love,
Hillary

I smiled, picturing her write the words. I picked up Josie's letter.

Dear XXXXXXX Jason,

It doesn't seem right calling you that. I'm having a hard time getting used to us being Jody and Hillary. We are practicing at home, so that we don't mess things up once we get to school. The school seems fine. It will be nice not having to borrow anything at school. I hope the same is true for you. I miss you so much. I wish they hadn't split us up. I ask Mr. Costas to let us be together every time I see him. He's told me it is to keep us all safe and I understand that, but it still seems wrong. J.R.'s still ruining our lives, even when he's far away. At least I hope he's far away. Either that or they catch him. The people taking care of us are okay. I hope the people you live with are good to you. We have a cat, which I like. Do you remember the cat I tried to keep, that J.R. chased away? At least he can't chase this cat away. I'm still scared and wish they would catch J.R. I want this to all be over and for us to all be together again.

    Love,
    Jody

I ached for Josie. It didn't surprise me that she struggled with the living arrangements. I pulled out the pen and paper and quickly wrote both of my sisters back. The names were crossed out in Missy's letter, probably for safety reasons, so I left names out of my own letter, merely describing Mr. and Mrs. Winters and their children. I tried not to let my own frustration seep into my words, and reassured them that I remembered my promise, and would do everything possible to make sure we saw each other again soon. I wrote that J.R. would be caught and that our nightmare would one day be over. I hoped they believed me. I rubbed the stubble on my head. Did *I* still believe?

CHAPTER 16
STARTING OVER

The bus would arrive any minute. I chewed on a strawberry Pop-Tart while I looked out the smudge-free front window. Normally the bus stop would be two blocks down the street, but Mr. Costas had arranged a special stop right at our door for safety.

McKenna was bursting with excitement as she curled her long orange hair in front of the bathroom mirror. Michael was still in bed, refusing to get up until the last possible moment. Their schools started later than mine, so he still had some time left.

I rubbed my newly close-shaven head. My mind swirled with mixed feelings of apprehension, dread, and excitement. I didn't know anyone at Lincoln High, which made me nervous, but it was also appealing to have a clean slate. I hadn't *earned* a bad reputation back home, except for being a little reckless, but too many people judged me guilty and pitiful by association. I was J.R.'s boy, and couldn't escape the stigma. J.R.'s only friends were his whiskey brewing and drinking buddies, and even they were guarded around him. Lots of the ladies enjoyed looking at him, but they would rarely risk talking to him for long. His sweet honey words soon turned rancid like vinegar. His temper was well-known and feared.

The chatting about Mama abandoning us had settled down years ago, but occasionally we'd still hear comments.

"I can see why she left that man. Don't blame her none."

"But those kids. Pity she didn't take them with her. That's what I wouldah done."

"Irresponsible leavin' young'uns with the likes of him."

I still saw people shake their heads and give the girls and me sympathetic looks. Sometimes it felt like we were being labeled unworthy, because our own mother hadn't valued us enough to stay with us.

Our run-down shack didn't boost people's opinion of us either. The houses around us certainly weren't mansions, but they weren't in the same eye-sore category as ours.

What would it be like to only be judged by who I was? Not J.R.'s son, or Grace's abandoned kid, or a poor, lazy shack dweller, but JaDon Chambers. I choked on a bite of Pop-Tart and grimaced. Even my name wasn't good anymore. I had to be Jason Williams. And I would have to be careful about revealing anything about my family or past. Most of it I would be glad to keep hidden, but how hard would that be?

Blinking white and red lights signaled the approach of the long yellow-orange bus. I opened the door at the sound of escaping air from the brakes.

"Bye, everybody!" I called over my shoulder.

"Have a good day," Mrs. Winters said.

"See you soon," McKenna shouted.

I took a deep breath before climbing up the bus steps. Some kids eyed me as I got on, but most ignored me while they talked to their friends or zoned out to music through their earbuds. I found an empty seat near the middle of the bus and sank into it. The bus lurched forward.

After multiple stops, we pulled in front of the high school. Students jammed the aisles and inched forward out the bus door. I allowed myself to be caught in the current as we flooded into the school.

I knew where my locker was, but figured there was no point heading that direction since I didn't have any books or homework yet. Besides, I would probably need extra time to find my first class. My jittery hands pulled out my schedule. Geometry was first. Room 202. Was it on the second floor? I climbed the stairs and began my search. Wrong end of the hall. The numbers started in the upper 200s and were gradually getting lower. I picked up my pace and breathed a sigh of relief when I found 202 before the bell rang.

All of the seats were taken except for in the front row. I groaned but slid into a seat near the left side. A girl with straightened blond hair walked in soon after me. A cloud of perfume floated around her, nearly making me sneeze. She wore a tight dress and heals that looked uncomfortable to me but didn't seem to bother her. She eyed the seating arrangement.

"Really?" she said. "This is going to have to change."

She managed to shimmy into the seat beside me and arranged her purse and book bag on the floor and her phone on the desk. After running her fingers through her hair, she glanced around the room.

"Hey, Rachel," she said to a girl in the back.

She caught me watching her. Her eyes travelled from my head down to my feet. She snorted. "Nice shoes." Then she turned her back on me as she resumed looking around the room.

I looked down at my feet. I really didn't care much about clothes, but I had worn the best jeans and t-shirt that I had. My shoes were old and scuffed and almost revealed the tip of my toe on the right. It wasn't the first time someone had noticed their sorry state. I steeled my mind, refusing to let the painful memories connected to my shoes distract me.

I snuck a subtle glance at the other shoes in the room, particularly on the guys. Most of them were clean and looked new. Many had the Nike swoosh or Adidas lines or some other popular mark. I felt like concealing my feet further under my desk, but I stubbornly left them right where they were.

The teacher walked in and gave us an overview of the class. We had the option of a textbook or using the online version. I preferred holding a book in my hand, so walked to the front to grab one. I sensed eyes following me, but when I looked up, I didn't notice any hostile stares. Good. I was already ahead of some of my classes back home.

The bell rang. Fortunately my next two classes were near my first, so I found them easily. I gathered a syllabus in each class and received my first homework assignment in Chemistry. Lunch was next.

I was curious about eating school food. Mr. Costas said I had money on my account so that I could eat a hot lunch every day. He cautioned me that if I ever chose the ala carte line, I would have to be careful to stay on budget. Mrs. Winters was thrilled that she didn't have to have lunch food available. *I* was thrilled to be able to eat a real lunch during the school day. J.R. never gave us money, so we just grabbed whatever leftovers we could find at home. My school secretary and counselor had both called J.R. repeatedly about signing papers because we qualified for free lunches. I took messages for him, but he refused to call them back. It made no sense to me. He would take advantage of people on a regular basis but was too proud to admit we needed lunch assistance. Of course, the girls and I were the ones who had to suffer for it, not him.

After a long wait in line, the lunch lady scanned my card and directed me to a stack of recycled cardboard trays. I continued walking in line until I could see the food choices. Rectangular stainless steel bins held assorted sandwiches, fruits, and vegetables. There was also yogurt, chips, and pizza. I selected a spicy chicken sandwich, broccoli, mandarin oranges, and chocolate pudding and then looked around the lunchroom. There was an empty circular table near the corner, so I slid into a seat and quickly took a huge bite of the sandwich. I smiled. The chicken wasn't as spicy as I had hoped, but it was still good. I sampled the broccoli and oranges. Students always complained about school food, but I was enjoying it.

A guy with dark hair and light brown skin sat across from me. "Hey," he said.

"Hey," I said back.

He stuffed down an entire slice of pizza, took several bites of a second slice, and chugged some pop before he looked up again. "I'm Miguel."

"Ja..Jason." That was close. I should have practiced my name like my sisters had mentioned.

"What? JaJason?"

"No. Just Jason."

"Oh." He looked up at the big clock on the wall and jammed the rest of the pizza in his mouth. The bell rang. "See ya."

"Later." I spooned the last few bites of chocolate pudding in my mouth and dumped my tray.

The crowd surged out of the lunchroom through two different hallways. I pulled out my schedule, unsure of which hall to choose. After being jostled around for a minute I selected a hallway and hoped for the best. I searched for room 107. No classes were in the triple digits. I groaned and

121

made a detour towards the opposite hallway. The bell rang before I had even reached room 103.

"Figures," I said aloud.

I rushed past the last few classrooms until I reached 107. All eyes turned on me as I stumbled into one of the only remaining seats. The teacher ignored my late arrival and walked to the front of the class.

"Welcome to English. I'm Mrs. Jane Arsenault. However, most people manage to butcher my last name, so you're welcome to call me Ms. Jane." She placed a stack of syllabi on each front desk, including my own. "Please pass these back to your classmates."

"You'll find I'm quite easy to get along with, as long as you follow my guidelines. I expect you to be on time..."

I felt heat rush to my cheeks and rubbed my head.

She looked directly at me and smiled. "...with the exception of the first couple of days as we're all trying to find new classes. I expect your work to be your very best and turned in on time. And I expect you to show respect by being quiet while I'm talking. I, in turn, promise to give you my best, return your papers on time, and to respect you when you're talking *with my permission*."

She showed the syllabus on the screen and discussed the upcoming assignments and test dates. At the end of the list was a daily journal rubric.

"You're probably no stranger to classes requiring a daily journal. Raise your hand if a teacher has asked you to keep a journal before."

Most of the class raised their hands. I did not.

"I thought so. I listed a notebook on your supply list to be used as your journal. I will try to give you some class time to write in them, but you're encouraged to write at home as well."

"How much do we have to write?" asked a guy with a brown crew cut.

"The minimum requirement is seven sentences. But remember to give me your best, not the bare minimum. This is the one time where I won't be counting off for spelling or grammar. I want you to develop your own style. Pour out your thoughts. If they're far too personal for a particular entry, write private on the top and I won't read it that day and will give you a completion grade only. Now, don't try this too often or it will affect your overall score. I'll keep your thoughts confidential."

"So if we talk about a teacher who annoys us, you aren't going to tell him what we said?" asked a girl near the back.

"I will not. Odds are, it would do more harm than good anyhow. Occasionally, I'll have you write on a specific topic or in a certain format, but most of the time it can be whatever comes to your mind." She looked at the clock. "You have six minutes left in class. Go ahead and pull out your journals and write about your impressions from the first day of school."

I grabbed one of my black notebooks and opened to the first blank page. I hadn't journaled since we left the shack. All of my journals had been deeply personal. I didn't know what to write knowing that someone else could read it. I looked around. Many of my classmates stared at their blank paper as well. Minutes ticked by.

"It doesn't have to be deep every time. Just write about the day so far," Ms. Jane told the class.

I stared at my pen and finally began writing.

Today I hold my own pen and write on my own notebook. I have yet to borrow a single thing. I am independent and need nothing from classmates. I couldn't find all of my classes immediately, but I am finding my way. I ate a normal lunch and briefly had someone to eat it with. Eyes told me that my shoes are worn out, yet words have yet to hurt me. I am out of place, far from home, but the day was good.

Seven sentences. Good enough for now. That described my entire day—good enough for now.

CHAPTER 17
SOMETHING LIKE THAT

The next day at school was less about learning the rules and more about getting to work. By the time seventh hour arrived, I was already burdened with homework. At least I knew I wouldn't have homework in Gym. I was ready to release some pent-up energy.

The locker room was packed and smelled like sweat and cheap cologne. I changed into the required black shorts and white t-shirt with *Lincoln High School* spelled across the front in black letters. I was grateful for the uniform. One less time I had to be judged for my faded clothes.

We ran laps around the gym to warm up, and then sat in lines while the gym teacher reviewed the rules for kickball.

"Now everybody up," said Coach Ruttledge. "Let's take advantage of the warm weather and play the game outside."

A few girls grumbled, but most students seemed eager to get back in the sun. We numbered off and split into two teams. I adjusted the sling on my arm, grateful we were playing something where my injury wouldn't interfere.

The coach approached me while I was waiting for my turn to kick. "Are you going to be okay playing with your injuries?"

"Yeah. My arm doesn't slow me down much anymore."

"Good. Do you know how much longer you have to be in a cast?"

"Not yet. Hopefully I'm almost done with it."

He glanced at my stitches. "Were you in a car accident or something?"

I cringed. Obviously, I couldn't tell the truth, but outright lies were a pain to maintain. "Something like that," I finally said. I averted my eyes until he took the hint and walked down the field. It was better if I kept my distance. I couldn't risk getting close to another gym teacher. I still had frequent nightmares about what happened to my last coach.

As soon as the game was over, we returned to the locker rooms and changed clothes, rushing to beat the bell and avoid crowded hallways. I grabbed books from my locker and got on my bus.

Most of the bus was still empty, so I was able to sit wherever I wanted. I headed toward the back seat and slumped down. I stared out the finger-smudged window and tried to imagine what Josie and Missy were doing. Were they getting on a bus, too? Did they even ride a bus?

Someone tapped my shoulder. I jolted in surprise and turned toward the aisle. A tall, muscular guy with spiked blond hair towered over me.

"You're in my seat," he said.

I studied his face to see if he was joking. His expression was blank and cold. "What?"

"You heard me. You're in my seat. Now move."

I pretended to look for something. "Oh. I'm sorry. Does it have your name on it? I can't seem to find it."

"I'm not laughing. Move."

I motioned toward the front of the bus. "There's lots of empty seats. Why don't you choose one."

"I am choosing one. This one."

He glared down at me. His eyes were ice blue like J.R.'s. "You a freshman or something? I always sit here. Move."

I clenched my fists and stood up. It was suddenly J.R.'s face I imagined in front of me and I began to see red.

"Oh. You think you can take me on?" He smirked. "I'll…"

"Relax, Troy. That's my cousin," I heard a voice say. "Don't be messing with him. I forgot to tell him where we were sitting. Come on, Cuz. I've got us a seat up here."

I forced myself to turn her direction and nearly choked. A short, but insanely beautiful, girl was motioning for me to follow her. I grabbed my backpack, slid past Troy's bulging arms, and followed her up four rows.

She sat down and patted the space beside her. "Have a seat, Cuz," she said.

I dropped beside her and snuck a closer look. Her large brown eyes were framed with long lashes and her kinky curly black hair draped past her shoulders. I had to concentrate to keep my mouth from dropping open.

"You're staring," she whispered.

I nodded vacantly.

"Don't. He may still be watching us, and you're supposed to be my cousin, remember?"

I looked away. "Sorry. I didn't mean…Why did you…" I wanted to kick myself. My tongue was tangled and couldn't even produce a normal sentence.

"*Are* you a freshman?" she asked.

I shook my head.

"Then this must be your first day on the bus. You would have found out soon enough. Troy always sits in the back seat. He's like crazy weird about it, and you don't want to get him upset. He's got an insane temper and once he goes off…it gets brutal. The good thing is he's suspended half the time for fighting, so if you really want to sit there, just wait until he's kicked out of school for a few days."

"Okay."

"You're not like that, are you?" she asked, pulling back.

"Like what?"

"A fighter. I mean, you weren't backing down like most people would, and you're covered in stitches and have a cast and…"

"I don't pick fights with people," I said. "He just reminded me of..." I shook my head. "He just annoyed me."

"I get it. But he's *so* not worth it. If you want my advice, just avoid him. That's what most people do."

"I'll do my best," I said.

"So what year *are* you?" she asked.

"Sophomore."

"Me, too." She turned to look at me. "But I haven't seen you before. Where are you from?"

I paused. "Just another part of town."

She smiled. "I guess since we're cousins and all, I should know your name."

I smiled back. "Jason."

"I'm Shania."

The bus came to a stop and several people shuffled through the aisle. I heaved my bag out of their way and accidently bumped the stitches on my chin. I winced.

"You're still in pain, huh?"

My hand flew up to the stitches self-consciously. "Not bad."

"How'd you get hurt?" she asked.

I bit the inside of my cheek. "It's a long story."

"Oh. Yeah. Sorry. I shouldn't have asked."

"No. You should have. I mean…I understand why you'd…" I sighed. "It's just…"

"It's okay. You don't have to tell me. I mean, we just met." She looked out the window and sat quietly for a moment. "My stop is next."

"Oh," I said. Keeping secrets stunk.

The bus came to a stop again. I stepped out into the aisle so she could pass. "Thanks for keeping me out of trouble, Shania."

"You bet." She shouldered her simple turquoise backpack and managed to glide down the aisle.

The bus driver closed the door. I watched Shania until the bus turned the corner. It was hard enough talking to a beautiful girl without having to second guess everything I said, wondering if I was telling anything that would reveal too much. Of course, if all went well, I'd be back with Aunt Sophie soon, and Lincoln High would just be a memory.

Several stops later, I grabbed my bag and walked toward the front.

"See ya, Cuz," Troy shouted in a sarcastic voice.

It was tempting to make a comment, but I heeded Shania's advice and ignored him.

"Thanks for that," said the bus driver as I walked down the steps. "I wasn't looking forward to breaking up another fight."

"No problem."

I glanced quickly up and down the sidewalk before ringing the doorbell.

Mrs. Winters answered. "Welcome back, JaDon." She opened the storm door and stepped aside to let me enter.

"Jason," I corrected.

"Oh, yes." She grabbed her forehead. "I should have called you that from the start so I wouldn't forget. How was your day?"

"Decent. I think I'll get my homework over with."

129

"Good idea."

McKenna was walking down the stairs as I started to walk up. "Hey, JaDon!"

"Jason."

"Oops. Boy, that's hard to get used to."

"Tell me about it."

"Guess what! My fourth grade teacher showed us the class pet today. We have a Guinea pig named Wilbur! He's adorable! He's tan and white with these beady black eyes and crumpled ears and he's fat and loves apple slices. If we're quiet, we can have a turn holding him, and guess who was quiet? Me! I was one of the ones who held him today! His fur was soft and silky and he just sat in my lap and let me pet him!"

"That's great," I said.

"I know, right? I don't think the other two fourth grade classes have a pet. I am *so* lucky."

"You are."

"Maybe she'll let her students take turns pet-sitting over the weekends. I'll have to ask. He could stay in my room and…"

"I think you should just enjoy him at school," Mrs. Winters said. She stood in front of the stairway with her arms crossed. "That way you have something extra special to look forward to on weekdays, and the rest of us won't have to smell him…or clean up after him."

"He has his own cage. He wouldn't get things messy," McKenna protested.

"A wire cage, right?"

"Yes."

"Bedding and food and…stuff can fall through the wires. Keep the pig at school, please."

"Fine." McKenna stomped the rest of the way up the stairs to her room.

I followed her but headed to the guest room, where I stacked my textbooks on the bed and looked over my assignments. So much for easing into the work. These teachers were already pushing hard.

I managed to complete one geometry problem but then found my mind wandering. What if Josie or Missy needed help with their homework? Would their foster parents be willing to help? Missy would probably be starting middle school. Could Josie teach her how to open a locker? I reached under the bed and reread their letters. I pictured them walking home from school. My throat got tight. I should be there for them.

I completed two more math problems. Then I pictured *Shania* walking home from school. Lincoln High sure had pretty girls. She was smart, too—getting me away from psycho Troy without making him blow up. Would she talk to me tomorrow? I stared blankly at my Geometry. Getting homework done was harder than I thought. At least this distraction wasn't painful.

CHAPTER 18
ELEPHANT'S
TOOTHPASTE

Chemistry. Yet another class I did not share with Shania. It was third hour already, and I was disappointed when I couldn't spot her curly hair.

Mr. Zandini pointed to the white board. In red dry erase marker it said:

H_2O_2 (aq) + I- (aq) –> H_2O (l) + OI- (aq)

H_2O_2 (aq) + OI- (aq) –> H_2O (l) + O_2 (g) + I- (aq)

"Go ahead and write this reaction sequence into your composition notebooks. Make sure it's clear enough you can read it later." He paused to let us write. "In our experiment, hydrogen peroxide is catalytically decomposed by the potassium iodide. By the iodide ion, actually. Oxygen gas is rapidly formed. Now, for the fun part. I need one brave volunteer."

Most of the class looked down at their shoes or became very interested in the writing in their notebooks. I raised my hand.

"Name please."

"Jason."

"Come on up here, Jason."

I stood beside him. He handed me some plastic goggles and a heavy apron. A glass beaker tall enough to reach my chin was centered on the table.

"We're going to make some Elephant's Toothpaste. Are you still willing to help?"

"Yes, sir."

"Excellent. I have 50 mL of 30% hydrogen peroxide in this beaker. I need you to put a squirt of dish soap into this beaker, and then add a drop of food coloring."

I did as asked and stepped back. Nothing happened.

"Now in this flask, I have 2 grams of potassium iodide. Can you pour it into the beaker, please?"

"Sure."

I dumped it in. Immediately a huge amount of foamy suds sprouted from the beaker like an attacking snake, reaching well past my head and then twisting down onto the table. The girls (and a few guys) in the front of the room screamed and scooted back. My first impulse was to touch the snake. Which I did.

"Thanks, Jason. Word of advice for next time—ask if it's safe before you touch a chemical reaction. In this case you're fine, but just keep that in mind, all of you, for future reference."

"Got it," I said, touching the foamy snake again.

"Now, what happened here, was when we added the potassium iodide, the released oxygen gas was trapped in soap bubbles, which resulted in the snake, or Elephant's Toothpaste. Thanks, Jason." He handed me a paper towel. "You can go back to your seat."

I slid into my chair. Chemistry had potential, even if Shania wasn't here.

"The iodide ion is not consumed by the reaction. Think back to yesterday's lesson. This means it is a..." Mr. Zandini paused with his hands out, waiting for an answer.

"Bubble snake?" asked the boy beside me.

"No. A little deeper. We talked about it yesterday."

133

Nothing.

"It begins with a "C" and rhymes with fist?" he tried again.

A girl in the second row raised her hand. "Catalyst?"

"Yes!" He looked up to the ceiling. "Thank you! What's your name?"

"Katrina."

"Thank you, Katrina. The rest of you, look over your notes, before tomorrow."

The bell rang and we swarmed out the door. I was eager to see my lunch choices for the day. I juggled my cardboard tray again with my good arm, and selected lasagna and a breadstick, with a romaine lettuce salad, and sliced strawberries and bananas. Miguel was already sitting at the table I usually chose, along with a tall guy with brown hair and freckles. I joined them.

"Hey, Jason," Miguel said. "This is Parker."

"Hey."

Parker nodded my way. He was eating lasagna as well. Miguel was back to pizza. We all inhaled our food without saying a word, until the bell was about to ring.

"You just came from chemistry, right?" Parker asked.

"Yeah."

"You dumped stuff into the tube to make the snake, right?"

"Yeah."

"Interesting."

"Yeah, it was."

The bell rang. We all nodded at each other, dumped our trays, and went our separate ways. English was easy to reach on time, now that I knew the right hall.

Ms. Jane greeted us at the door. "On your way in, please pick up our first book of the year."

Three large stacks of paperback books lined the front of her desk. I grabbed one and glanced at the title. It was *To Kill a Mockingbird* by Harper Lee. I'd already read it, but didn't mind reading again as it was one of my favorites. I scanned the room, prepared to be disappointed yet again. Instead, I spotted Shania settling into her chair across the room. My heart beat a little faster.

Ms. Jane waved her hand, pointing to the classroom walls. "I have five different quotations taped to the walls in the room. I want you to walk around reading them, until you find a quotation that speaks to you, or is similar to something that's happened in your own lives. Stay standing by the quote. Got it? Now move."

Students slowly got to their feet and moved around the room. I read each quote and then returned to two quotes that I could relate to. The first quote was, "You're too scared to even put your big toe in the front yard." I'd felt that way many times, but if gathering by the quote led to a discussion, I might be in trouble.

The safer option was, "You never really understand a person until you consider things from his or her point of view." I stood by the card, waiting for the other students to make their decisions. I was pleasantly surprised when Shania stood beside me. She smelled faintly like vanilla.

"Hi, Jason," she said.

"Hey."

The rest of the students finally stopped milling around.

"I see no one stopped at card number three," Ms. Jane said. "I'm guessing I know which card it is." She walked over and laughed. "I thought so. In case you're wondering, it says, "I realized I would be starting school in a week. I never looked forward more to anything in my life." No huge school fans?"

Shania grinned. I didn't notice the reaction of anyone else.

"Now I want you to share why you selected the card you did with the rest of your group."

Shania spoke up first for our group. "This is kind of like the saying about walking a mile in someone else's shoes. I like to imagine what other people are thinking." She looked at me. "Like what someone might be thinking when they stand up to a huge crazy guy who could beat them to a pulp."

I smiled. "Or what someone is thinking when they step in to prevent the beating, even though they're half the size of the crazy guy, and have never met the guy about to get beat up who is possibly crazy as well."

"What?" said a girl with braces. "Am I missing something?"

The rest of the group talked for a few more minutes until Ms. Jane asked us to return to our seats. She had us discuss what the stories we heard in our groups told us about our own lives, and whether we had similar or different stories.

"If you haven't already guessed, the quotes you discussed are from the book you just picked up as you walked into class. How many of you have heard of *To Kill a Mockingbird*?"

A few people nodded.

"How did you hear about it?"

A girl in the back raised her hand. "My parents were watching a really old movie of it."

"Good. It *is* old—it was made in 1962, and was considered one of the best movies ever made. It even won three academy awards. Now, how many of you have actually read the book it was based on?"

No one raised their hand. Was that for real, or was it just too embarrassing to admit? I didn't care what they thought, so I raised my hand.

"Oh, good. Thank you for admitting it…"

"Jason."

"Thanks, Jason. And what did you think of it?"

"Good stuff."

"Oh? And why is that?"

"I liked that the main girl, Scout, had this amazin' dad who took a stand by defendin' a black guy who was accused of a crime he didn't commit."

Ms. Jane looked me in the eyes and smiled. "Excellent." She turned to the class. "And what made it even more profound, was that it was during a time when the south was poisoned by prejudice." She motioned to the cards taped around the classroom again. "What do you anticipate about the stories to be found in the book from the quotations we considered today?"

A few people answered, but I was distracted. Shania was looking at me. Next thing I knew, the bell rang. I took my time gathering my books until she walked by.

"So do we have any other classes together?" I asked.

"Don't know. What do you have next?"

"History and then P.E."

"That would be a no and a no. At least we have one class together," she said, pushing a black curl out of her face.

"And the bus ride."

"Most days. I catch a ride with my friends a couple times a week. Speaking of friends…" She motioned towards the door. Two girls were waiting for her. "I need to get going. I'll see you later."

"Yeah. Later."

Later wound up being even later than I thought. She wasn't on the bus. Unfortunately, Troy *was* on the bus, and made his presence known.

"Hey, *Cuz*. You on your own today?" he yelled from the back seat.

I didn't bother turning around.

"Where's Shania, *Cuz*?"

I gritted my teeth, and tried to distract myself by scratching under my cast with a pen.

"Hey. I'm talking to you, *Cuz*. Turn around."

Troy's voice morphed into J.R.'s voice mid-sentence. I even imagined his Arkansas accent. J.R. yelled for me to do things on a regular basis. If I didn't respond right away, he'd smack me on the side of the head. Once when I was much younger, I saw his hand raised before he hit me, so I ducked. He missed my head, but threw me against the wall instead. I learned it was better to just take J.R.'s hits as they came rather than ignite a bomb.

"Stop ignoring me, *Cuz*."

I wondered how long *my* fuse was? Had J.R.'s temper contaminated me? How long could I let Troy taunt me before I exploded? I wanted nothing in common with J.R. so I closed my eyes and took deep breaths, waiting for the next comment.

"Whatever," Troy said.

Several minutes passed and Troy remained quiet. The tension in the entire bus seemed to release. I smiled. A small victory had been won. Troy was done spouting for now and I had remained cool. I was distancing myself from J.R.'s personality. How long would J.R. keep his distance physically?

CHAPTER 19
BEHIND DRYWALL

Mr. Costas came to visit after dinner. "There's nothing new to tell you about the manhunt," he said when we were alone. "But I do have more letters from your sisters."

"Thanks." I dug through the top dresser drawer in the guest room and removed letters I had written a few days ago. "Can you give them these?"

"Of course." He squeezed my good arm. "Hang in there. J.R. can't hide forever."

"I'm not so sure about that."

The moment he was gone, I unfolded Missy's letter.

Dear Jason,

I miss you. I don't mind it so much here, but I wish you were with us. School is good so far. We don't stick out here cuz we got nice clothes and pencils and all we need. I've already made two friends who sit with me at lunch and walk home with me sometimes. Josie just mopes around behind us on the walk home. She still seems sad lots. I think her only friend might be the cat. It likes her more than me. Don't know why."

Love,
Hillary

I immediately read Josie's letter next.

Dear Jason,

I know J.R.'s sneaky, but why can't they catch him and get this over with? I'm getting tired of looking over my shoulder, wondering if he's watching us. I don't mind living here, but I want you with us. They shouldn't split up family. My teachers are real good, but I'm not sure about making friends. As soon as I do, we may be leaving, right? I like the cat here. They call it Mr. Whiskers. I'm not crazy about the Mr. part, so I just call it Whiskers. It sneaks into our room at night and sleeps in my bed. I'm glad because I don't have as many nightmares when it's with me. Thanks for the last letter. I read it whenever I get lonely.

Love,
Jody

I put their letters under my pillow and shook my head. We'd been apart far too long. I wandered into the bathroom and brushed my teeth, being careful to wipe down the countertop when I was done. It was hard work keeping everything neat enough for Mrs. Winters. I changed into pajamas and crawled under the covers. The letters crinkled under the pillow and I read them again. They would get my letters soon, but I wanted to talk to them in person.

I leaned back on the pillow and closed my eyes, trying to picture my sisters. Their curly hair, their tentative smiles, their pale gray eyes…I drifted into another dream.

"Shh." I whispered in Missy's ear.

She tried to stifle her sobbing, covering her little mouth.

There was a narrow crack where we slid the chunk of drywall back in place. It cast a sliver of dim light on Josie. Her thin arms wrapped around her knees as she huddled beside us. She chewed on her lip and rocked back and forth.

I silently squeezed her hand.

The yelling had stopped several minutes ago, but we could still hear J.R. stomping around in a drunken rage.

"I can't believe that woman," he hissed.

Something glass smashed against the wall next to us. Missy jolted. I stroked her hair, trying to calm her. Josie scooted closer, until she was pressed against my side. I could smell whiskey through the crack. Was it dripping down our walls?

"Why she want to leave me?" J.R. yelled.

More glass shattering, followed by wood splintering. I imagined the mess we were going to have to clean up when he was done. Mama would probably cry as we worked. She cried quietly, thinking we didn't hear her, but I knew what her shaking shoulders and hidden face were doing. She always did the first cleaning, picking up the broken pieces of plates and glasses before we could help.

"I don't want any of you gettin' glass in your feet or hands," she'd say.

I'd wash up the spilled whiskey or beer. Josie and Missy were only four and five, so their job was to take turns sweeping what we missed. It sounded like I was going to be scrubbing walls this time.

J.R. started grunting and grumbling, dragging something through the hallway. He paused by our hiding place. He was so close I could hear his heavy breathing. Could he hear *us* breath? Had he discovered our hiding place? I wanted to peek out of the crack, but I was too afraid to move. Josie's eyes were wide in terror.

At last he began grunting and dragging things again. "Gotta hurry," he said.

The front door opened and slammed shut. We heard the truck roar to life and peel out.

We sat frozen for several minutes and then each breathed a collective sigh of relief.

"When's Mama gonna come?" asked Missy.

"Shh," said Josie.

"But it sounds like he's gone," Missy whispered.

"Mama always says to stay put. She'll get us when she's sure it's safe," I said.

They nodded at me, but their faces shifted. Their chubby cheeks were replaced by gaunt faces. Older faces. Defeated faces. They were still hiding behind the drywall, but I wasn't with them. I couldn't open my eyes. Where was I?

Finally, I forced one eye open a crack. I saw the fringe of my quilt where it nearly touched my bedroom floor. My mouth tasted salty. I spit. Blood spattered the quilt. I tried to sit up, but couldn't move. Every part of me ached. My mouth parted, but no words worked their way through my puffy lips. A soft moaning sound drifted to my ears. My muddled head tried to focus. Was I moaning? I was dizzy and desperately wanted to detach from my body. To escape from the pain. More moaning. It wasn't coming from me after all. I tried to scoot towards the sound, but the pain was too great. Especially from my arm. Who was moaning? It sounded like ghosts. I cringed. Were they coming to take me away? Where were they? I pushed myself on the linoleum floor with my feet, sliding on a pool of blood. I looked out my door. Pale eyes fixed on me, watching my every move. White wispy shapes drifted towards me. The moaning intensified.

"Stop!" I yelled.

The moaning grew louder.

"No more! Stop!" I covered my ears, trying to block out the moans.

Hands grabbed me, sucking me toward…

"JaDon! Wake up!"

I forced the hands off my shoulders as my eyes sprang open. Mrs. Winters was shaking me. Her normal perfectly arranged short hair was sticking out all over her head. Mr. Winters stood behind her, his eyes puffy and alarmed.

My heart thundered in my chest and my pajamas were soaked with sweat. Michael and McKenna tumbled through the doorway.

"What's going on?" asked Michael.

"It's okay," Mrs. Winters said. "He just had a nightmare."

A nightmare. I noticed the clean dresser. The waterfall picture on the wall. The clock. I wasn't in the shack. The reality of my past could not reach me. Or could it? I took a deep breath and then clamped my mouth shut. Had I been yelling out loud?

"You're all right, JaDon," said Mrs. Winters, releasing her grip on my shoulders.

I pushed myself up in bed. "But that's just it. I won't be all right until they find him."

"Find who?" asked Michael, pushing forward. "Who are you talking about? Why do they need to find him? Who needs to find who?"

Mr. Winters snapped to attention. "That's it, kids. Back to bed."

"But we want to know what he's talking about," protested McKenna.

"It was just a bad dream," said Mrs. Winters. "He's still waking up. You know how it is. Sometimes dreams seem real and get stuck in our heads." She herded them out the door. "Come along. I'll tuck you in bed."

"But…" Michael began.

"No buts," said Mrs. Winters. "To bed."

Mr. Winters stayed by my side and waited quietly until the kids were gone. "She's probably right about a nightmare just being stuck in your head, so I'm going to give you a minute or two for it to fade away."

I nodded. I tried to focus on the framed photo on the wall, hoping the sound of moaning and the image of ghosts in the hallway would fade away. My nightmares were getting worse.

Mr. Winters rubbed the stubble on his chin, watching me carefully. "I know there are secrets about your past that we aren't supposed to ask about, but I need to know. Are you in danger?"

I wanted to yell yes, but Mr. Costas had warned me to be very careful if I wanted to keep a protected place to stay. "I'm safe as long as I stay hidden."

"Someone is looking for you?"

I looked down at the blue blanket and nodded.

"Is my family in danger with you staying here?"

"Marty!" Mrs. Winters exclaimed as she returned. "We're not supposed to ask questions."

"I have the right to know if my family is at risk. It's my job to keep all of you safe."

I closed my eyes. Where would I go if I couldn't stay here? Would I have to change schools and start over again? Would I just have to keep running? "I'm so far from home that I'd be nearly impossible to find, and Mr. Costas has made sure I can't be traced. The man looking for me would have no reason to harm you anyhow. You're safe."

Mr. Winters looked me in the eye. I forced myself to keep my eyes locked on his. It was the truth. Almost.

"Come on, Marty. Let's let him get back to sleep." She studied my face. "If he can."

Mr. Winters stood, but continued to look at me. "Okay. But can you promise me something?"

I nodded.

"If you ever feel like we *are* in danger, can you let me know?"

I swallowed hard. "Yes."

"You promise?"

"Marty!" Mrs. Winters tried to herd him to the door like she had done with her children.

He pushed her hands away. "This is important, Michelle." He looked back at me. "Do you promise?"

This was a good reminder that my time here was short. One way or another, I would probably have to move soon. "Yes. I promise."

CHAPTER 20
BIKE RIDE

Three weeks passed slowly without a word from Mr. Costas or letters from my sisters. I had no way to reach them or protect them. I was completely cut off from their lives. So much of my existence had wrapped around keeping them safe. Now I struggled to find meaning. Life didn't seem to matter. My reckless nature intensified to the point that teachers began to notice.

The weather was still warm, so we continued to play outdoor sports in P.E. I was glad. Kicking and throwing balls were great ways to release my pent-up frustration. Today we were practicing tossing the football before heading out to the field. I could throw with one hand, but found my control was lacking. I would be so glad when the doctor could finally remove my cast.

My throwing partner for the day was a husky football player named Dave. He was intentionally throwing the ball hard. We had to spread out further than the other pairs. I watched the way he threw and started copying his technique. The football went farther and faster than I had ever thrown it before. I smiled. The competitive nature in each of us flared and our practice became intense.

"Nice throws, gentleman," said Coach Ruttledge. "Make sure you don't invade the space of those around you though. You're making some of the other groups nervous about getting hit in the head."

"Got it, Coach," said Dave.

We shifted closer to the school, freeing up a large area between us and a pair of girls. Dave threw even harder. I barely managed to catch it. I threw harder in return, my grip slipping slightly as I threw. The ball went hard to the left, landing on the school roof.

"Really?" Dave exclaimed. "Go grab another ball from the bag before Coach can notice. Hurry! Otherwise we have to go find the janitor to get it down."

I ran toward the ball bag, but paused. The steel trash dumpster was close to the brick wall. It couldn't be that hard to get the ball off the roof. Granted, two fully functioning arms would make the climb easier, but it was worth a try.

I pulled my arm out of the sling and wiggled my fingers. My arm didn't hurt any more. It seemed like it was time to remove the cast, but Mr. Costas had probably forgotten about me. Was he that busy? The dumpster smelled like rotting green beans and wet paper towels, so I held my breath as I climbed to the top. Thankfully the lid was closed. I pulled myself up the wall's drain pipe, using the indentations between bricks for a little extra support. My cast arm was clumsy and weak, but I managed to pull myself to the top of the roof.

"You have got to be kidding me!" exclaimed Coach Ruttledge, shielding his eyes as he looked up. "What are you doing up there?"

"I just had to get our football!" I shouted back. I grabbed the ball and threw it to the ground.

The rest of the students from our class gathered closer, watching me. Comments began to float up about how stupid but brave I was.

Coach smacked his head. "The janitor could have done that. Wait right there and I'll have him get a ladder so you can get down."

"It's okay," I said, returning to the pipe and swinging my legs over the ledge. "I got this."

"Wait! Don't go down…"

I was already sliding down the pole. My hands were sweaty by now, so I slid a little faster than I'd hoped, but I managed to land on the trash dumpster. I jumped down to the ground.

"Are you okay?" asked Coach.

I looked myself over, wiped my hands on my jeans, and stuck my arm back in the sling. "Yeah. I'm fine."

He rubbed his forehead and adjusted his baseball cap. "You could have been killed. I could have been fired. Don't ever do that again."

"I was just trying to get the ball."

"I get that, but the janitor can do it—with a ladder." He tossed Dave the ball. "Let's have you and Dave practice on the other end of the field, *away* from the school."

"Got it, Coach," said Dave.

We started running. Dave smacked me on the back. "You're crazy. But that was great."

In Chemistry, I was called on whenever we had an experiment that seemed risky to the rest of the class. I obviously didn't mind, as I was the one volunteering. Besides, I knew Mr. Zandini wouldn't do anything so risky that I would actually get hurt. Of course, there was an instance where we could have been hurt, but it wasn't the teacher's fault.

A student in the back of the class named Rick managed to catch his green plaid sleeve on fire while he was working over a Bunsen burner. Panicking, he started waving his arms.

"Put it out! Put it out!" he yelled to the boy next to him.

His partner froze. "How?"

Meanwhile the fire quickly spread up his arm.

"Drop and roll," yelled Mr. Zandini. He grabbed a fire blanket from the supply closet.

Rick started running around the classroom in terror, oblivious to the fact Mr. Zandini was trying to reach him with the blanket. The extra oxygen fed the flames, causing them to spread down his shirt toward his jeans.

I instinctively tackled him and tried to make him roll. The fire nipped at my cast until Mr. Zandini caught up and smothered him with the fire blanket. He checked us both for injuries. Rick had mild burns over his arms and chest. My sling was singed, but I was unharmed.

"That's the first time I've been glad I still had a cast," I said.

Mr. Zandini inspected my arm. "It certainly came in handy today. I still want the nurse to look you over. Can you escort Rick to her office?"

"Sure."

"And Jason?" he called as we walked to the door. "Thanks. That was risky, but helpful."

I nodded and kept walking.

"For the rest of you, let's review fire safety procedures *again*," Mr. Zandini said.

Another week passed without me hearing from Mr. Costas. In my frustration and anxiety, I began to take risks after school as well. Troy rarely tried to pick a fight with me anymore. He would still punch my arm when he walked on the bus and call me, "Cuz," but if I ignored him he let it drop.

One day, Shania wasn't on the bus. She told me she would be riding home with friends again. It had already been a bad day and now my feeling of loneliness and depression was reaching critical mass. I passed my usual seat and walked to the back of the bus. As soon as I dropped into the last seat, the chattering stopped. A bus load of faces turned toward me with puzzled expressions. I ignored them and looked out the window, searching for Troy's hulking frame. I just needed a distraction from my life. Talking to Shania sometimes gave me an escape, but with her gone, drastic measures were in order. I figured today even a beating would do. It might make me feel like I was back home. The talking began again, largely about how I was asking for trouble.

Minutes passed. I tensed my body, ready for a blow. The grief bomb inside my chest needed to be diffused before it exploded. I began to wonder if I was tempting disaster. My bruises were finally gone and my stitches had dissolved. Did I really need more? The bus engine roared to life. I looked up in surprise. No Troy. He must have been suspended again, or just missed school. A mixture of disappointment and relief washed over me. How long could I contain my frustrations?

The next day, all eyes were on me as I walked on the bus.

"Where are you sitting today?" asked a freshman near the front.

I ignored him and dropped in the seat by Shania.

She turned to me, pushing stray curls out of her eyes. "Why'd he ask that?"

"I guess I sat in a different seat yesterday."

150

"Okay."

The girl in back of us added, "Yeah. The *back* seat. Troy's spot."

Shania's forehead crinkled. "Really?"

I shrugged.

"Why would you do that? Did you catch a mind-eating disease?"

"No. I just needed a change."

"So wear a different shirt. What happened?" She looked me over. "You don't have any new bruises or bandages. Did he rebreak your arm?"

"Troy didn't show up."

"Good thing. Do *I* need to knock the sense back into you?"

I snorted. "That would be fun to see."

"I'm serious. You've been acting strange lately. Is something going on?"

"No."

"Oh, really? Then why the sudden death wish?"

I scowled. The anger and frustration building inside of me slammed into my mouth and pushed its way out. "How would you know if I was being strange? You barely know me. Nobody here really knows me. I'm not allowed to see the only people who know my normal."

"What is that supposed to mean? Who aren't you allowed to see?"

"Nobody. Just forget it." I gritted my teeth.

"You're cutting me off, just like that?" Shania's voice went up in pitch. "So I barely know you, huh? I've been sitting beside you in this seat for over a month talking to you, and you don't think I know you at all?"

"Not really."

"Fine." She grabbed her backpack. "It was nice not knowing you." She climbed over my legs and threw her stuff in a seat six rows back.

I punched the seat in front of me and fumed until the bus whined to a stop for her. She stomped past, purposely not looking my way. I had just blown off the one person I could talk to.

Something snapped in me, like a smoldering fire combusting. I felt J.R.-quality rage burn away my outer shell. The bus stopped. I stormed down the stairs, skipping my usual search for J.R. and pounding on the Winters' storm door. Mrs. Winters opened it, barely getting out of the way in time for me to barrel inside.

"What's wrong?" she asked.

"Did Mr. Costas call yet?"

"No. I'm sorry. Still no word…"

"Then that's what's wrong."

Michael sat at the table, munching on a handful of chips.

"Can I borrow your bike?" I asked as I flung my backpack on the floor.

"But I thought you weren't…"

"Thanks." I stormed into the garage, grabbed his bike from a rack on the wall, and pushed the garage door opener.

"Wait, Jason," said Mrs. Winters. "You know you can't…"

"My name's not Jason!" I yelled. "I have to get out of here." I climbed on the bike and pedaled out of the garage.

"Stop!" yelled Mrs. Winters. "Come back."

I ignored her and pedaled as fast as I could. Who cared if J.R. saw me. At least I would know I wasn't forgotten. At least I wouldn't have to keep waiting and pretending to be part of this family and part of this school. I was done being

152

fake and alone. I wanted to see my sisters. I promised them we'd be together, and I was being forced to break that promise. Who did Mr. Costas think he was to keep them from me without a single phone call or letter? It had been a month with nothing.

The fresh air blasted my face, but I soaked it in. It wasn't school air. Or bus air. Or house air. It was free, out-in-the-open, unguarded air. I biked on the sidewalk next to the street, tempting fate. "Go ahead and find me!" I yelled. I pedaled faster until sweat began to drip down my stomach.

Flashing red lights blinked far up the road. A train whistle sounded. I kept pedaling. The railroad crossing gates began to lower and the bells started clanging. Adrenaline surged through me. Could I beat the train? I had to try. Did I care if I made it? Not right now. I saw the train pound down the track, blowing its whistle and spouting smoke. I didn't care. I just didn't care.

Second thoughts raced through my mind right as I flew over the track, mere seconds before the train thundered past. I squeezed the hand brakes, clinging to the handlebars until the wheels squealed to a stop. Dropping to the ground beside the bike, I started hyperventilating, holding my head between my knees.

"What am I doing?" I shouted. I struggled to catch my breath and calm down. "I'm falling apart. How do I make my nightmare end?"

CHAPTER 21

THREE LEGS

The garage door was closed when I finally returned. The code box taunted me. Of course I didn't know the code. I wasn't truly part of this family. They were good to give me a place to stay, but I was just a visitor.

I leaned the bike against the garage, and knocked on the front door. Mrs. Winters opened quickly. She had clear latex gloves on her hands and was holding a scrub brush.

"There you are!" Her voice wavered. "I'll open the garage door for the bike, and then you need to come inside quickly."

"Okay," I said. I expected her to yell at me for taking off. Maybe that would come later. I wheeled the bike back to the rack in the garage and walked inside.

Mrs. Winters closed the garage door behind me and motioned to the couch with shaking hands. "Have a seat."

I slumped onto the couch and prepared for a verbal beating. She seemed very agitated. At least she probably wouldn't talk with her fists like J.R.

She peeled off her cleaning gloves and rested them on her apron. "I'm guessing you know how foolish it was to take off like that," she said.

I nodded.

"You scared Michael, and had all of us worried. I almost called the police. I know things are hard for you but you can't just take off like that. Understand?"

154

I nodded again and risked looking up at her. Her face was flushed and the lines between her eyebrows were furrowed deeper. Would she get mad enough to kick me out? Would I have to go to another foster family? I felt like punching myself.

"Right before you left, you mentioned Mr. Costas not calling. You were obviously mad about it. I got to thinking that it had been a really long time since he had checked on you, so I called him."

"You had his number? He told me it was safer if I didn't call."

"He gave it to me in case of emergencies. I figured you taking off *was* an emergency—especially if it had to do with him not calling." Her frown deepened and she adjusted her glasses.

I scooted to the edge of the couch. "What? Tell me."

"He said not to call that number again. It wasn't safe anymore. He'll call tonight on a secure line to see if you're back."

"And then what? Did he say anything else?"

"No. He hung up." She started twisting the gloves nervously. "He was…Well, he was rude, and sounded stressed, and he's never been anything but calm and polite."

"You're right," I said.

She got up quickly. "I'm going to finish cleaning inside the oven. I think it will help calm me down. We'll eat dinner once I'm done."

"Okay."

She pulled the wrinkled gloves back on and returned to the kitchen. I sat for a moment. No hitting or yelling. Why did I still feel like a bomb had dropped? I grabbed my backpack and trudged upstairs.

Michael stood in front of my door. "Are you okay?"

"Yeah."

"Is my bike okay?"

"Yeah. Sorry about that. I shouldn't have taken off with it. I just had to let off some steam."

"So did you let it off?"

"What?"

"Did you let off the steam?"

"Enough."

"Good." He stuck his ear buds back in and returned to his room.

I dropped onto the bed and started to unzip my backpack. Who was I kidding? I wasn't going to be able to do any homework until Mr. Costas called. I had to know what was going on. I stared at the wall instead. My mind started bouncing around from painful memories to possible things Mr. Costas might say. I was going down a dangerous spiral, so I decided to journal and attempt to get back on track. I let the thoughts flow onto paper until we were called for dinner.

Mrs. Winters placed a big blue bowl of macaroni and cheese onto the center of the table. "Does anyone want me to dish them up?"

We each let her spoon heaping spoonfuls onto our plates. I was very familiar with boxed macaroni and cheese. It was one of the few things I could make at home. I could picture my sisters eating it with me. I wondered what they were eating tonight.

Mrs. Winters kept quiet at the table. She looked at her husband and opened her mouth several times as if to say something, and then stuffed in a bite of macaroni and cheese instead. The rest of us followed her lead and sat in awkward silence. I shoveled food into my mouth until my plate was merely coated with an orange shadow.

The phone rang. Mrs. Winters jumped up and scurried to the phone. "Hello? Yes, he's back. I'll let him take it to his room." She handed me the phone.

"Thanks." I walked quickly to the room and closed the door.

"Are you there?" Mr. Costas asked.

"Yeah."

"I'm on a secure line at the police station."

"Okay. So what's goin' on? Why has it been a month since I heard from you?" I tried to keep my voice calm and steady, but irritation weaved through my words.

"I planned on it, but my world turned upside down a few weeks ago."

"How?"

"J.R. reappeared. I came home from work one day, and he was in my home waiting for me."

I sucked in a breath.

"I walked in the door, and he was sitting on *my* couch with a hunting rifle pointed straight at my chest. There was an open beer beside him—on *my* side table, but he was sober. He demanded to know where all of you were. I told him I wasn't sure. That we were moving you around a lot. But he didn't believe me. He said it was lucky for me that I didn't have a family, because he'd have taken them by now as payback. Then he told me to look out my back door." Mr. Costas started choking up. "He still had the gun pointing at me, so I did. He turned on the porch light." He stopped talking as he struggled to keep control.

"What? What was on the porch? What did J.R. do?" I asked, afraid to hear the answer.

"On the cement slab by my lawn chair he had written *Give me JaDon* in huge letters...in blood."

I closed my eyes and dropped to my bed.

"I've seen some awful things with my job but…but this…My dog's leg…it was right beside the writing." Mr. Costas could barely talk now. "I asked him where my dog was. He led me to my bathroom and opened the door. My dog was covered in blood, lying on my bath mat, but he was still alive. He whined when he saw me and struggled to stand—on his *three* legs." Mr. Costas paused. "He tried to limp to the door. I bent down to hold him. The blood had clotted, but when he moved the blood started flowing. I grabbed…I grabbed a towel and tried to stop the bleeding. J.R. asked where you were again. I told him if he just waited I'd look it up. He laughed and said that wasn't good enough…and he…then he…aimed his gun and shot my dog. Right in my arms. If he had been off by an inch, he would have killed me, too. That dog was my best friend."

Tears rolled down my cheeks. "I'm so sorry."

He was quiet for a minute as he fought for control. "He dragged me back to the kitchen and crammed a pencil and paper in my hand. He told me he knew I had gone to visit and probably had the address memorized. He told me to write where the three of you were staying. I still refused, but then he put the barrel of the gun to my forehead. I made up an address for somewhere on the other side of Arkansas. He told me that if it was right, he'd leave me alone, but if I'd made something up, he'd be back to kill me. He swung the gun at my head, and the next thing I knew, it was the middle of the night and he was gone."

"I'm sorry. Your dog…your head…now you're not safe. This is all my fault…"

"No," Mr. Costas said firmly. "It isn't. It's all on J.R. Don't even let your mind go down that road."

"But what do you do now? You haven't gone back home have you?"

"No. The police arranged a safe place for me to stay for now, with strict instructions not to call you. It took a lot of convincing for them to even let me call you tonight. It sounded like you had taken off. Mrs. Winters was concerned."

"Yeah. I guess I lost it for a moment."

"That's understandable, but there's too much at risk for you to do that again. You've got to keep it together."

"I try. But I want to see my sisters—or at least hear from them."

"I know. I'm not allowed to visit either you or the girls for a while, so I'm afraid I can't deliver letters. I know that's hard on all of you. But maybe you'll be together soon. The police are investing more resources and time into the search."

I wanted to say something appreciative or hopeful, but nothing would come out. Finally I asked, "Are you gonna tell the girls what happened…with you and your dog?"

"I wasn't planning on it. You don't think I should, do you?"

"No. Their heads are already full of stuff like that. They don't need more."

"That's what I was thinking. And it seems like they're adjusting to their new life. At least Missy is."

"Their temporary life," I insisted.

"Yes. Their temporary life. I don't think we need to disturb that. I'll call them though, so they aren't confused. Hopefully they won't do anything crazy like you did today."

I winced. "Sorry. I thought you just forgot about me."

"Do you understand now?"

"Yes, and I feel awful about it."

"Me, too. I'll try to keep you updated from now on. Hopefully it won't be for much longer."

"We've been saying that for over five weeks."

"I know." Mr. Costas sighed over the phone. "But J.R. gave us a new lead. Police are watching my house now in case he comes back to finish me off for lying to him."

"Seems like everyone involved with J.R. gets kicked out of their home."

"True—for now." Mr. Costas was quiet for a moment. "Is there anything you need? Well, besides your sisters and your freedom?"

"No."

"Good night, then."

"Good night."

I flopped back on my bed. Now Mr. Costas was suffering thanks to our insane lives. I felt horrible about his murdered dog. As shocking as it was to Mr. Costas, I knew J.R. was used to cutting up animals. It probably hadn't pricked his conscience in the least. Mr. Costas had talked about his dog during our long drive out here. It was a golden retriever. Images of a bloody, three-legged dog were now stuck in my mind and weighed heavy on my heart.

This was far from over.

CHAPTER 22
HIGH DIVE

A few days later, Ms. Jane had another weekly journal check. We passed our notebooks to the front of the class. Up to this point, I had been careful not to mention J.R. by name, and if anything about my past seeped onto the pages, I labeled it Private. She had honored her word, and only made comments on the unlabeled pages. I was surprised she actually read anything I wrote. How did she find time to read journals from so many students? I looked forward to reading her comments. She didn't just write, "Great job," or "Write more," like I had expected. Her comments were specific and encouraging.

I glanced over at Shania. She eventually turned my way, but immediately diverted her eyes when she caught me looking at her. We hadn't talked since my explosion on the bus. My sisters had been mad at me many times, but they never held a grudge for this long. Maybe because they needed me. Shania obviously did not.

"Now that you've passed your notebooks forward, you can pass the tests backward," said Ms. Jane.

Most of the students groaned.

"I warned you that our final test on *To Kill a Mockingbird* would be today. You're welcome to keep your books on your desks in case you need to mention a quote or specific example in an answer. You have the entire class period to complete it, so take your time and do your best."

The test was entirely made up of essay questions. I heard more complaints as my classmates realized there weren't just multiple choice answers to circle. I actually preferred essay questions. Even if I wasn't sure of an exact answer, I could write my way around it and sound convincing. I hoped that ability didn't come from J.R. He could be quite convincing when he set his mind to it. He was a horrible writer though, so I eased my mind with that differentiation.

Ms. Jane read journals while we worked on the test. By the time class was nearly over, she had read the journals from my entire row and passed them back. She began to read journals from the next row. I placed my test on her desk and sat back in my seat. I was glad I had a few minutes to flip through my journal pages and read the comments.

One page had a bright yellow sticky note on it. Unusual. It said, "Can you please come to class early—right after you finish lunch? I'd like to talk to you."

The sticky note clung to the page I wrote after my bike ride. My stomach dropped. I forgot to label that day as private. I avoided Ms. Jane's eyes and looked at the clock. Thankfully, it was only a minute until the bell would ring. I scowled. Ms. Jane was my favorite teacher. I actually cared what she thought, and didn't mean for her to know about me at my worst.

The bell rang and I dashed out of my seat. I accidently cut off Shania in the process and mumbled an apology. She ignored me and talked to some of her friends instead. Not surprising. I merged with the crowd until I reached my history class. I sat near the door because I knew I had to leave quickly. P.E. was next, and Coach Ruttledge told us to bring a swimming suit and towel today. I needed extra time to grab them from my locker.

The history teacher was talking, but nothing registered in my head. I was already thinking about P.E. I'd never actually swam in a swimming pool before. I'd been in creeks and ponds, but our school didn't have a pool, and there wasn't a neighborhood pool nearby. J.R. wouldn't have taken us anyhow. He figured a creek was just as good.

As soon as the bell rang, I slipped out the door and rushed to my locker. I grabbed my suit and towel and walked as quickly to the locker room as I could without being yelled at for running. I changed into my faded blue swimming trunks. They were tighter and shorter than I remembered. Was it possible I had grown since swimming with my cousins? Of course, now that I thought about it, they were tight then too, I just hadn't really cared.

Some of the guys glanced my way and smirked. Let them. I'd just get into the water as quick as possible. I bumped my arm on the locker and groaned. I'd forgotten to bring a bag for my cast.

Coach Ruttledge had us sit in two rows by the pool while he reviewed the rules he had shared yesterday, and threatened us about causing trouble or being careless.

"Everyone in the pool," he said at last.

I followed the mob to the ledge.

"Whoa. Not you, Jason. Do you have a bag for your cast?"

"No. But I should get it off soon anyhow, so it's okay."

"I don't think so. I don't want a phone call from Mom or Dad about you ruining your cast later. Run to the nurse's office. She'll have something to cover it."

I looked down at my swimming suit. "You mean, go down the hall like this?"

He looked at my swimming suit and his eyebrows shot up. "Did you bring a towel?"

"Yeah."

"Wrap that around you, or change back into your clothes. Just hurry."

I returned to the locker room and eyed my towel. Clothes were probably the better choice. I jammed my t-shirt over my head and pulled my jeans over my trunks. My legs felt cramped and stiff, but I managed to walk to the nurse's office.

"Do you have a bag or something I could use to cover my cast?" I asked.

She was holding her breath while tying a knot in the top of a plastic sack. I immediately plugged my nose and felt like gagging. Another student sat on the narrow vinyl bed holding a bag-lined trashcan under her face.

The nurse put the sack in a small dumpster with wheels and washed her hands. She pulled a plastic bag off a roll from her cupboard. "Here you go."

"Thanks." I grabbed the bag and rushed out, not releasing my plugged nose until I had stiff-walked way down the hall.

Once in the locker room, I quickly yanked off my outer clothes and wrapped my cast with the bag. I rushed back to the pool. The rest of the class was already in the water.

"Much better," said Coach Ruttledge, eying the bag. "Jump in."

Without a second thought, I stepped off the rough cement ledge. The water was cool, but not nearly as cold as the creek usually was. It was clear and clean and had an unfamiliar chemical smell. I dived underneath anyhow.

Coach had us try different strokes. I'd never had lessons before, but watched my classmates closely until I could do a rough imitation. Near the end of class, he told us we could have some free time in the water.

Most of my classmates started splashing each other or racing. I eyed the diving board, wondering what it would be like to jump off of it. The divers on TV made it look easy. I waited until no one was swimming right under it and pulled myself out of the water. Dripping and cold, I quickly climbed the stairs so I wouldn't draw more attention to my swimming suit. It seemed like divers sometimes got a running start, so I ran to the edge, bounced, and leaped.

My stomach dropped as I sailed through the air and plunged into the water head first. I bobbed to the surface and sputtered for a moment.

"What are you doing?" demanded Coach Ruttledge.

I wiped the water out of my eyes. "Diving?"

"I said we would work our way up to that."

"Oh," I said. "That must have been while I was getting a bag."

He smacked his forehead.

"Sorry. I've just always wanted to give diving a try."

"That was your first dive?"

"Yeah."

"Have you had any training?"

"No."

"Swimming lessons?"

"No."

He rubbed his head. "Yet you have no fear of water. Or roofs. Do you have a death wish?"

"Not really." My mind flashed to the yellow note on my journal. My bike ride made me wonder.

"How about from now on, ask before you do something."

"Got it," I said.

I was relieved to change out of my swimming trunks and into clothes that fit. By the time I'd walked to the bus, my head was dry. That was one of the benefits that came with having a nearly shaved head. I walked down the bus aisle and sandwiched myself between the seat I used to share with Shania and Troy's seat. I wasn't in the mood for a fight or drama.

Troy caught my eye as I sat down. "Stop staring, *Cuz*," he growled.

I turned my back to him and slid into my own seat. He snarled at a couple more kids who made the mistake of looking at him, and smacked one for getting too close. At least he stayed in his seat.

I flipped through my journal again, reading the page about my race with the train. Had I been so upset that I couldn't even remember to label it private? I had tried to distance myself from teachers this year. Partly to protect myself so it would be easier when I returned home. Partly to protect them. The last time I told a teacher, my coach, too much it had not ended well. There was no chance of Coach Ruttledge becoming close to me. He probably thought I was crazy. I didn't want Ms. Jane to think I was crazy. For some reason, I cared what she thought.

The bus braked in front of the Winters' home. I grabbed my backpack and walked straight to the door. Mrs. Winters answered before I could ring the doorbell.

"I have good news," she said.

My heart started beating faster. "What?"

"Mr. Costas just called."

"Yeah? Did they catch him?"

She looked taken back for a moment. "He didn't say anything about catching someone." Her puzzled expression morphed into a smile. "But he did say he'd talked to the doctor near us and set up an appointment for Friday to get your cast removed."

I tried to wipe away traces of disappointment and focus on the good news. "That's great."

"Soon you can take a regular shower again and scrub where the cast is. Not washing under all that plaster would drive me crazy."

"Yeah. It makes me crazy all right."

I wandered upstairs. Maybe thinking I was crazy was safest for Ms. Jane, too. Anyone who cared for me got hurt. I didn't want to add her to the list.

CHAPTER 23
CAST SAW

"Ah, Jason. Have a seat." Ms. Jane wheeled her chair next to where I usually sat.

I dropped into my chair.

"So…How are you?" she asked.

"Fine."

"How's school going for you?"

"Good."

"Everything's okay at home?"

"I guess."

She studied my face for a moment. "Should I get right to the point then?"

"That would probably be best."

"Did you really ride your bike over the tracks right as a train was coming?"

"Well, technically it wasn't *my* bike, but yes."

She took in a sharp breath. "Why?"

"Because I'm crazy." I looked down at my feet. It was better if she kept her distance from me. I cared what she thought, but if being labeled crazy kept her safe, it was worth it.

"Not buying it." She leaned back in her chair and crossed her arms. "Reckless I might believe—especially after talking to some of the other teachers."

"You guys get together and talk about me? That's weird. Do you do that to all your students?"

"No. Just the ones who stand out."

"Lucky me. What do they say?"

"That you're reckless but brave. I heard about how you put out the fire when a kid was running around in flames in Chemistry. I also heard how you climbed onto the roof to get a ball and dived into the pool without any experience—or permission."

"So what do *you* say?"

Ms. Jane shoved her shoulder-length hair back behind one ear. "I say you're willing to take risks that others avoid. That you think and feel deeply. What I don't say, to the other teachers at least, is that I'm concerned about you. I told you I wouldn't share anything you wrote in your journal unless it was a danger to you or someone else. Is the bike incident something you plan to repeat?"

"No."

"Do you intend to do anything else that endangers your life?"

"Not that I know of."

"That's not good enough."

"Why does it matter to you? I'm just one of hundreds of your students."

"I care about all of my students. And I think you have amazing potential. Your answers in class are profound, and your writing is...well it's not the type of writing I usually read in a sophomore journal. It's deeper, and captivating and...poetic."

"Please don't say that to anyone else. The other students would never let me hear the end of it."

"I won't." She got an evil twinkle in her eye. "Unless I hear about you trying another race-the-train stunt. Then it's all out in the open."

I rolled my eyes. "I said I wouldn't do anything like that again."

"Good. Then you have nothing to fear from me."

A couple students walked in the door. Ms. Jane immediately wheeled her chair back to the desk. "Welcome," she said.

I pulled out my books and reviewed our conversation in my mind. She didn't seem scared away by my crazy angle, but at least nothing had been said that should make her want to snoop into my past. I exhaled. This time, I would keep my teachers safe.

Friday came at last. Mrs. Winters drove me to the Medical Center as promised. I sat in the doctor's office, scratching under my cast for what I hoped would be the last time.

A short man with a receding hairline walked in. "I'm Dr. Edwards. Sounds like you're ready to get rid of a cast. Right?"

"Very," I said.

He looked at my singed sling. "Did you have an accident after your initial accident?"

I should have just thrown my sling away after the chemistry fire. "Something like that." I pulled it off and stuck it behind my back.

He nodded. "Okay then. I need you to sit on the exam table and rest your arm on a pillow in your lap."

I sat as instructed and watched as the doctor pulled out a small cast saw. "This won't hurt. It's just loud," he said.

The saw had a vacuum hose attached, and a flat circular metal blade with teeth. He turned it on and it started vibrating back and forth, buzzing loudly. He made a long cut on the top and bottom of my cast, and then traded the saw for a special tool resembling pliers. He used them to spread the cast pieces, and then used scissors to cut off cast padding and the stockinette.

My arm was a different shade of brown and was slightly thinner than my other arm. A layer of dead skin was peeling.

"It kind of smells, doesn't it?" Mrs. Winters wrinkled her nose.

"That's normal," said Dr. Edwards as he rubbed off some of the dead skin.

"But the smell will go away, right?" she asked.

"Yes." He examined my arm, turning it in different directions. "It looks good. I'd still recommend elevating it and icing it occasionally, but it's healing well. Just take it easy for a while. No lifting heavy objects."

I wiggled my fingers, marveling at the freedom. "Got it."

"I'll send papers up to the front and you can check out."

"Thanks," I said.

I enjoyed flexing and twisting my arm on the ride home. Michael and McKenna raced downstairs when we walked through the door.

"Can we see your arm?" asked McKenna.

I extended it in front of them.

"Nasty," said Michael. "Your skin's peeling off in chunks!" He couldn't stop staring.

"Should I make us a cake to celebrate?" said Mrs. Winters.

Mr. Winters walked in the room. "Cake sounds good."

She tied an apron around her waist and pulled a yellow cake mix out of the cupboard. I sat on the couch, elevating my hand on the arm rest. A smile tugged at my lips. I couldn't remember the last time someone had baked a cake to celebrate anything related to me. The girls tried a few times for my birthday, but J.R. never bought cake mixes, so they had to struggle with creating one on their own.

McKenna sat down beside me. She couldn't take her eyes off my arm. "So now can you tell us how you broke it?"

"I heard that," said Mrs. Winters. "No questions. Go do your homework."

"I don't have homework."

"Then go clean your room."

"It *is* clean," McKenna protested.

"My type of clean, or your type of clean?"

McKenna rolled her eyes and dragged herself off the couch. "I'll go clean it again."

I followed her upstairs. My journal topic for tonight would be the escape from my cast. I sat on my bed and started writing. This would be a safe entry that Ms. Jane could read without any growing concerns.

That night after dinner, Mrs. Winters cut into the cake. It was lopsided, but it was covered in thick chocolate frosting, so it looked beautiful to me. She gave us each a thick slice.

"Can we watch a movie while we eat?" Michael asked. "It's Friday, you know."

"And get crumbs and frosting on the couch?" Mrs. Winters shook her head. "I don't think so. *After* you're done eating we can watch a movie though."

Michael turned to me. "What kind of movie do you want to watch?"

I shrugged. "I like about anything." I thought for a moment. "Well, except horror movies." I'd lived through enough horror on my own without being reminded about it.

Michael and McKenna debated for a long time, but finally decided on *Inside Out*. I wasn't excited about watching a cartoon, but I kept my opinion to myself. It turned out to be much better than I thought.

That night, I put my arm on a pillow, just to be safe. It wasn't long before I drifted to sleep. Soon I heard the cast saw. I opened my eyes and found myself back in the doctor's office. Dr. Edwards was still cutting my cast. I looked up to smile at him for setting my arm free, only to discover that it wasn't Dr. Edwards at all. It was J.R.

"You thought you could get away from me, didn't you?" He smirked. "You know that's not possible." He looked back down at my cast and pushed harder with the saw. Instead of tickling, it started to cut into my skin.

"Stop!" I yelled. "You're hurting me!"

"I am? But at least I'm using a saw." He held the whirling blade up to his face. "I just used a dull knife on the last limb I cut off. Remember Mr. Costas? That girly-man? He needed to be taught a lesson, thanks to you. His dog sure howled when I cut off its leg." He pressed the saw back into my arm. "Will you howl, too?"

I woke up with a start. My arm was tangled in the covers, so I freed it and rubbed the chafed skin. My heart was beating fast. I glanced at the door, hoping I hadn't yelled again. No one came running, so I sank back into the pillows.

On Monday morning, I rushed to the bus, cramming a blueberry Pop-Tart into my mouth as I climbed up the steps. Several stops later, Shania walked down the aisle. She still avoided sitting in the empty space next to me, but she gave me half a smile.

"Your cast is off," she said. "That's great."

She walked two rows further and sat down.

Maybe the ice was thawing. That would have to be good enough for now.

My cast removal was mentioned several times throughout the morning. Even my continual lunch companions, Miguel and Parker, commented on it. Normally we were so busy eating we didn't say more than a few words. Today, they were full of questions. Well, a couple questions.

"Does it still hurt?" asked Miguel.

"Some."

"Can you lift weights or something to make it look like your other arm?" asked Parker.

"Eventually. I have to ease into it."

Then it was back to devouring pizza and chicken nuggets. That was fine with me. Our silence was comfortable and expected. Eating was our priority.

The sole of my disintegrating shoes flapped as I walked into English, causing me to trip. I caught myself on a desk.

"That was close," said Ms. Jane. "Congratulations on the absence of your cast. I'm glad you didn't actually fall and need a new one."

"Yeah."

"Would you like some tape?" she whispered.

The blood rushed to my face. I nodded.

She dug through her desk and selected a roll of duct tape. She slipped it under the papers on my desk. I was grateful no one seemed to notice. The rest of the class found their seats.

"October is finally upon us, so we're going to read some stories by Edgar Allan Poe. Who can tell me something about this author?"

Soon we were in a deep discussion about the man. He was not one of my favorite authors. It seemed like Poe would be more to J.R.'s taste, if he actually liked to read.

174

"On your way out today, please take a book off the stack. It's a collection of Poe's short stories and poems. Start by reading *The Fall of the House of Usher*. We'll discuss it on Wednesday."

As soon as the students were out the door, I hurriedly wrapped tape around my shoe three times, hoping it would hold. I returned the tape to Ms. Jane.

"Thanks."

"No problem. Have a good day, Jason."

The rest of the day was as good as it can get at school. I stayed awake during history, and was able to swim in P.E. without wrapping a cast. Shania smiled at me on the bus again, and Troy was nowhere to be seen.

Even better, after school Mr. Costas called. "I've been talking to the police," he said.

"Okay."

"I told them how hard it was on the three of you not to be able to contact each other. They still won't let me visit you because J.R. could be watching me, so I can't deliver letters…"

"Great," I said with sarcasm.

"Let me finish. But they said it was okay for you to call the girls."

"What?!"

"They will give your foster parents the phone number. You can call them every Thursday night at 7:00."

My jaw dropped. I didn't know what to say.

"Are you there?"

"Yes. Thanks! That means a lot."

"I know. The only condition is one foster parent will have to be in the room with you."

"Why? What if they hear something they shouldn't?"

"That's just it. The police want to make sure you're careful with what you say. It was the only way I could get them to agree to the calls."

I thought for a moment. "Okay. It's still better than nothing."

"Good. I'll let Mrs. Winters know. Have a good night."

Yes, it was a good day and a good night. Could I dare to hope that things were improving?

CHAPTER 24
PASSED OUT

The next morning, I walked into first hour, hopeful for another good day. The girl with straight blond hair (I still hadn't bothered to learn her name) looked down at my shoes.

"Nice tape. Those things just get better and better."

"Hello to you, too," I said, starting to sit in my typical seat in the next row. Surprisingly, a seat was actually open in the back of the room. My luck was holding out. I changed course and headed to the back seat.

Blond hair girl spun around to see where I sat. I dropped my book onto the desk and waved, glad to have some distance from her. Not only could I avoid her snarky comments, but I could also avoid breathing in perfume-laden air. She crossed her arms and turned back to the front.

As soon as the bell rang, our geometry teacher gave each person in the front row a stack of papers. "Take one and pass it back. These are study guides for your test tomorrow. Make sure you fill them in during class. If you have any questions, ask me today so you do well on the test."

I read the first question and started looking up the required formula in my book. The assistant principal, Mr. Veatch, stuck his head in the room, and motioned for the teacher to come to the door.

Soon after the teacher left, the guy sitting by me elbowed me in the ribs. "Check this out."

Two guys in the seats next to him were out of their chairs, bending down at the waist, and taking rapid deep breaths. Another student was counting out loud for them.

"What're they doin'?" I asked.

"You've seriously never seen this before?"

"I guess not."

"It's the pass-out challenge. We found a video of it from years ago. Watch."

The two guys stood straight, holding their breath while the guy who had been counting pushed hard on each of them right at the chest. One collapsed onto the floor. The second stood for a couple more seconds and then fell, smacking his head on the desk on his way down.

"No way!" the guy next to me said.

I jumped out of my seat to check the guy's head. "He's bleeding!" I yelled.

The teacher came running in. "What happened?"

The blond shoe-appraiser in the front said, "Some imbeciles in the back were trying to pass out and got hurt."

He ran to my side. "Wake up," he said, patting the injured boy on the cheek. He pulled out his phone. "I need help in room 202. We have an unconscious boy with a head injury."

The guy on the floor next to us started reviving. "What's up?" he said in a groggy voice.

The teacher's shoulders slumped. "Make that two kids down."

Mr. Veatch rushed into the room. "The nurse is on her way. What's going on?"

"This group was trying to pass out while I was talking to you. It looks like this one hit his head on the way down."

Mr. Veatch grabbed the box of tissues and handed a thick stack to the teacher. He pressed them to the student's head. Blood immediately soaked through.

"Anybody else hurt?" asked Mr. Veatch.

"What?" asked the guy still recovering.

"Can you stand up?" Mr. Veatch asked him.

He pushed himself to his feet, but started swaying. His friend caught his arm. "I can't feel the side of my face," he said, slurring his words.

"Then sit back down," said our teacher.

The nurse hustled into the room carrying a supply case. After listening to a brief explanation she opened the case and pulled on plastic gloves. She removed the tissues and held a thick bandage to the student's head. She checked his eyes with her other hand. "I think we should get an ambulance, just in case."

The teacher made the call while the nurse wrapped the student's head.

"All of you, come with me," Mr. Veatch said, motioning to those of us in the back row.

"But we didn't do anything," a student protested.

"We'll figure out who did what in my office. The rest of you, back to your seats. These boys need some air."

I followed Mr. Veatch down the hall. He had us stand against the wall in his office while he walked back and forth in front of us.

"Whose idea was it to pass out on purpose?"

Most of the guys looked down at their feet.

"Did any of you join in?"

Everyone shook their head.

"Did any of you help the boys pass out?"

We all shook our heads again.

Mr. Veatch stopped pacing. "I find it hard to believe that you were all innocently doing your work while two boys were hyperventilating right next to you. Especially from those of you who have been in my office before. Do you realize how dangerous that is—even if you don't crack your head on the way down?"

A few of the boys shrugged.

"Is it worth risking impaired vision or speech or gross motor skills, or just killing off brain cells altogether?"

None of us responded.

"Well, is it?" He crossed his arms and glared at us. "One last chance to tell me about your involvement."

No one budged.

He sighed. "I guess I'll have to ask your classmates." He pulled out a sheet of paper. "Write down your name and student ID. I'll be in touch with you later."

He looked over the list of names while we filed out of the room. "Jason Williams. Are you the Jason who climbed on the roof to get a ball?"

I looked up in surprise. "Yes."

"Hmm." He squinted his eyes and pursed his lips.

Hmm? What was that supposed to mean? Heat rushed to my face. I hadn't done anything. I wasn't even involved in the stupid challenge.

I was still steamed at lunch, and angrily tore into my hamburger.

Miguel dropped his pizza onto his plate. "Did you guys hear about the ambulance coming this morning?"

"Yeah," said Parker.

I nodded. I didn't feel like sharing my so-called involvement.

"Those guys didn't have enough brain cells to spare," said Miguel.

"Nope," Parker agreed.

We finished eating and headed to our lockers. I was glad English was next. I needed a good distraction from the day. My heart sank. What if Mr. Veatch shared the names of everyone on his list? Would Ms. Jane think I was being reckless again? I grabbed my books and slammed my locker shut.

Ms. Jane had written a quote on the dry erase board. It said, "Be wise enough not to be reckless, but brave enough to take great risks."

Once we were settled, she said, "The quote on the board is by Frank Warren. I'm sure you've heard about our ambulance visit by now. I'm not going to dwell on how irresponsible or reckless I think that old pass-out challenge is, because all of you are smart enough to know better. If you didn't know it was dangerous, you should by now. An update in case you were concerned—I was told the student who hit his head had eighteen stitches and will be in the hospital overnight for his concussion and for observation. If anyone needs further convincing about depriving your brain of oxygen, see me after class."

I watched her eyes, looking for condemnation. I didn't normally dwell on what other people thought, but for some reason she seemed to care, and I didn't want to let her down. Her eyes rested on me for a moment, but her expression did not give a clue to what she was thinking.

"Now, back to our topic. Edgar Allan Poe and most of his fellow authors were good at writing descriptions. We're going to try writing good descriptions as well. If you look around the room, you'll notice some peculiar objects."

I scanned the classroom. A full length rectangular mirror was propped against the front wall. Two yard sticks were taped to the side wall, one on top of the other, making a tall stick. A piece of butcher paper was on the floor with a foot size chart on it. A scale was in the corner.

"In your journals, I want you to first describe your physical description. Give me specific details using the objects around the room. I want it so clear that a blindfolded person could picture you. I want to know eye color, if you have freckles, your hair style…everything. Then I want you to describe your personality. Once again, I want so many details that a friend could pick you out just by reading it."

"Are you going to read these out loud?" asked a girl in the second row. "I mean, that's kind of personal stuff."

"No, I won't read them aloud—unless you give me your permission. I know it seems risky or embarrassing, but not only does this assignment strengthen our writing skills, it lets us get to know each other better. I'll even demonstrate. Here's the one I wrote."

She walked over to her desk and grabbed a piece of paper. She read, "My name is Jane Arsenault. I am 5'4" and even though many of my students tower over me, I refuse to wear high heels. My flat, comfortable shoes are size seven. My hair is brown and shoulder-length with just a touch of wave. Thankfully I have only found two gray hairs, which I quickly plucked. My eyes are hazel. I wear contacts because my vision is atrocious, possibly due in part from reading whenever possible. My skin is the color of pastry dough, except in the summer when I have more time to venture outside. I am thirty-seven, and am getting laugh lines around my eyes and two deeper lines on my forehead. I weigh 125 pounds with problem areas I conceal with clothing and choose not to discuss."

The class snickered, and she continued. "I am an English teacher and enjoy what I do, except when students misbehave. I love kids and was hoping to have a few of my own by now. I'm married but have learned adoption may need to be my path to a family. I'm calm and loving, but also a perfectionist and stubborn. My pet peeve is laziness."

She looked up at the class. "Remember that." Then she continued. "I read every night before I go to bed and spend time studying the Bible, strengthening my relationship with God in the mornings. My favorite food is Italian, even though the pasta adds to my mentioned problem areas. Dark chocolate makes every day better and might help you as well if you need extra credit and have some to spare."

She returned her paper to her desk. "And on that fine note, I will let you begin on your own descriptions. Pull out your journals, and you may start writing. At the end of class, place them on my desk."

We sat in silence for a moment. I couldn't remember my previous teachers sharing that much about themselves. I hoped even more that she wasn't disappointed in me, especially for something I hadn't done.

Students started milling around the classroom. I walked straight to the scale. I was glad Ms. Jane brought the evaluation props. There was a mirror in my room, but I couldn't remember the last time I had been on a scale or measured my height or foot size. Mama used to take us to the doctor each year for a checkup, and the nurse would tell us our height and weight, but we hadn't gone at all since she left. As far as the girls and I knew, the only thing wrong with our health was brought on by living with J.R.

CHAPTER 25

GHOST STORY

A forgotten geometry book almost caused me to miss the bus. By the time I managed to climb back up the bus steps, there were no empty seats. I started looking for someone who wouldn't mind me invading their space.

Shania looked up and scooted towards the window. "You can sit here if you want."

I raised my eyebrows in surprise and dropped into the seat, careful not to crowd her too much. "Thanks."

The bus began its bumpy journey. We sat in silence for several minutes. I crammed my geometry book into my backpack with my other homework. She busied herself by pulling her curly hair into a ponytail.

"So, how's life been treating you?" she asked at last.

"Good," I answered. "How about for you?"

"Good."

She looked out the window. An awkward silence hung over us.

Finally, she said, "Crazy about the ambulance having to come for those guys."

"I know. Right?"

"I knew kids were doing stupid things like making themselves pass out, but I didn't think anyone would try it at school."

"Yeah."

"You've never tried it, have you?" she asked.

"No. Why? Did someone say I had?"

She cocked her head to the side. "No. Relax. Why so defensive?"

I forced myself to back off. "I was sittin' near the guys who did it, and Mr. Veatch thought I was involved. He called me to his office and everything."

"Ouch. Did you set things straight?"

"I don't know. I guess he just assumed the worst 'cuz teachers think I'm reckless."

She bobbed her head.

"What? You think I'm reckless too?"

"Only from the way you handled Troy. Twice."

I shrugged. "Yeah."

"And from things I've heard you did at school…"

"Okay. You made your point."

The bus slowed to a stop. "Stay safe, Cuz," she said, trying to hide a smile.

"Whatever."

That night I dreamed J.R. was beating on me and wrapped his muscular hands around my throat. I tried to fight him off, but my arm hurt too much and I was too weak.

He laughed at me. "Look at those girly arms. Is that all you have?"

I started to lose consciousness and felt myself float out of my body. Familiar moaning came from the hallway. I floated towards it and tried to open my eyes wider. I couldn't see clearly in the dim light. Shadowy figures in the hallway beckoned me closer.

"You weren't choking him," said a familiar voice from my bedroom. "He was choking himself."

I stopped drifting and floated back to my room. Mr. Veatch was talking to J.R.

"What're you talkin' about?" asked J.R.

"It's a game the kids play," said Mr. Veatch. "They choke themselves. And you know your son. He's reckless. We've all seen it."

"I'll teach him a lesson," said J.R. "Just let me get my hands on him."

Ms. Jane walked into the room. "Be wise enough not to be reckless, but brave enough to take great risks." She grabbed my hand and pulled me off the floor. "Time for class, Jason."

"Who you callin' Jason?" J.R. pointed a rifle at her. "Get your hands off my boy, or I'll teach you a lesson too."

I woke up with a start and turned my light on. It was only 2:30. It didn't matter. I wasn't going back to sleep. I grabbed a book, needing a safe place for my thoughts to settle. I was afraid to let them roam about on their own.

The next day trudged by slowly with me in a sleep-deprived fog. I returned to my original seat in the front of the room in Geometry and had to shake my head repeatedly so I wouldn't fall asleep during the test. Blond hair girl caught me nodding off and rolled her eyes. Or maybe she rolled her eyes because of my shoes. The duct tape was starting to peel off. It didn't matter. Her disapproval was constant anyhow.

I allowed myself to zone out during Introduction to Psychology. In Chemistry, Mr. Zandini looked at my glazed expression and chose someone else to help him demonstrate his explosive experiment. I woke up a little during lunch, always eager and awake enough to eat a full plate of food.

A full stomach added to my drowsiness in English. We discussed *Fall of the House* of Usher as promised. I failed to contribute much to the conversation, mainly because I was tired, but also because of the images the story triggered.

186

Many of Poe's stories were too dark for me. As someone who lived in darkness and horror, I wanted to read to escape madness, not to be drawn back into it. Something about Roderick Usher's sister Madeline reminded me of my own sisters. When the narrator and Roderick heard sounds from her vault, it made me revisit my dreams with ghosts moaning, putting me on edge.

Ms. Jane removed a flashlight from her top desk drawer. "I'm going to read one of Poe's shorter stories, *The Tell-Tale Heart*. I thought it might be fun to read it like a ghost story, since we're getting close to Halloween." She wheeled her chair to the front of her desk, switched on the flashlight, and turned off two sets of overhead lights. "Go ahead and scoot your chairs closer."

We crammed our chairs together, appreciative of the change in routine. She sat in the chair and began to read, "TRUE! --nervous --very, very dreadfully nervous I had been and am; but why will you say that I am mad? The disease had sharpened my senses --not destroyed --not dulled them..."

She continued to read about the narrator and his mad desire to destroy the old man's pale blue eye. I pictured J.R.'s cold blue eyes. They became embedded in my mind. I nervously began tapping my pencil on my desk until my neighbor elbowed me in the ribs.

Ms. Jane read about the narrator stalking the old man each night until he finally killed and dismembered him, then stashed his body parts under the floorboards. I pictured J.R. cutting off the dog's leg. My sleep-deprived mind struggled to maintain control. Escape was necessary. I forced myself to start coughing and raised my hand.

Ms. Jane paused in the middle of a sentence. "Yes, Jason?"

"I'm sorry. I know I'm making it hard to hear with my coughing. Can I go get a drink of water?"

"Of course. Go ahead," she said.

I walked into the hallway and closed the door behind me. Once I reached the drinking fountain, I took a quick sip and then leaned against the wall. The cool cement blocks felt good against my neck. I slid to the floor, rubbing my shaved head. I concentrated on regulating my breathing. I needed J.R. out of my head for good. His calloused fists seemed to reach me even if we were states apart. Had he twisted my brain into madness like the characters Poe seemed to enjoy writing about? The bell rang. I pulled myself to my feet and stumbled back to the English classroom to get my books.

The students were pushing their desks back into place and walking out the door. I shoved my own desk into its original spot and grabbed my books and backpack.

"Jason, can you stay after for a moment?" asked Ms. Jane.

"Yeah." I sank into my seat.

She smiled as the last student left the room. "Do you have a cold?" she asked.

"Oh. Maybe. Or I might have just had somethin' caught in my throat." I stifled a yawn.

"Late night?"

"Not really. I just couldn't sleep."

"I'm like that sometimes." She leaned against her desk. "You seemed a little agitated when I was reading the story. Did it make you feel uncomfortable?"

I looked down. "Poe isn't my favorite author. His stories creep me out."

"He's not my favorite either. His work is part of my curriculum however, so I figure October is a good time to squeeze him in."

188

"Makes sense."

The bell rang. I jumped to my feet.

"I'm sorry I made you late for your next class. I'll write you a pass. Can you stay just a couple more minutes?"

"Don't you have a class comin'?" I asked.

"It's my planning time." She reached under her desk and pulled out a bag. "I know this is weird and awkward, but the real reason I asked you to stay after, is I have something for you. Please don't be offended when you look inside." She handed me the bag.

My brow raised in confusion. I opened the bag and pulled out a long shoebox. I removed the lid and stared at a pair of new black and white Adidas.

"Is this why you had us describe ourselves yesterday? So you could get my shoe size?"

"Not entirely. I already planned the description lesson, but I added the shoe chart element for you. I didn't want to ask your size straight out."

Mixed feelings flooded over me. I looked at my own shoes, outgrown and falling apart. They barely stayed on my feet. But then I pictured my old gym teacher giving me shoes.

"I can't take these," I said at last.

"Why not?"

"I just can't." I put the lid back on the box and stuffed it back into the bag.

"Jason. I'm not trying to hurt your pride. I just see you sit in my class every day with a need that I can actually fill. Please let me help."

"It's not about my pride."

"Then please take them. I don't think your shoes will last much longer. I care about you, Jason."

I gritted my teeth. "That's the problem right there. I don't want you to care about me."

She stepped back, her face looking stricken as if I had slapped her. "Why not?"

"I had a teacher care about me at my old school. He gave me shoes too. Evidently he was embarrassed about this worn-out pair, even back then. I took the shoes. I was too pathetic to let pride stand in the way. I wanted the shoes. I needed the shoes. I get that. But it came with too high a cost."

She sank into her chair. Fire blazed in her eyes. "Did he step over a line? Did he hurt you, or take advantage of you?"

"No. Nothin' like that. He only tried to help me."

She sighed in relief. "Then what's the problem? I'm afraid I don't understand."

"I'm not allowed to talk about it." I looked her in the eyes. "You're a good teacher, Ms. Jane. But don't go wastin' your time or money on me. It's not safe. *I'm* not safe." I pressed the shoe bag back into her arms. "It's better if you just keep your distance from me."

I turned and escaped before she saw the water in my eyes that threatened to drip down my face.

CHAPTER 26
PHONE CALL

After an average night's sleep, my drowsy fog lifted, but I still had a hard time focusing during any of my classes. I wasn't sure if my Geometry teacher believed I was innocent in the drama from a couple days ago, and I knew I had hurt Ms. Jane. I needed J.R. caught quickly so I could leave before making things even worse.

I was relieved when I finally returned to the Winters' home. I rang the doorbell, and Mrs. Winters quickly opened the door.

"How was your day, Jason?" she asked.

"Okay, I guess." I automatically untied my shoes and lined them up against the wall. She had managed to train even me.

Mrs. Winters glanced at my shoes and crinkled her nose. "Would you like to go shoe shopping? I think those things have died."

It felt like someone had punched a huge bruise. I pictured Ms. Jane's hurt expression. "No. I'm good."

She bent over and picked up three deep orange leaves that I had tracked inside. "The trees are sure pretty this time of year."

"Oh. Yeah. I hadn't really noticed. I don't get outside much."

"I know," she said, her smile fading. "I wish that wasn't the way it had to be."

191

"Yeah. At least I get to talk to my family tonight. Right? That hasn't changed, has it?"

"It's all set. Mr. Costas said 7:00."

"Good." I turned and headed up to my room. After several failed attempts at homework, I threw my backpack on the floor and started to write in my journal. It was a free topic night, so I wrote about my frustrations, careful to label it private when I was spent.

Michael walked into my room with a ball and glove and flopped on the bed. "Are you good at sports and stuff?"

I shrugged. "I guess so. Why?"

"We're playing baseball in P.E. and the guys said I throw like a girl. I play baseball great on my phone but can't seem to get it in real life. Father probably isn't any better than I am. I was just wondering if maybe you could help me…you know…throw the ball around."

"I'd be glad too, but I'm not allowed to be outside, remember?"

His head hung low. "Yeah. I just thought maybe with you going on a bike ride that one time, that maybe it wasn't as risky as Mother said. I wondered if maybe things were getting better now." He started to leave the room, the glove drooping from his hand.

"Wait."

He turned in my doorway.

"Maybe I can give you some pointers if we sneak out the back and we keep it quiet."

His face brightened, highlighting his orange freckles. "That would be great. I'll stay quiet, I promise."

"Go on out back. I'll slip out as soon as it's clear."

"Got it!" He rushed down the stairs.

I shook my head and tried to rationalize my decision. J.R. was a good hunter, but if he knew I was in Missouri, he would have grabbed me by now. And my venture outside was for a good cause. Michael needed my help. Besides, the teachers thought I was reckless at school, even when I wasn't involved, so why not live up to my reputation.

I closed the bedroom door behind me and crept downstairs. My shoes were still in their morbid state resting against the wall. I stuffed them under my shirt and returned to the stairs to put them on. I peeked around the corner. Mrs. Winters was in the kitchen attaching a can opener to a chicken noodle soup can. I waited until she turned her back to search for something in the refrigerator, and then snuck out the back door.

"You made it," whispered Michael.

"Yeah. But we probably don't have long. It looks like she's gettin' dinner ready."

"Okay."

After I gave a brief explanation on how to throw and catch the ball, we started tossing it back and forth. We practiced until we heard Mrs. Winters call for dinner.

"I'll go in through the front door and distract her," said Michael. He grabbed the hose and sprayed the ground.

"What're you doin'?" I asked.

"I need mud if I'm going to get her attention," he said, smiling.

I grinned. "Good idea."

He stomped in the mud, and then turned off the water and returned the hose. "Here goes."

He ran around to the front door. Soon I heard Mrs. Winters yelling at him to take off his muddy shoes and start cleaning up his tracks. I pulled off my own shoes, crammed them back up my shirt, and slipped through the back door. Mrs. Winters was on her hands and knees with a washcloth. I dodged her and returned to my room, stashing the shoes behind my bed.

"Dinner!" Mrs. Winters repeated once the floors were clean.

I followed McKenna down the stairs. Michael was drying his shoes by the sink. We all sat down just as Mr. Winters opened the garage door. We munched on carrot sticks while Mrs. Winters poured the soup into our bowls. Michael grinned at me.

"I don't see what you have to smile about," snapped Mrs. Winters. She turned to her husband. "That son of yours tracked mud all over the house."

Mr. Winters didn't even look up from his bowl. "Oh, really."

"Yes. He knows better."

"Sorry, Mother," said Michael, still smiling.

"Don't just be sorry. Learn not to do it again," she said, glaring at him.

"I will."

We slurped our soup and ate our carrots without as much conversation as usual. Mrs. Winters was clearly still fuming and didn't feel like asking questions to get us talking. We cleared the dishes, and she began scrubbing down the table and washing dishes.

Mr. Winters dropped into his recliner and began watching the news. I sat on the couch. Every few minutes, I looked at the clock, longing for 7:00 to arrive so I could finally call my sisters.

At 6:55, I walked into the kitchen. "Where should I make the phone call?"

Mrs. Winters looked at the clock. "Oh. It is almost time, isn't it." She wiped her wet hands on her apron. "Mr. Costas told you that I have to be in the room, right?"

I nodded.

"Okay. I feel bad about invading your privacy, but rules are rules. He asked me to remind you to only use your fake names. Let's go to the library."

I followed her into the room. She sat at the desk and pulled a piece of paper from the middle drawer. "Are you ready?"

"Yes."

She started to punch in the number on her cell phone. "Oops. I must have left the ringer off today." She turned it back on. "I have some voice mail. Remind me to check my messages when you're done." She completed entering the phone number and handed it to me. I sat on the floor in the corner, listening to the phone ring.

"Hello?" a woman's scratchy voiced answered.

"Can I speak to…Jody or Hillary?"

"Just a moment."

"Ja..son? Is that you? It's me, Hillary."

My heart swelled. "Yeah, it's me. It's good to hear your voice. What's new with you?"

"I'm just sad. Did Mr. Costas tell you what happened?"

"Yeah. I didn't know he was going to tell you though. Are you okay?"

"Not really." She started to sniffle.

"I'm sorry," I said, wishing I could hug her. "I know how much you like animals. But at least Mr. Costas is okay."

"What?" She paused for a moment. "What does me liking animals have to do with anythin'?'

I smacked my forehead. "Sorry. I assumed you meant that he told you everythin'. He didn't mention anythin' about a dog?"

"No. What dog?"

"Nevermind. Forget I brought it up." I had to distract her. "How's school goin'? Are you still makin' friends?"

"School's okay, but my two best friends don't like me anymore."

"Why not?"

"They kept askin' me questions about my family and stuff from my old school. Mr. Costas said we couldn't tell any of that stuff, so I came up with a great story and told it to them. The only thing is, it's hard to remember all of the details from a made-up story. I mixed up some parts the next time I told it, and they figured out I was lyin'. Now they avoid me."

"I can relate. Even without lyin', keepin' our past a secret causes trouble."

"Yeah. Hey, Jos…Jody keeps pullin' on my arm. She wants to talk to you. I love you. Here she is."

"Hey, Jason," said Josie. "Are you okay?"

"Yes. Are you hangin' in there?"

"Yes." She lowered her voice. "What were you talkin' about with a dog?"

"If Mr. Costas didn't tell you, it's better you don't know. Besides, it's not a story I can tell with a listener."

"Oh. Okay. Can you just tell me if it's about Mops?"

"Mops? No. Why?"

"I just figured the dog story was related to the news about Aunt Sophie. They only have one dog."

I rubbed my head. "What news about Aunt Sophie? I don't think we're even on the same page. What exactly did Mr. Costas tell you?"

"He said that Aunt Sophie was back in the hospital. Her chemo treatments haven't been helpin' this time around, and the doctors don't think she has much time left." Josie started crying. "He just told us a few hours ago."

196

My stomach churned. "He didn't tell me that."

"I don't get it. She seemed so strong and healthy when we saw her. I thought she was beatin' it." She cried harder. "What do we do if she doesn't make it? She's the closest person we got to Mama."

"I know. Maybe she'll get better after all."

"I hope so," she choked out. She pulled herself together enough to say, "I'm being told it's time to get off the phone. We get to talk again next Thursday, right?"

"Definitely. Stay strong, sis."

As soon as I hung up, the phone started ringing. I handed it back to Mrs. Winters. She answered it and then handed it right back to me.

"It's Mr. Costas," she said.

Mr. Costas confirmed the news about Aunt Sophie. He had tried to call earlier, but no one answered. I told him about the ringer being off. We didn't talk very long. I was devastated about Aunt Sophie and needed time alone. Had the stress from our whole adventure played a part in her health falling apart? What if she died before we got to see her again? I felt like I was in some island penitentiary and the ocean just got a little wider—and the land a little further away.

CHAPTER 27
COLORED MARSHMALLOWS

The following week, I dropped into a seat near the back of the bus. Shania was gone, but Troy was back from his latest suspension. He looked up briefly when I sat down, but didn't greet me with his usual insult. Instead he muttered to himself and looked out the window. His face was bruised and his lip was swollen.

I had enough on my mind without wondering about Troy. The knowledge that I could call my sisters again had implanted the idea we could actually meet. I wanted to see them face to face. Our calls were monitored, so I knew I couldn't ask for their address straight out, but I saw Mrs. Winters place the girl's foster home phone number in her desk. If I could somehow tell them to answer the phone on the first ring on a different night or time, I could ask them for their address and set up a time for us to see each other. Maybe we could all get away for long enough to see Aunt Sophie. I couldn't stand the thought of her dying without us even getting the chance to say goodbye.

Aunt Sophie was still on my mind when I was in Chemistry class. We were discussing atomic mass numbers, and I tried to find a way to tie in questions about cancer cells. Not knowing enough about atoms to connect the two subjects, I waited until the teacher finished his lesson, and then just blurted out, "Can stress make cancer cells grow faster?"

Mr. Zandini scratched his balding head. "How did that question pop in your mind?"

Heat rushed to my face. "I know it doesn't fit into what you were teachin', but I just wondered."

He paused to collect his thoughts. "Well, I'm no doctor, but I have read that when you're stressed, you're body makes stress hormones to help deal with it. If you already have cancer, the hormones can bind with cancer cells, and make them more invasive and protected, so the tumor can grow and the cancer can spread. So, if that research is correct, then the answer would be yes. Why? Do you know someone with cancer?"

I nodded.

"I'm sorry. At least now there's hope for some types of cancer that are caught early."

"Yeah. Thanks."

I could feel eyes resting on me and it made my neck itch. I was glad when the bell rang and I could escape to lunch. Well, almost escape.

Parker asked, "Who do you know with cancer?"

"My aunt." At least I could tell the truth about something.

"Sorry. My grandma had it. That stinks."

"Yeah."

We returned to silence. I had decided to join Miguel with the pizza option today, and was quick to finish it off before rushing to class.

Two large silver canisters, five boxes of milk chocolate packets, several white Styrofoam cup towers, and a stack of plastic spoons rested on the edge of Ms. Jane's desk. Intriguing. I sat down quickly.

Ms. Jane waited until everyone was seated. "I graded your Edgar Allan Poe tests last night, and was very pleased with the results. For the first time this year, everyone in this class scored an 80% or above. It's cold out today, so I thought we'd celebrate with some hot chocolate."

Several students cheered.

"I'll call you up one row at a time. You can fill your cups with hot water, grab a packet and spoon, and return to your desk."

Soon everyone had a steaming cup of hot chocolate. I blew into my cup and took a sip, burning my tongue but enjoying the taste. I took several more sips. Ms. Jane began walking up and down the aisles. She had a bag in her hands and was spooning something into each student's cup. She finally reached my chair and dropped five mini marshmallows into my hot chocolate. Colored mini marshmallows.

I froze.

Memories washed over me, sending back to my shack. I pictured Mama removing the chunk of drywall that kept my sisters and me hidden in the hallway wall.

"He's gone. You can come out now," she'd say, often with new cuts and bruises all over her body.

We would crawl out into the open and stretch. She'd hug us long and hard, and then lead us to the kitchen. We'd sit at the table while she warmed up a saucepan full of hot water. My sisters were often still shaking and didn't talk much at first. Then Mama would stir in the hot chocolate packets and place the steaming mugs in front of us. We'd actually start to smile when she dropped colored marshmallows into each cup. She often made a cup for herself and would sit with us while we sipped. Once the hot chocolate warmed our insides, we would start talking again. The terror from hours hiding would melt away.

I stared at the colored marshmallows floating in the hot chocolate. Tears welled up in my eyes, but I refused to let them fall. I pushed the Styrofoam cup to the corner of my desk and rested my head into my hands. The special treat made my heart ache. I couldn't even look at it, let alone drink it. I tried to picture Mama's face, and realized the image was blurred and fading. It had been too long since I had seen her.

Ms. Jane began discussing our next unit. I looked up in time to see her glance at me and then at the hot chocolate that I'd pushed aside. Her smile faltered. I looked away, realizing I was hurting her feelings again. I grasped the cup, but couldn't make myself drink anymore with those marshmallows floating on top.

Near the end of class, she gave us time to update our journals. I tried to write about school, but could not focus beyond my current feelings. After a brief struggle, I gave in. I wrote private along the top of the page, and spewed out my pain related to the hot chocolate. Ms. Jane had us turn in our journals as we left. I added my journal to the stack, and carefully placed my full cup into the trash, burying it down deep so it wouldn't get knocked over or be visible to anyone else. I wanted to apologize to Ms. Jane, but knew I couldn't explain. Instead I slipped into the crowd of departing students and walked to History class.

There was nothing in History that could distract me from my sense of loss, so I endured the hour and then escaped to P.E. Once I had changed into my swimming trunks, I jumped into the pool. We practiced more strokes and then had several races swimming the length of the pool. As usual, we had free time at the end of class.

Dave orchestrated a competition holding our breath under water. I volunteered immediately. My chances at winning were high. I had years of practice breathing quietly or holding my breath whenever J.R. and I were in the woods hunting, or when I was hiding from him in the house.

A girl who wore her long red hair in a braid named Cami looked at the clock. As soon as the second hand reached twelve, she shouted, "Go!"

Twelve of us dipped our heads under water as we held our breath. I waited until I saw the other students around me float to the top. When I was sure most people were out, I bobbed to the surface.

"One minute and twenty-eight seconds!" exclaimed Cami. "The three of you beat some of the others by a whole minute."

Dave and a slender girl with short hair were the other winners. I grinned at them both.

"This time just the winners," Dave demanded.

Cami watched the clock again and told us when to begin. We immediately went under water. I calmly watched the other two clench their eyes and mouth shut as they struggled without air.

Dave opened his eyes and watched the girl float to the surface. He then turned to wait for me. He struggled for eighteen more seconds and then began to thrash about. Finally he popped up, gasping for air. He smacked the surface of the water. I started to follow him to the top, and then decided to test my limits.

I felt powerless over so much of my life. It felt good to be able to dictate something, even if it was just holding my breath. My body started craving air, but still I held myself down. I wondered how long someone could survive without oxygen.

Finally, I felt two calloused hands pull my shoulders up out of the water. "That's long enough," said Coach Ruttledge. "You already won. You don't need brain damage."

I shook the water out of my ears and looked around. A crowd had gathered. Dave crossed his arms and looked annoyed.

Cami's eyes were wide. "Four minutes and nineteen seconds. Wow!"

"Yeah. Wow. Now everyone go change. The bell's about to ring," Coach said. "That goes for you, too, Jason. Let's take it down a notch. You're going to give me gray hair."

I nodded and pulled myself out of the pool. The coach followed, and began gathering stray towels as the other students headed to the locker room. I inhaled the chlorine-filled air as deeply as I could in my tight trunks. This coach would have no desire to interfere in my life. He would probably be relieved if I disappeared. Maybe I could make that happen, at least for a few days.

Mr. Costas called later that night. Mrs. Winters gave me the phone, and let me talk in the library alone.

"I just wanted to give you an update on your aunt," Mr. Costas said.

"Is she doin' any better?" I asked.

"No." He was quiet for a moment. "Her doctor told your uncle and cousins to stay by her in the hospital, because she could pass away any time now."

"What? So quickly?" I tried to shake off the shock. "This is my fault," I muttered.

"And how could you possibly think that?"

"If we hadn't drawn her into our crazy lives, she wouldn't have had extra stress. She could have fought off the cancer like she did before."

"I don't think that would have made any difference."

"But you don't *know* that. I need to tell her I'm sorry. I need to tell her thanks for trying to help us and—"

"I'll call her and tell her for you."

"That's not the same. I want to tell her face to face. My sisters will want to see her again, too."

"I can't imagine the police allowing that."

"But can you at least ask?" I pleaded. "This is important."

He sighed. "I'll ask."

"Thanks," I said.

One way or another, we needed to see her before it was too late.

CHAPTER 28
BUS SILENCE

I spotted Shania as soon as I climbed on the bus. She smiled at me. I wasn't sure if that was an invitation to sit in her seat. Just in case, I sat in the empty seat in front of her.

The chatter on the bus rose in pitch soon after the bus started moving again. Nothing surprising. It was always loud.

"Be quiet," Troy growled from the back seat.

No one paid attention. They continued laughing and talking as usual.

"I said for you all to SHUT UP!"

I turned around in my seat. Troy was covering his ears and had a crazed look in his reddened eyes. His lip wasn't as swollen as yesterday, but he still had bruises on his face. The tiny portion of restraint that kept him corralled in his seat was missing. My scalp tingled, but no one else seemed concerned. They continued their oblivious chatter, evidently accustomed to his tirades, and confident they were far enough to be safe from his fists.

His jaw clenched and he stood up. As if in slow motion, I watched as he pulled a small black object out of the back of his jeans. A gun. My breath caught. He aimed at his window and fired a shot, shattering the glass.

The bus grew deathly still, except for the bus driver. "What was that?" he shouted.

Troy's eyes were wild. "I want it quiet!" He fired a shot at the driver. The bullet missed his head by inches, and splintered the windshield.

"What in the…" The bus driver swerved to the side of the road and braked hard, forcing us all to grab our seats. He ducked down behind the tall chair.

"No one pays attention," Troy said. "Now you all have to listen to me. I'm in charge. No one moves or talks unless I say so."

We froze in our seats, transfixed as he waved the 9mm back and forth. J.R. had a 9mm as one of his many guns. I tried to remember how many rounds were in the magazine. I figured it was sixteen or seventeen. Troy had only fired two shots. The disturbed look in his blue eyes reminded me of J.R. We were in trouble.

A student near the center of the bus turned around towards the back.

Troy pointed the gun at him. "Who told you to move?"

"No one, I just…"

Troy squeezed the trigger. A bullet fired into the student's shoulder, driving him backwards. Blood started seeping through his shirt. He clutched the wound and curled into a ball, clearly in shock. Several kids started screaming.

"I said to be quiet!" Troy shouted. He shot two of the kids who were screaming. Panic engulfed the bus. More people started to yell.

Shania ducked her head lower, but started talking in a soothing quiet voice. "Everyone calm down. We'll be okay, but we need to stop screaming."

The crowd gradually grew quiet.

"Is that you, Shania?" asked Troy.

"Yes," came her muted reply.

"Sit up so I can see you," he commanded.

Shania slowly scooted back to her upright position.

"I've always liked you," he said, his voice strained. "You know me." He motioned towards the kids he shot. "I didn't plan on shooting them. They just wouldn't be quiet."

"I know," she said calmly. "It was an accident. Can you lay down your gun so there aren't any more accidents?"

"But then no one listens," he said. "I want people to do what I say."

"We'll still do what you say."

"Oh, really? Then come back here."

"Put down your gun first and I will," Shania said. The tremble in her voice was barely noticeable.

Troy started to lower his gun and then gritted his teeth, aiming the gun at her. "No. Don't tell me what to do. *You* come here. Now."

Shania took a deep breath and stepped into the aisle.

"No," I whispered.

She started to walk toward him. He reached into the aisle and grabbed her arm, pulling her closer. "Much better. Now you can see up close what he did to me."

"What who did?" Shania asked.

"My dad. He was mad because I was suspended again. So he hit me. I told him to stop, but he wouldn't listen. He never listens."

"I'm sorry," said Shania.

"Yeah. Me too." He pointed the gun at her head.

"Whoa," I said, sitting up slightly. "Shania's not the one you're mad at. You like her, remember?"

He swung the gun in my direction. "Who asked you, *Cuz*?"

"No one. No one wants to listen to me either. But I get where you're comin' from."

Troy laughed. "No you don't."

"But I do. Remember how I had a cast on my arm and my face was all tore up?" I stood slowly and pointed to some of my scars. "That was from my pa. He beat me so bad the ambulance had to take me to the hospital. He was always beatin' on me, especially when he was drunk. It got so bad the police had to arrest him and me and my sisters had to move out."

"Is that supposed to mean something to me?"

"It means you're not in this alone." I stepped forward. "If you want someone to take your frustrations out on, choose me. I'm used to it. I'd prefer you use your fists instead of a gun, but we can work on that. Just let Shania go."

"I can't."

"Sure you can." I took another step. "I doubt if you really want to hurt anyone. You're not like your pa."

"But I did hurt someone." He waved his gun towards the kids he shot. They were moaning and bleeding. "I hurt lots of people. Now I'm in too deep."

"I don't think so. We can still work this out." I took a third step towards him, not allowing the trembling in my body to make its way to my skin.

"Don't come any closer." He aimed the gun at my chest. "I don't want to shoot anyone else, but I will."

I put my hands up in the air and froze. "Okay. I'm not movin'. I'm listenin' to you. See?"

Sirens started blaring in the distance, gradually growing louder.

"Who called them?" He started waving the gun wildly.

"No one," Shania said. "They probably just saw the bus on the side of the road with broken glass everywhere."

Troy's flushed face began to pale as despair washed over him. His hand started shaking and he dropped Shania's arm. "It's all over now, Cuz. There's no point to keep trying." He slowly turned the gun until it pointed at his head. He closed his eyes tight.

"No, Troy!" I tackled him right as he pulled the trigger. Blood trickled down his face as a bullet grazed his cheek. The gun slid out of his hand. I pinned his arms to the floor and kicked the gun out of his reach.

A police officer banged on the door. "Is everyone okay?"

The bus driver peeked out from behind his seat and reached for the door release lever. "We're so glad you're here. Kids have been shot. We need an ambulance."

The officers boarded the bus and shoved their way down the aisle, pausing when they saw the blood. One officer called for an ambulance and back up. The other officer continued towards the back. Troy leaned up enough to see them and stopped struggling. I felt the fight drain out of his body but I kept him pinned just in case. One of the officers grabbed the gun while the other put cuffs around Troy's wrists. The officer with the gun pulled me to my feet and twisted my arms back to cuff me as well.

"What are you…" I began.

"Wait, officer," said Shania. "Jason's the one who saved us."

"There was only one person shooting?" he asked.

She nodded. "Jason just got the gun out of his hands."

The officer released me. "Sorry about that, young man." He turned to his partner. "Let's get the shooter off the bus and get the medics up here." He pulled Troy to his feet and escorted him down the aisle.

More sirens began blaring as an ambulance sped up to the bus. The officers met the paramedics on the bus stairs and told them quickly how many were injured. The medics rushed onto the bus and began checking the vital signs of those wounded. The student who was shot in the shoulder had passed out. Two other students had been hit, one in the leg and the other in the arm. The paramedics stopped the bleeding with pressure and bandages, put them on gurneys and carried them off the bus.

Shania sank into a seat and started shaking.

I wrapped her in my arms. "Hey. It's gonna be okay."

"Thanks to you," she said into my sweaty shirt. "That was crazy. He just snapped."

"Yeah."

She pulled back for a moment. "Was that all true about your dad?"

I nodded. "But I'm not supposed to talk about it."

"Maybe it's good for you to talk about it. Keeping it bottled up can't be healthy."

"Much healthier than letting people hear about it. If word gets out, I'm in trouble."

One of the officers climbed back up the stairs. "We're going to stay here for just a little longer. We need to do some questioning, and then we'll let you continue to school. If you would prefer to go home, you can have your parents meet you there. I'm guessing most of you have phones. If not, borrow one."

The eerie silence broke. Students who hadn't already called their friends and family, began to place their calls and take pictures. A kid across the aisle held up his phone and snapped a shot of me. I covered my face.

Officers called us off the bus two at a time, starting with Shania and me. We told our story twice, and then we were grilled with numerous questions. Finally, we were allowed to stand by the bus. Row after row of students were escorted out for questioning. Once everyone had told their story, they began walking around the bus, growing restless. I felt drained and just wanted to crawl into bed.

A lady dressed in a suit with perfectly styled straight hair walked towards us. She held a microphone in her hand and was followed by a guy holding a large video camera.

"Are you Jason?" she asked.

"Yes."

"We heard you were the one who disarmed the gunman. Is that true?"

"I guess."

She motioned to the cameraman, and began talking into the microphone. "Here we have Jason Williams, the young man who tackled the gunman, saving the lives of a packed bus full of students. What inspired you to risk your own life by standing up to your crazed classmate?"

She shoved the microphone into my face.

"I don't want to talk about it," I said, immediately covering my face.

Her eyes twitched but she kept smiling. "Still in shock, I'm sure, since it just took place a few minutes ago." She thrust the microphone at Shania. "How about you? Shania Rogers, isn't it? I heard the gunman grabbed you after you tried reasoning with him. Is that correct?"

"Yes."

"Can you tell us what happened?"

Shania tried to step away, but the reporter blocked her path. Shania sighed. "You basically said it. He was stressed and shot out some windows and then some kids. I tried to calm him down. He grabbed me, and Jason talked him out of hurting me. He tackled him when it looked like he might shoot himself."

"And is it true he shot at the bus driver, narrowly missing him?"

"Yes."

"And he shot three other students. Can you tell us about that?" The reporter shoved the microphone back in my face.

I kept my hands up. "I'd rather not."

She turned back to Shania. "How about you?"

"I'm sure the police can fill in the details. We just want to get back on the bus."

"But I only have a few more questions."

An officer walked up. "I'd be glad to answer any questions. Let them get on the bus. We need to make sure all of the parents have been contacted before you show students on the air."

She backed up. "Of course."

"Thanks, officer," I said. "I don't want to be on the news."

"I don't blame you. At least not so soon," he said, patting me on the back.

The reporter smiled again. "We'll be around most of the morning. I'm sure you'll be up to it soon. You're a hero, after all."

The cameraman kept recording as we climbed back up the bus steps. We sat in our old seat together.

"That reporter was annoying," said Shania.

"Yeah."

She turned her head to me. "What was the big deal with keeping your face hidden?"

"I just don't like the attention."

"Seriously? You're like an attention magnet with all your crazy stunts. There's more to it than that."

"I don't want to be on the news."

"Well, you made that clear." She grinned. "Did you see the expression on the reporter's face when she couldn't get

212

an interview out of you? She was fuming! I thought steam was going to come out of her ears."

"Yeah."

"Thanks, by the way. I was scared when Troy grabbed my arm. He was freaking out. I was actually thinking he was going to shoot me. And then I was afraid he was going to shoot you, and then…"

"You're welcome. You were the first one to try calmin' him down though."

The rest of the students climbed on the bus, avoiding the seats where students had been shot, even though the blood was washed away and the shattered glass was swept up. Continuing to school seemed so bizarre. I felt a connection to the others that I had never felt before. I now wasn't the only one forced to see how fragile life really was. Shania rested her head on my shoulder. Did she feel it too? An odd hush fell over everyone, only interrupted by the bus driver starting the engine. Troy finally got his request.

CHAPTER 29
NEWS REPORT

The bus driver parked in front of the high school. The parking lot was jammed with cars and news vans. Parents were packed on the sidewalks, straining to see their child through the bus windows.

We were still so quiet I could hear the bus driver clear his throat. He stood up. "I'm glad you guys are okay. You were brave. Be careful as you get off the bus." He dropped back into his seat and opened the door.

The silence was broken. Students began talking as they swarmed off, but it was a different kind of discussion. The light-hearted chatter had been blown away. Their standard coolness towards their parents melted away as they rushed off the bus. I hung back, watching the news crews tape the tearful reunions.

Shania stood up. "Are you ready for this?"

"Not really."

"I don't see my parents yet. If you still want to avoid reporters, we can run to the front doors together."

"Sounds good."

I followed her down the aisle. The bus driver looked up as we passed him. "Thanks you two. I'm guessing that would have gone much worse if you hadn't helped."

Shania patted him on the shoulder. "I'm glad Troy's aim was off. We would have hated it if you'd been hurt."

He choked up and nodded.

Shania grabbed my hand. "Ready?"

"Ready."

We stepped off the bus and threaded through the crowd with our heads low.

"There he is," I heard someone say.

We started running and didn't stop until we burst inside the building. I looked around the main hall. No reporters. I exhaled.

The school counselor, Mrs. Garcia, rushed to our side. "The police have been updating us on everything. Do you two want to come into my office until your parents arrive?"

We both nodded.

We sat in padded chairs with Mrs. Garcia sitting directly across from us. "Would you like to talk about what happened today?"

"Not yet," said Shania.

I shook my head.

"Is there any way I can help you?"

"Just keepin' us away from reporters is helpful," I said.

Mr. Veatch poked his head through the door. "I thought I saw you two come in here." He strode up to us and patted me on the shoulder. "I heard you got the gun out of Troy's hands. I'm proud of you. I knew you were a good kid."

My eyebrow shot up. Was this the same man who found me guilty by association last week?

"The reporters have been calling us all morning. They'd really like to interview you. What do you say? I'm guessing some good publicity for the school would be helpful about now. One of our students being the hero, keeping fellow students safe. It would help everyone focus on the positive instead of Troy's...mistake."

"I can talk to them, but no cameras," I said.

Mr. Veatch scowled. "Why not?"

"I have my reasons."

"Could you share those with us?" he asked. "Most students enjoy their fifteen minutes of fame. Given your record the last month or so, I would think that would be especially true of you."

So much for his claim that I was a good kid. "It's complicated," I said.

The secretary walked in. "Shania, your parents are here and want to take you home."

Shania squeezed my hand. "Good luck," she whispered, and followed the secretary out of the room.

"Care to share the complication?" asked Mr. Veatch.

The counselor cleared her throat. "He's probably emotionally wrung out. Maybe now is not the time–"

"We had reporters here for that pass-out challenge, which you took part in, but I shielded you from that. Why not go on camera for something positive?"

Something in the way he stood, reminded me of J.R. and his arrogance. I felt heat flood my face. I had reached my patience limit and wanted to leave. Now. If answers were what it took to escape his glare then that's what he would get. I gripped my arm rests. "I don't want to be on camera, because I can't have my face on the news. My pa could see it, and then he would know where I am."

The secretary was standing by the door with wide eyes. She said quietly, "Mrs. Winters is here for Jason."

I turned my back on Mr. Veatch, eager to escape. Ms. Jane was in the hallway talking to Mrs. Winters. Had they heard my explosion? I searched their faces but found no answers.

"I heard what you did on the bus today," said Ms. Jane. "That was brave. I'm so proud of you."

216

"Me too," said Mrs. Winters. "Do you want to go rest? I would think you've had enough for one day."

"Yes. Definitely."

I followed my foster mom out the front door, ducking down and covering my face once more. The crowd had thinned. Most of the bus students and their parents were gone. Reporters were packing up their gear—until they saw me.

"Jason, can you answer a few questions?" I heard someone ask.

I kept my head low and kept walking. Mrs. Winters guided me to the car and we quickly drove home.

"Thanks for getting me," I said. "I really didn't want to answer questions all day, and Mr. Veatch…well, he was on my case. Do you mind if I go to bed?"

"Not at all."

I dragged myself up the stairs, flopped on the bed and closed my eyes, craving an escape through sleep. Instead, my mind replayed the entire episode with Troy. I fixated on his crazed blue eyes. They morphed into J.R.'s eyes. I shook my head. It was over. I had to let it go. Finally I slipped into a fitful sleep.

The sound of the garage door opening woke me up. Mr. Winters was home. I rubbed my eyes and wandered downstairs.

Mr. Winters turned to look at me. "I heard about the shooting on the bus." He walked over to the TV, switched it on, and began scanning through the stations. "One of the guys at work said it was on the news."

"There," I said, once our bus appeared on the screen.

Mrs. Winters joined us.

"What are you so interested in?" asked Michael.

"Shhh!" said his mother. "Just watch."

A news reporter recounted the story, showing clips of emergency personnel wheeling the injured into the ambulance, police questioning students, and kids talking to the reporter about their ordeal. They showed a brief clip of me walking by with my face covered. The reporter described me as a humble hero who asked not to be filmed.

I sank into the couch, breathing a sigh of relief.

"Nicely done," said Mr. Winters.

"That was you?" asked Michael. "You tackled the guy with the gun?"

I nodded.

"That is so awesome. McKenna! Come down here! You've got to see this."

Another news station replayed a similar story.

"You're a hero!" said McKenna. "The kids at school aren't going to believe this!"

We sat down for a dinner of spaghetti and meatballs. My relief was so great that my hunger returned. The reporters hadn't shown my face and they had used my false name. I was safe. Everyone around me was safe.

After dinner, Michael wanted to watch the news again. It was amazing how many times the stations aired the story. I sat and watched it with him again. Only this time the story was more thorough. After the initial story, including Shania's brief interview, one reporter elaborated.

"Our humble hero, Jason Williams, refused to talk on camera. After further investigation, we have learned more about the brave teen who saved the lives of so many."

My school picture appeared on the screen while the reporter's voice narrated. I scooted to the edge of my seat. "Jason is a Sophomore and is new to Lincoln High. Many of his classmates describe him as a bit reckless, but brave. One classmate even recounted a story of him saving a friend from

218

a fire in Chemistry class. How grateful we are that young men like Jason are willing to help those in need, regardless of the danger."

"Thanks for the update, Kristen. And now on to weather…"

It felt like someone had punched me in the stomach. I slid off the couch and sank to my knees. I had been so careful. What if J.R. watched the news? A close up of my face had been plastered on the screen. He would know the town I lived in. The high school I attended. My stomach churned.

"Are you okay, Jason?" asked Mr. Winters.

I shook my head. "No. And neither are you." I swallowed hard. "You asked me to tell you when your family was in danger. If my pa sees this newscast, it's all over."

"What?" His face grew serious. "Go upstairs, Michael."

"But, I want—"

"Now."

Michael kicked the couch but turned and left the room.

Mr. Winters said, "Tell me more."

I closed my eyes. Secrets wouldn't protect them anymore. "My pa is hunting me. He didn't know where to find me, but now he might. I can't risk stayin' here. He's dangerous, and not just for me. All of you are at risk if he thinks you're standin' in his way."

"We need to call Mr. Costas." He pulled out his cell phone.

I looked at the clock. It was 7:05. "Wait. It's time for my call to my sisters. They're probably waitin' on me. I need to warn them first. We'll call Mr. Costas afterwards." I held out my hand for the phone.

He hesitated.

"I'll make it quick."

He handed me the phone. I raced to the library, dug for the number, and dialed it. The same scratchy voice answered.

"You're late," she said.

"I know. I'm sorry. It has been a crazy night. Can I talk to Jody?"

"Yes. Just a moment."

"Josie?"

"Don't say my real—"

"Don't worry about that now. I need you to listen carefully. I don't have much time. No one's in the room with me. I need to get your address."

"Why? I thought—"

"My picture was on the news. If J.R. sees it, he'll know where I live. I don't know what's goin' to happen, but if I need to get away, I want to know where you are."

"Does Mr. Costas know?"

"Not yet. I'll call him next. Are you in Missouri?"

"Yes."

"Okay. Start talking about something, but in the sentence slip in the city. Be careful so your foster mom doesn't catch on."

"School was okay, but this kid named Barnard, we call him Bernie, was rude. He kept making fun of me."

"Barnard? Is that right?"

"Yes."

"Good. Now talk about somethin' else for a moment."

"I miss you. How's school?"

"That'll do. Now see if you can sneak in the street name."

The line grew quiet.

"Josie? Are you there?" I started to panic.

"Yes. I'm thinkin'. I wish I had *more* time with you."

"More? More Street?"

"Wait. I think this *house* is nice."

"House. Housemore? Housemore street?

"Flip it."

"Morehouse Street?"

"Yes."

"Okay. Let's try house numbers. Sneak in the first number only."

"Yes, I love you *too*."

"Two. Excellent. Next number." I looked up. "Oh wait. Mrs. Winters is coming. I'll call right back." I hung up.

"Sorry, Jason. I just remembered it was time for your call. Here you go." She handed me her phone.

"Oh. Your husband gave me his. I was just waiting for you to dial the number."

"Just a minute." She started to dig through the desk drawer for the paper. Her phone rang.

"Hello, Mr. Costas. We were just about to call the girls. Here's Jason."

She handed me the phone. "Hi," I said.

"Did you see the news?" he asked.

"Yes. I'm guessin' you did too. I tried to keep my face covered. I can't believe they showed my school picture."

Mrs. Winters looked up. "They showed your school picture? But they didn't in the story I saw."

"It showed up in a story later on," I told her. I returned the phone to my mouth. "What should we do?"

"The police are discussing that now. We have no idea if J.R. has been watching the news. We may get lucky. Still, I would suggest packing tonight, just in case. I'll try to let you know more in the morning. Just keep your eyes open for

221

now, and don't leave the house. Not even to go to school. I don't want you to call your sisters tonight either."

"Why not?" I asked. "I've been waiting all week. I just need to talk to them for a few minutes." My throat went dry. I needed a few more numbers for their address.

"The police think they're safe. You, however, they don't know about. They don't want you to contact them and jeopardize their position. If this blows over we can start the calls again."

"But I just want—"

"I know this is hard, but that's what they told me. I'm sorry. Go ahead and put Mrs. Winters back on the line."

I delivered the phone. Mrs. Winter's face looked more serious the longer she listened. "We'll wait for your call in the morning. Good-bye." she finally said.

"What did he say?" I asked.

"Probably the same thing he told you. We have to wait to hear what the police want us to do. In the mean time, you need to stay in the house. And we all need to be ready to leave."

"They want you in hiding, too?"

"Possibly. Just for a few days."

"I'm so sorry. I really thought you'd be safe since we were so far away from my house."

"Not your fault. But it looks like it's time for you to pack."

My shoulders slumped. I trudged up the stairs. Yet another family I was endangering and throwing into limbo. When would this stop? I walked into the guest room and pulled my black trash bag out of the drawer. A heavy weight pressed on my shoulders as I stuffed clothing into the bag.

What should I do? Should I wait and let the police decide my fate? Where would the police send me if they decided I had to move? Obviously nowhere near my sisters. I didn't want to be separated from them anymore. And we wanted to see Aunt Sophie before she died. But how would I get to Bernard?

And what if they didn't move me in time and J.R. came to the house? The Winters could be at risk. If I left right away, would he still come to their house and threaten them? How could I prevent that? What would J.R. do to me if he found me? Kill me? He had to make sure I didn't share his secrets and he was furious with me for my betrayal.

My thoughts ran around crashing into each other. I needed to write in my journal to sort things out. Too bad it was still in class. I clutched my head. No matter what I did, someone could get hurt.

I finished stuffing everything I owned into my bag. I kept my clothes and shoes on and sat on the floor weighing my options. There was no point going to bed. I knew I wouldn't sleep.

CHAPTER 30
TIME OFF

The next morning, reporters waited in front of the high school, hoping to be the first to capture the elusive Jason Williams on camera. Parents pulled up in cars, and said their goodbyes through windows. Drivers pulled up in buses, waited until students streamed out, and then drove away. No one spotted Jason. Had he managed to slip by all of them?

An hour passed. Finally, the principal stepped outside. "If you are waiting for Jason Williams, you might as well leave. He's not at school today."

The reporters grumbled as they packed up their gear and left.

The principal returned to the office, pausing at the front desk. "Did Jason Williams' foster mom say how long she was going to let him stay home?"

"No," answered the secretary. "But I would assume just for today. Most of the kids who were on that bus are taking the day off. Can't say that I blame them. I'd need time off if I'd had a gun pointed at me."

"I suppose I would, too."

"Sounds like Jason wants to avoid reporters, too," the secretary continued. "I'm glad he missed the mob outside. I hope they don't wind up at his house."

"Let's keep his address confidential, so we can give him some space," said the principal.

The assistant secretary grimaced. "I wish I had known that earlier. A reporter called first thing this morning and asked for his address. Sorry. I figured by today he might want to talk."

The principal sighed. "They can probably chase off one reporter. But let's not send any more his way."

The next afternoon, Ms. Jane stopped by the office. "I noticed Jason was gone again today. Do we know when he's coming back?"

The secretary shook her head. "Mrs. Winters called yesterday to say he wasn't coming in, but we haven't heard from her today. I tried calling, but didn't receive an answer. I wonder if they were getting calls from reporters and stopped answering their phone for now. I left a message for her to call the school as soon as she can."

"I see. Thank you." Ms. Jane took a left and stepped into the counselor's office. "Do you have a moment?"

Mrs. Garcia looked up. "Of course. Come in."

Ms. Jane sat in a seat beside the desk. "I didn't mean to eavesdrop, but two days ago I was in the hallway and I heard Jason talking to Mr. Veatch."

Mrs. Garcia closed her eyes. "Yes. That didn't go how I'd hoped."

"Jason is one of my students, and, well, I was concerned when he mentioned not wanting to be on camera because of his dad. Do we know anything about his dad? Does he really not know where Jason is staying?"

Mrs. Garcia pointed to the open file on her desk. "I wondered about that, too, but there really isn't much in his file. He moved in with a foster family right before school started. I thought about calling his old school for

225

information, but all of his previous information was left blank."

"Do you think that was an accident?"

"No. It was approved. I was concerned so I made some calls. His records are sealed."

Ms. Jane leaned back in the chair. "Oh, my. Do you think he ran away from his home—wherever it was?"

"Maybe. A social worker is involved and he has a foster family, so at least he isn't living on the streets. I set up times to talk to each student involved in the bus shooting, just to see how they were coping. I hoped to talk to Jason today, but he still isn't back."

"I noticed that. Should we be concerned?"

"Not yet. Though I would feel better if we could reach his foster mom. Odds are, he just needs time on his own."

"But did you watch the news? Some of the reports showed his picture. Isn't that what Jason was trying to avoid? What if his dad saw it?"

Mrs. Garcia thought for a moment. "If I don't hear from Mrs. Winters by tomorrow morning, I'll call the social worker listed."

"Can you let me know when you hear something?"

"Certainly."

After the last class of the day, Mrs. Garcia called Ms. Jane. "You asked me to keep you updated on Jason. Mrs. Winters finally called back. She said Jason will be out for the rest of the week, but should be back to school on Monday."

"Thank goodness," said Ms. Jane. "At least we know he's safe."

Monday arrived at last. Ms. Jane stood at her classroom door, eager to welcome Jason back to class. The bell rang, but still no Jason.

Shania walked up to her. "Any news on Jason? I'm surprised I haven't seen him around yet."

"You two are friends, right?"

"Yeah. I think we're back to that."

"He hasn't been in contact with you since the shooting?"

"No. But then we just talked on the bus or at school. We never called or texted each other."

Ms. Jane erased her frown. "He'll probably be back tomorrow. But if you hear anything, let me know."

"Sure," Shania said. She took her seat.

Ms. Jane began her lesson, but her eyes continually drifted to the classroom door.

Reports and rumors about the shooting spread through the hallways. Troy had outpatient surgery on his cheek and was being held in juvenile detention while his lawyers determined how to plead. Versions of the story ranged from Troy being in jail for life to him being released the following week and returning to school. The three students who were shot were all still in the hospital, but were in stable condition. Several classes had banded together to make them get-well cards that Mrs. Garcia delivered.

Mrs. Garcia met with each of the students who witnessed the shootings. Most of them would need time for the memories to fade, but they were all back in school. Except for Jason.

Ms. Jane was walking to Mrs. Garcia's office after her last class of the day. Coach Ruttledge stopped her.

"Hey, any word on Jason? He missed P.E. again."

"No. And I'm getting concerned."

Coach Ruttledge shook his head. "He's brave, I'll give him that. But he's almost too brave. Has anyone checked to make sure he didn't do something crazy and get hurt?"

"Mrs. Garcia talked to his foster mom, but he was supposed to be back today."

"He's a foster kid, huh? Maybe that's why he's a loose cannon. Maybe Mrs. Garcia should check on him again."

"I'm headed to see her right now," Ms. Jane said. She turned the corner and knocked on the counselor's door.

"Come in," said Mrs. Garcia.

"Jason still isn't back. This just doesn't add up. The Jason I know, or at least thought I knew, wouldn't stay down for this long. Should we call him?"

"I think you need to have a seat," said Mrs. Garcia. "The office called Mrs. Winters when he didn't show up this morning. She said things were complicated right now and that we needed to start directing our calls to Jason's social worker, Mr. Costas."

"Did you call him yet?"

"Yes." Mrs. Garcia rubbed her forehead. "They want to keep this quiet, but police are searching for Jason right now. He actually went missing the morning after the bus incident. They aren't sure if he ran away or if he was taken by his dad."

"But Mrs. Winters called and said…"

"I know. The first day, she called early in the morning, before he left. The next day, police told her to say he was coming Monday because they didn't want anyone to know he was missing. They hoped to find him by now."

"So he's been missing almost a week?" Ms. Jane sank into a chair. "He could be long gone by now. Or seriously hurt."

Mrs. Garcia sighed. "I know. Mr. Costas told him to pack the night the news aired, because he might have to relocate. Evidently, his dad is extremely dangerous and they have been looking for him for a long time. The next morning, Mrs. Winters checked on him after taking her kids to school. He was gone. His backpack and some clothes and a bike were missing too. His garbage bag was left behind."

"Garbage bag?"

"Everything he owned was packed in a garbage bag."

Tears filled Ms. Jane's eyes. "He could be biking around on his own, or he could be kidnapped by a dangerous dad. Neither option sounds good."

"I agree."

"So what do we do now?"

"Mr. Costas said if we think of anything helpful, to let him know. I'll give you his phone number, too." She scribbled the number onto a paper and tore it off the pad. "Otherwise I guess we just wait and pray."

Ms. Jane returned to her classroom. She tried to grade papers, but ended up staring at the paper with the phone number instead. She sighed and started checking journals. Jason's was at the bottom of the stack, since he hadn't written any new entries for the week. She flipped through the pages. Many of them were labeled private. As tempting as it often was, she had respected his privacy. But now that he was missing...Could there possibly be anything written that might help police find him? She stuck the journal in her bag, turned off the lights and went home.

She made a quick dinner of chef's salad, much to her meat-loving husband's dismay. He was very understanding, however, after she explained the mystery surrounding Jason's disappearance, and her desire to read his journal, searching for any helpful information.

She curled up on the couch with a light blanket and a cup of cinnamon honey tea. Her German shepherd circled three times and then sprawled on the floor at her feet. She skimmed over the entries that were not labeled, that she had already read.

She paused at the page with his description of himself. Surely the police already had a thorough description. Had they posted it so other people could call in if they spotted him, or was that dangerous since they weren't certain he was already with his dad? She stuck a yellow post-it note on the page just in case. He mentioned his favorite color being dark blue, and that he loved watching and playing sports. His favorite food was chicken gumbo, and he liked abstract art. A faint smile crossed her lips as she reviewed the way he had described his personality. The words certainly weren't funny, but she loved his perception. Now the description made even more sense.

I am a case of opposites. I'm determined yet discouraged. A basically honest person forced to lie. I love deeply but have someone I hate even deeper. I have scars inside and out. I'm good at sports, but reading is my distraction and writing is my release. I'm reckless with my own life, but protective and careful with others.

Ms. Jane cared about all of her students, and she knew playing favorites was unprofessional. But Jason had a special place in her heart. If only they could find him.

The first page labeled private stared back at her. She had never read a private entry before and felt tremendous guilt as she considered breaking her promise of confidentiality.

"He's in danger. This is an exception," she whispered out loud.

She hoped she had to answer for what she was about to do, because that meant she would see him again.

CHAPTER 31
PRIVATE JOURNAL

There were no journal entries that were labeled private for the first two weeks. Then the private entries became more and more frequent.

August 28

I'm still not sure what to think about Lincoln High. The building is way better than my old school. I don't have to get wet or cold going from class to class, since it's all in one building. The teachers and students don't treat me much different than anyone else, which is a nice change. Sure, I get looks because my shoes are falling apart and my clothes are faded, but I don't care about that—much. I just like that I don't have to prove myself. I don't have to convince everyone that I'm nothing like my pa. They don't have to fear me. No one here knows who I'm related to. How could they? My name is changed. Ask me about my name change and I might actually tell you some of my story.

September 1

We got our journals back yesterday. I thought you might ask me about my name change. I guess that means you really don't read our private pages. I have to admit, that was a test. I wouldn't blame you if you read it. I would be

232

tempted to read something handed to me that was labeled *private*. I guess that means I really can write what I feel. I'm glad because my other journals were full, and I won't ask Mrs. Winters for anything extra. It's enough that I actually have every school supply that was on the list. I know my social worker would still want me to be careful and not write anything that would endanger me, but sometimes I just get this urge to take risks. Besides, I'm tired of writing Jason Williams on everything. My name is JaDon Chambers. Chambers I don't miss. I could lose that name forever and be glad of it. But JaDon, well, Mama gave me that name. She based it on my pa's name, James Donald Jr., so I should hate it too. But she put her own twist on it and when she said it, it was like she was hugging me. I know she loved me. J.R. tells me different, but I know the truth. Me and my sisters don't call J.R. Papa. He doesn't deserve that name.

September 10

Today on the bus, I felt like blowing up. A guy who bullies everyone is trying to run me down too. I almost went off on him. I could feel the anger bubbling up, but then I realized I could stop it. I could cool down and ignore it. I didn't have to be like J.R. just because I'm related. I have Mama's blood in me too, and she had a long fuse. J.R. could rip her up with his words and his fists, but she stayed calm. Unless he hurt one of us kids. Then she'd fight hard. I have hope. I can be who I want to be, not some monster just because I have monster blood in me.

September 22

How much missing can a body take? I miss my sisters. I wish I knew where they lived so I could visit them. Mr. Costas didn't deliver their letters to me this week. I've

233

reread their other letters so much, I have them memorized. Who's helping them with their homework? Who's calming them when they're scared? That's my job. I should be there. I miss Aunt Sophie, Uncle Ron, and my cousins, too. I wonder if they got to go back home yet. I hope they aren't still suffering because of taking us in.

October 6

I'm wondering why you seem to care about me, Ms. Jane. Lincoln High has good teachers. I get that. And most of them seem to care about their students to an extent. But you're different. I can't believe you shared so much about yourself in your example of a description. The physical description I get, but when you read about your personality, well you sounded like a real person. A real good person. I forgot to label my journal about my bike ride private. Maybe that wasn't a bad thing—forgetting to label it private, not the bike ride. I know taking off on the bike and racing the train was crazy. I was just frustrated about not being able to talk to my sisters. I take risks as it is, but not being with my sisters pushed me over the edge. It felt good to know you cared enough to talk to me about it. You're probably just doing your job, and maybe you're like that with everyone, but you make me feel like I matter and that maybe I'm worth something.

October 9

I found out J.R. hurt my social worker. Everyone who knows me gets hurt. He cut off Mr. Costas' dog's leg to write a message about getting me. Then J.R. killed the dog in front of him. He demanded to know where I was. Mr. Costas gave him a fake address, and had to go move out of his own place, so J.R. wouldn't come back and kill him when he found out.

Another person with a ruined life thanks to me. What if my foster family is next? I have no idea why they even took me in. They've been patient with me and have given me space. I told Mr. Winters that if I ever thought his family was in real danger, I would let him know. The thing is, anyone who knows me could be in danger. If I ever find out J.R. is on his way, I'll have to leave. I don't want him to harm the Winters family.

Ms. Jane put a sticky note on this page.

October 14

Somehow, whenever you don't give us a specific topic for our journals, my journal becomes more of a letter to you, Ms. Jane. I don't know why. Maybe it feels good to vent to an actual person for once. I've always tried to be careful about what I said to my sisters. They've had too much to deal with as it is. They don't need to hear my negative thoughts. It's not like I can talk to them now anyhow. And I can't talk to my foster family about much, because they aren't supposed to know the details of my case. I can't talk to my friends, which is too bad, because I'd like to tell Shania. I'm not supposed to talk to you either, but writing it in a private journal makes me feel better.

October 23

You tried to give me shoes today. I think I hurt your feelings when I refused them. Believe me, I wanted to take them. I know my shoes are falling off my feet. They've been in bad shape for a long time. The thing is, I already had a teacher try to replace them. My gym teacher at my old school. He really knew me and treated me like I mattered. I was excited when he gave me shoes and I wore them home. It felt so good to have shoes that fit and didn't have holes. But J.R. got mad when he saw them. He said we didn't take pity offerings. He threw them out. The next day, my gym teacher asked why I wasn't wearing the shoes. I was mad and told him the truth. I was tired of covering up for J.R. Everyone knew J.R. was beating us, but they chose to look the other way, because they knew how dangerous J.R. could be. My gym teacher decided it was time to do something about it. He talked to the counselor, but she said we didn't have proof of abuse. She saw our bruises and black eyes. Did she really think the three of us were so klutzy that we fell down and ran into things every day? He decided to talk to J.R. I begged him not to. I told him I could take it. But he said he'd seen me come in hurt too many times. He came to our house one night. Soon he and J.R. were arguing. He told J.R. if he ever hurt me again, he'd report him and call the police. J.R. snapped. He pulled out a knife and plunged it into my teacher's stomach. He twisted it while my teacher doubled over. I yelled. I couldn't help it. But then J.R. knew he had a witness. He yanked the knife out and put it to my neck and said he'd kill me and my sisters if I ever told. He dug around in my teacher's pocket for the car keys. Then he threw the body into the car, drove it to the lake and sank it. He shot a deer on the way back and skinned it right where he'd killed my teacher to cover the blood. Whenever I'd cause trouble, he'd ask if he needed to get another deer carcass. That's why he can't let me be. I know too much. That's also why I couldn't accept the shoes from you and why I keep labeling some of this stuff as private, even when deep down I want you to know the truth. But I have to protect you. You remind me of my gym teacher. You probably wouldn't be able to ignore my abuse, and might somehow get tangled up in J.R.'s web. I have to protect you.

236

October 26

I'm guessing you don't know why I don't like reading things by Edgar Allan Poe. Most teenage boys are likely into his stuff. I'm sorry I left when you were reading Tell Tale Heart. You were trying to make it fun for us. I get that. My story is just too much like a creepy ghost story. I already have nightmares all of the time. Usually they are about J.R. Sometimes they're about ghosts in my old house. I like to read books to escape my horror, not remind me of it.

November 3

I found out today that my Aunt Sophie is dying. I knew she was fighting breast cancer again, but I thought she was beating it. Aunt Sophie took us in after J.R. nearly beat me to death. It was the first time I felt loved and like I was part of a family since Mama left. J.R. said Mama left because of us kids whining. Maybe that's partially true, but I think that if she left it was mainly because of him. Aunt Sophie thinks he either forced her out or killed her. I don't know which is better—to know your ma could turn her back on you and leave you with a monster, or to have her killed at the hands of your own pa.

November 6

You gave us hot chocolate today, and I hurt your feelings again. I know I did, and I hate that. I love hot chocolate and I could have drank it all, but then you gave us the colored marshmallows. When J.R. was drunk and in a violent mood, Mama would have us hide in the hallway behind a piece of broken drywall. When he finally left, she'd remove the drywall and tell us to come out. She was usually beat up, but she would hug us and have us sit at the table while she made hot chocolate. She'd always give us colored marshmallows. I haven't ever had colored marshmallows since she left, and that was over seven years ago.

November 9
My social worker said Aunt Sophie is doing worse and may die in the next few days. I want to see her before she goes. I didn't get to say good-bye to Mama. Aunt Sophie's the closest person to her. I've got to say good-bye. I know my sisters want to see her too. I've got to figure out where they are and then find a way to see my aunt before it's too late.

Ms. Jane added another sticky note. She turned the page and was disappointed to discover there were no more entries.

CHAPTER 32

WHERE IS HE?

Ms. Jane wiped her tears on her sleeve and got up to get another tissue for her nose. Her heart was aching and her protection instinct was flaring. She pulled out a piece of paper and wrote each possible scenario.

Did he leave to get his sisters and see Aunt Sophie?
Did he leave to keep the Winters safe?
Did J.R. find him and take him?
Did JaDon do something reckless and get hurt?

She looked at the clock. It was 3:00am. She wanted to talk to Mr. Costas, but knew it would have to wait until morning. Her blanket had slipped to the floor and her dog was stretched out on it. She gently pulled it out from under his legs and pulled it up to her chin. She didn't have the energy to go to bed, and soon fell asleep on the couch.

The next morning, she finally made her phone call. "Hello, Mr. Costas? Is there any news about JaDon?"

"JaDon? Who is this? Where did you get that name?"

"Oh. Sorry. I must still be half asleep. This is Jane. Jane Arsenault. I'm his English teacher. Mrs. Garcia and I have been concerned about him, and she gave me your number. She said you told her to call if we had any information."

"That still doesn't answer my question about his name. All of his records are under Jason Williams."

Ms. Jane took a deep breath. "Yes. Of course. I only got a few hours of sleep so I'm not handling this correctly. Let

239

me back up. One of his assignments was to write in a journal each day. They had the option of labeling some of the pages private, so they would learn to write freely. Up until last night, I made a point of not reading the private pages. But I decided that in desperate circumstances, it was worth breaking that trust."

"Go on. I'm still waiting for the connection."

"In one of the entries, he shared that his name wasn't Jason Williams, and that it was JaDon Chambers."

"That was a risky thing for him to do. He was supposed to keep his name and his past secret. The police and I tried to make that point clear."

"He was very careful about that in school," Ms. Jane said quickly. "But journaling seemed to be a good release for him. He's quite the writer…and reader."

"I gathered that from going through the garbage bag of stuff he left at the Winter's home. He had several journals where every page was filled."

"Did you read his journals?" asked Ms. Jane.

"Yes. I felt it might help the case. Like you said, these are desperate circumstances."

"That makes me feel better. I felt very guilty reading the private pages, especially at the beginning. Then it was almost like he was writing for me."

"Interesting. So did you find anything that might help us find him? All the journals I read were dated before school started, so they didn't tell me what he was thinking right before he went missing."

"Do you suppose it's possible he ran away?"

"We don't know."

Ms. Jane flipped through the journal, pausing at each sticky note. "He did write about wanting to protect the

Winters family, and that if he felt they were in danger, he would leave."

"We figured that was a possibility. He certainly had reason to believe they were in danger when his picture was posted on the news. The thing is, we don't know if J.R. was watching the news, or that it even aired wherever he was staying."

"Let's hope not."

"Anything else?"

"He mentioned wanting to get his sisters and wanting to see his Aunt Sophie before she died."

Mr. Costas sighed. "Sadly, he's too late for that. She passed away four days ago. Her family is having the funeral service tomorrow. I'll attend and will try to ask questions. I wanted to go anyhow. She was quite a lady."

"That's what JaDon said. I'm so sorry to hear she died. He'll be devastated."

"Yes. All three kids will be. They loved her, and hoped to live with her again after J.R. was caught."

Ms. Jane's throat tightened. "Will they stay with their foster families? I mean, if J.R. is caught?"

"I don't think so, but we'll have to cross that bridge when we come to it. Any other information that we should know?"

"I'm assuming you have a good description of JaDon already. If not, he wrote a very thorough one."

"We have that covered."

"Are you going to post it so people can be watching for him?"

"We'd like to, but until we're certain J.R. has him, we don't want to advertise the fact that he could be out biking around by himself."

"Makes sense." Ms. Jane rubbed the sides of her head. "Do you have someone watching where his sisters are staying?"

"Yes. But maybe since you read that he specifically mentioned getting his sisters in the journal, we might add a few extra."

"Does JaDon know where the girls are staying?"

"I'm not sure. The girls' foster mom mentioned a phone call that Mrs. Winters didn't know about. We think he may at least know the town they're in. We questioned the girls, but if they know anything, they aren't admitting it."

"Could J.R. get it out of JaDon?" asked Ms. Jane.

"I don't know that J.R. cares as much about getting the girls. We found something in the journals that explains why J.R. didn't want JaDon able to talk to police. I don't think the girls knew anything about it."

"Was it about the gym teacher?"

Mr. Costas inhaled sharply. "He mentioned that too? He was being awfully trusting in that journal. Yes. He described where J.R. sank the car. Can you believe he made JaDon help drag the body into the car and then watch it sink? Sick. We dragged the lake right after we read the journals. We found the car and some decaying bones."

"Oh, my."

"We also have men looking for Grace Chamber's body. After reading the journals, I have a feeling she might not have really left. Our detectives would have found some trace of her by now."

"This just keeps getting worse."

"Let's just hope we find JaDon soon. We knew J.R. was dangerous, but now we know he's a murderer too. I don't think his sisters could handle it if JaDon turns into one of his victims."

Ms. Jane's lips quivered. "No. I would think not."

"I have your number now. Do you want me to call you if we hear anything?"

"Yes, please. I'll do the same."

They hung up, each fearing the worst.

Later that night, two policemen began their shift patrolling the streets in Bernard, Missouri. They passed a black Ford Fusion parked in the Donut Hut parking space.

"Why do you suppose a car's parked there at this time of night?" asked one officer.

"I don't know. Maybe someone needed a late night sugar fix," said his partner.

"Then they went to the wrong place. It closes at noon. Believe me, I know. Their crème filled donuts are the best anywhere." He turned into the parking lot. "Let's just check it out."

They parked in the spot next to the black car. Both of them got out and checked the doors. They were all locked. They peered through the windows with their flashlights. The car was empty.

"Hey, come check this out. There's something on the back seat. Does that look like blood?"

The officer stepped aside for his partner. "Yeah. Grab the slim jim."

The policeman used the metal tool to unlock the back door and sucked in his breath. "That's blood all right, and it's still wet. You call it in. I'm going to pop the trunk."

He searched until he found the trunk release near the steering wheel and pulled it. He walked around to the back. A bike was crammed inside.

Within minutes more police arrived, along with forensics, and two detectives. Fingerprint testing showed a match to J.R. and JaDon.

The lead detective grabbed his phone. "I need road blocks within a five mile radius. We have confirmed our suspect and victim were at site two within the last three hours. I need extra men at site one immediately. For now, keep a low profile."

He thought for a moment and then made a second call. He frowned as an answering machine clicked on. "This is Detective Greer. I'm sorry to disturb you if you're sleeping. If you get this message, please call me back as soon as possible. You have my number." He turned to his partner. "They're either asleep or out."

He waited a few moments and called again. This time someone answered.

"Mrs. Salsman? This is Detective Greer. I'm sorry to call you so late. I'm just checking to make sure everything's okay."

"Yes."

"I don't mean to frighten you, but have you seen anything suspicious this afternoon?"

"No."

"Can you do me a favor, and please keep the girls inside with the doors locked?"

"Yes."

"Thank you. And once again, I'm sorry for calling so late. Goodbye."

The detective stood thinking for a moment and then looked at his partner. "Why didn't she ask me for details?"

"Does something seem off?"

He nodded. "Let's just pay her a visit to be safe. If it's nothing, I can apologize to her later. She's already awake, so she shouldn't get too upset."

They got back into their car and pulled into a gravel driveway that led to a tan house. All was quiet. The detective walked up to the front door and rang the doorbell. "It's okay. It's Detective Greer." He pressed his badge up to the peephole. "You can unlock the door now."

There was no response.

He rang the doorbell again.

Still no response. He knocked on the door. "Mrs. Salsman? It's Detective Greer. Please come to the door." The door opened a crack, but the chain remained in place. Mrs. Salsman peeked out. "Yes?"

"Good evening, Mrs. Salsman.

"Good evening."

"I know I just called, but I had to be sure. Are you okay?"

She winced, but said, "Yes."

He signaled to his partner to come closer, and then turned back to the door. "Can I come in?"

"I'm...I'm not dressed for guests. Can we talk in the morning?"

"I guess we can." The detective studied her wrinkled face. "But first I just wanted to give you something. Can you unlock the door?"

"Is this really necessary? Can't it w-wait?"

"I'm afraid not. It will only take a moment, and then I'll leave."

She looked nervously to her right, and then slid the chain back. She only opened the door a few inches wider. "What is it?"

The detective noticed raw skin around her wrists, as if tape had been removed. She was shaking and had tears in her eyes. He pulled out his gun and motioned for his partner to do the same. "Actually, I guess I do need to come inside. Just for a moment."

An arm shot out and grabbed the elderly lady, pressing a gun to her temple. "Turn around and go back outside quickly, or she's dead."

The detective hesitated.

J.R. fired his gun. "Too slow." Mrs. Salsman crumpled to the floor. He shoved her aside and grabbed JaDon, holding the same gun up to his head. "I think this is what you were lookin' for. Everyone pulls out now or he's dead too. And don't think I'll stop there."

The detective backed out of the house. The door slammed and locked behind him. He staggered down the stairs and yanked out his phone. "We found them. Send back up...and an ambulance."

CHAPTER 33
TIED UP

J.R. kept the gun pressed to my forehead. "Let's get you tied up again," he hissed in my ear.

He pushed me forward, forcing me to step over Mrs. Salsman's bleeding body.

I was shaking uncontrollably, barely able to stumble along as J.R. half-dragged me to the living room. Missy, Josie, and Mr. Salsman were each sitting with their hands taped together behind their back and their ankles bound tight. Missy was sobbing.

She looked up when we walked in the room. "JaDon!" She cried harder. "I heard the gun. I thought he shot you."

"No," snarled J.R. "But there's time for that yet if ya don't cooperate."

He threw me to the floor and twisted my arms behind my back. I felt duck tape being twisted around my wrists, chafing and pinching my skin. He then began taping my ankles.

"And Mrs. Salsman?" asked Josie. "Is she okay?"

"She would 'a been if she was a better actress," said J.R.

"Is she…dead?" asked Mr. Salsman.

"I think so," I said, avoiding their eyes.

"Can I check?" Mr. Salsman choked out. "Maybe we can still save her."

"It's too late, ol' man," said J.R.

Mr. Salsman started crying. Josie joined him.

"Quit yer blubberin'. What was I s'pose ta do? Jus' let that guy walk in?" He stuck the gun in his jeans, stomped into the kitchen and opened the refrigerator. "Ain't you got nothin' worth drinkin'?" He slammed the door shut. "How 'bout food? I ain't had me much to eat all day." He started opening cabinets, grabbing what he could find and dumping it on the counter. He stuffed some saltine crackers in his mouth.

We all stared at him. Anger bubbled inside of me and collided with my fear. He was a calloused monster. My hatred for him was growing by the minute.

"What?" he asked. Cracker crumbs fell out of his mouth. "Are you guys hungry? Oh, wait. You been here eatin' all you want while I was on the run. You get three square meals a day? Looks like it. You ain't skin and bones no more. I cain't hardly stay in one place for a meal thanks to you and your flappin' mouths, and here you been stuffin' it in."

He threw the box of crackers on the floor and grabbed a jar of peanuts. "So now we're jus' one big happy family again, ain't we?" He eyed Mr. Salsman. "Except for you. You don't belong." He grabbed his gun and aimed at the old man's head.

"No!" I shouted.

"What?" J.R. glared at me. "You don't even know him. You had yer own little family to fuss over ya. We get rid of him and we got us a house to ourselves. We need a house now that you got ours taken away."

My eyebrow shot up. Had he snapped?

He laughed. "What, JaDon? Didn't you get enough of us livin' in a car the last week? Do you miss it?" His face grew dark. "Or does it bother you that we got police all 'round us? You don't think we could just settle in?"

I glared at him.

"Don't you talk no more, boy?"

"Every time I talk you just punch me in the mouth."

"Me? I would never."

He punched me square in the jaw. I saw a bright light like a camera flash for a second, and could taste my lip bleeding again, but I steeled myself so that I wouldn't show my pain.

"Oh, wait. I guess yer right." He sat in a kitchen chair and wiped my blood off his hand and onto his jeans. "I gotta teach you not to talk—'specially to cops." He jammed the gun back into his jeans. "Well, since we can't stay here, I s'pose it's time to think of a plan for gettin' out. Any ideas?" He looked at me and smirked. "I don't want no ideas from you. You practically asked ta be caught."

I kept my swollen mouth shut. For once, he was right. Getting my picture on the news wasn't really my fault, but the failed escape the next morning was.

J.R. stopped talking for a moment while he chomped on peanuts. My sisters huddled by the wall, retreating into their former ghost-like selves. Even though I didn't know him, I ached for Mr. Salsman. Tears streamed down his wrinkled cheeks. He had scooted far enough to see his wife's still body on the hallway floor.

The phone started ringing. J.R. grabbed it. "What?" He listened for a moment. "I ain't interested in releasin' nobody and I ain't goin' ta turn myself in. I'm comfortable right where I am. Stop wastin' my time." He hung up. "I figured them negotiation calls were just from the movies."

249

He went back to the refrigerator, pulled out some sliced ham and started stuffing it in his mouth. "Guess I'd better load up before we get goin'. Anybody else want somethin'?"

None of us responded.

He shrugged. "Fine with me, but we won't be stoppin' to eat for a long time." He polished off the package of meat, and then walked to Mr. Salsman. "Okay, ol' man. Where's yer car keys?"

Mr. Salsman didn't answer.

"You deaf? Where are they?" J.R. kicked him in the ribs with his steel-toe boot.

Mr. Salsman doubled over, coughing. "Hanging on the wall by the back door," he finally managed to say.

J.R. grabbed the keys and pulled a rifle out of his bag. He walked towards the girls. Missy's whimpering turned into sobs.

"I can't stand that sound," he muttered. He snatched the roll of duct tape and stuck a piece over her mouth. He smacked one on Josie's mouth next. Then he grabbed Missy.

"What're you doin' with her?" I demanded.

He ignored me and strode into the garage. Seconds later, he returned and grabbed Josie. She was stiff and still. When he came back, he pulled out his knife. "Either of you try anythin' stupid, you're dead."

He cut the tape off our ankles and pointed the rifle at us. "Walk to the car."

We shuffled to an old gray Honda accord. J.R. opened the back door. He waved the gun at me. "Get in."

I slid in next to Josie and Missy. He pointed the rifle at Mr. Salsman. "Your turn. Get into the driver's seat."

Mr. Salsman cringed as he inched his way across the seat.

"Push your garage door opener when I say. Got it?"

Mr. Salsman nodded, but J.R. apparently did not see him.

"Answer me, ol' man. Do you understand what I said?"

"Yes."

J.R. kept his rifle pointed at us and checked for his handgun in the back of his jeans. He got into the other car and started the engine. I strained to see what he was doing. He put the car in reverse, and yelled, "Now!"

Mr. Salsman pressed the button and J.R. placed something on the gas pedal before jumping into the passenger seat of the Honda with us and ducking down. The car rolled down the drive way. Cops started to get out of their vehicles with their guns drawn. Once the car reached the street, J.R. opened his door a crack and fired his rifle three times.

The car exploded.

All of us ducked down, shielding our faces. Debris smashed into the back of the car we were in. Flames and smoke billowed down the street.

J.R. handed Mr. Salsman the car keys. "Now drive!"

Mr. Salsman's hands were shaking as he stuck the keys into the ignition and started backing the car out the driveway. "Where do I go? I don't want to back into the burning car."

"Drive over the grass! Go!"

He sharply turned and we bounced over the grass, headed toward the street. Four gunshots blasted. The car grated to a stop.

J.R. pounded on the car dashboard. "They shot our tires!" He started swearing in fury and then sense returned. "Lock the car doors!"

Mr. Salsman pressed the lock button. All of our doors clicked.

Our car was immediately surrounded by police aiming their guns at the car windows.

"Come out with your hands in the air!" the officer by J.R.'s window demanded.

J.R. stuck the tip of the rifle onto Mr. Salsman's cheek. "Or what? You know I'll shoot."

"Just put the gun down," said the officer.

"Why? So you can shoot me?" He kept the rifle trained on Mr. Salsman and started to reach for his handgun. I lunged for the rifle with my taped hands, pushing it towards the windshield. J.R. pulled the trigger, missing the old man and shattering the glass. The police officer by J.R. fired. More glass shattered. J.R. roared in pain, and swung the rifle at the officer, who fired again. I watched in horror as blood splattered all over Mr. Salsman. His eyes rolled back and he slumped in his seat. I couldn't see J.R. from where I sat.

I started to hyperventilate and looked at my sisters. Their ghost eyes were wide. I couldn't tell if they were screaming or moaning with the tape over their mouths.

The officer reached through the shards of glass in the passenger side window and unlocked the door. He yanked it open, and snatched the guns from J.R.'s hands. Another officer stepped forward and pulled J.R.'s limp body out of the seat and onto the concrete. Mr. Salsman was gently pulled from the car as well.

"We need the paramedics," someone shouted.

My sisters and I sat stunned in our seats. I tried to draw them close, but it was too difficult with taped wrists. Sirens blared as a firetruck raced to the driveway. Men were yelling, hoses were spraying, and we were fighting to make sense of it all.

A familiar face eventually appeared at the open car door. "Come on out, kids." Mr. Costas held out his hand to me. A small portion of relief trickled through my shock. I slid towards him. The girls did their best to follow.

"Can I have a knife or scissors over here, please?" he asked.

A paramedic handed him some scissors. He carefully cut the duct tape off our wrists and off the girls' ankles. He bent down and gently pulled the tape off their mouths. New tears joined the old, but they did not say a word. We shakily emerged from the car in time to see Mr. Salsman on a gurney that was being lifted into the ambulance. I looked down at the ground.

J.R. was lying in a pool of blood. His ice blue eyes were looking straight at me. For once they did not narrow in anger. They did not even blink. Somehow they still pierced through me and sent shivers down my spine.

"Can we get him covered?" asked Mr. Costas.

An officer covered the body with a blanket.

I finally pulled my sisters into an embrace and held them close. "It's over," I said, and hoped that it was true.

CHAPTER 34

STITCHES & TAPE

Mr. Costas drove us to the hospital. Missy became hysterical when the nurse tried to take her to a separate room. After a brief explanation of our situation, the doctor agreed to examine and treat us all together. I had to have more stitches on my face and arm, but the girls' cuts were small enough to be taped closed. I also had a mild concussion, so the doctor wanted to hook me up to an IV and keep me under observation for the night. When it became apparent that the girls would not leave without a meltdown, the nurses wheeled in two more cots covered with sheets and blankets.

"Is there anything else you need for tonight?" asked Mr. Costas.

We shook our heads.

"I'll be back first thing in the morning," he said. "All of you have been so brave. You can rest easy tonight. You're safe now." He smiled at us and turned off the light before he walked out the door.

"Turn it on," Missy begged.

I immediately got up and switched the light back on.

"Can we just leave it on all night?" she asked.

"Of course," I said.

The room was quiet for a few minutes. I focused on breathing. That was all I could handle.

"Is he really dead?" asked Missy.

"Yes," I said.

"What happens now?" asked Josie.

"I don't know yet."

"But we'll get to stay together this time, right?" Josie asked.

"Yes," I said. "No matter what."

Eventually, I heard their breathing become steady. I stared at the hospital ceiling, wishing sleep would claim me too. Instead, I pictured J.R.'s cold, unblinking eyes.

I finally must have drifted off, because I jolted when the nurse walked in the room. "Let's just check your vitals," she said. She shined a light in my eyes and then wrapped the blood pressure cuff around my arm.

Mr. Costas walked in as she was finishing. "How are you three doing this morning?"

I shrugged.

"Did you get any sleep?"

"A little," said Missy.

"Good. We'll see if we can get you out of here soon. Detective Greer is on his way, but I'll keep him out until you at least have breakfast."

"I'll go get that now," said the nurse.

Soon she returned with a tray holding a plate of scrambled eggs, an English muffin, a fruit cup and a glass of orange juice. She placed it in front of Missy. "I'll be right back with the other two trays."

My stomach growled when she walked back into the room. I realized how little I had eaten during the last week. J.R. had a stash of junk food in the car, but we never stopped anywhere for real food. My stomach had been in knots at the Salsmans, so I couldn't even eat there. I stabbed the scrambled eggs with my fork. They were a bit rubbery, but I was so hungry I didn't care. The girls picked at their food at first, but soon we had cleaned our plates. The nurse removed our trays while Mr. Costas left to get the detective.

Detective Greer followed Mr. Costas into the room and sat down on a rolling chair. "I know you three have been through too much, and you may not want to talk about it, but it would help if you could fill in some gaps for us." He faced me. "First we'd like to know what happened the morning after the news cast with your photo aired."

I hesitated, not excited to share what now seemed like a mistake. "I packed the night before, like Mr. Costas asked, but after stayin' up most of the night, I decided I couldn't put the Winters in danger. I thought if I left before J.R. could get there, he would leave them alone. I was goin' to try to make it to where Josie and Missy were stayin', and then go visit Aunt Sophie." I paused. It had been several days since I had thought about Aunt Sophie. I sat up straight and looked at Mr. Costas. "How is she? Can we visit her?"

He hesitated, pushing up his glasses and wiping his eyes. "I had hoped to tell you later, when you weren't already overwhelmed. She passed away several days ago. They just had her funeral."

My heart dropped. I watched Josie and Missy melt, tears flowing silently and heads dropping.

"We didn't get to say good-bye," Josie said.

Mr. Costas frowned. "I know. I'm so sorry. I really hoped we would catch J.R. before she died."

"Will we at least be able to see Uncle Ron and our cousins?" asked Missy.

"I'm sure we can arrange that." He turned back to me. "Can you tell us more?"

It was several minutes before I could stuff my pain in enough to go on. The men did not rush me. "I didn't really think through a plan, I just knew I needed to leave, so I waited until Mrs. Winters left to take Michael and McKenna to school. I stuffed food into my backpack and took Michael's bike and left through the garage. It turns out, J.R. was already in Missouri. He said he saw the newscast and immediately started driving to my school. He slept in his car and then called the school in the morning and got the house address. He was planning on breaking in. Instead he saw me bike down the street. He followed me in his car until I got to a stretch without houses. Then he pulled in front of me. All I remember is him jumping out and punching me over and over. I blacked out. Next thing I knew, I woke up with my hands tied together in the back seat of a car." I stopped again. "I don't know what happened to Michael's bike. I need to get it back to him. I didn't even ask if I could take it."

Detective Greer spoke up. "We found the bike in the trunk of the car J.R. stole. We can get it returned for you."

"Thanks." I leaned back on the pillow and continued. "J.R. wanted to find the girls. I told him I didn't know where they were, but he had already gone through my backpack and found the address I had written down. I'd printed a map off the computer so I could find them." Heat rushed to my face. "I'm sorry, Mr. Costas. I called Josie before Mrs. Winters came into the room and got most of their address. I just didn't know what was going to happen and didn't want to lose them forever."

Mr. Costas nodded. "We already figured that part out. That wasn't a great decision, but I understand now. Go on."

"We got close to their house and then stayed in a hotel a few nights, so J.R. could watch the news, and so he could find the best way to break in without being seen."

"Do you know how J.R. paid for the hotel?" asked Detective Greer.

"He said something about stolen credit cards and ATM machines. We didn't really talk about that kind of thing much, unless he was bragging." I took a deep breath. "Late one night, we ditched the latest car he stole and snuck to the back of the Salsman's house."

"I had their house under surveillance. How did he manage that?" asked the detective.

"He's a hunter. He knows how to move without being seen. That's one thing he actually taught me, too. Once we got to the back, he picked a lock. He tied the Salsmans up, and then we were going to leave in one of their cars. That's when you called Mrs. Salsman. He hoped you would leave it alone, but then you rang the doorbell, so he had to change his plans. I guess the rest you know."

"Is Mr. Salsman going to be okay?" asked Josie in a quiet voice. "Did he get shot in the head, too?"

Detective Greer turned to her. "No. He wasn't shot at all. The paramedics said the blood was from us shooting J.R. Mr. Salsman had a heart attack and had some damage to his ribs. I asked to be notified of his progress. I'll let you know as soon as I hear anything."

"And Mrs. Salsman?" Missy wiped away a tear. "Is she really dead?"

"I'm afraid so," said the detective. "She probably died instantly."

"I'm glad J.R. got shot, too," said Josie. Her voice was shaking. "He didn't even care that he killed her. He was a monster."

"A monster that can't hurt us anymore," I said. Except in our dreams. Would he ever let us sleep in peace?

Detective Greer asked a few more questions, and then closed his file. "Thanks, kids. I'm sorry you had to go through all this, but at least now you can move on." He shook Mr. Costas' hand. "It was nice working with you." He walked out the door.

"Now what?" I asked. "Where do we go?"

"I'm working on that. I talked to Mrs. Winters this morning, and she said you and your sisters can stay there for a night or two. She doesn't feel like she has the room for three kids on a long-term basis though. And honestly, the stress and danger of this case made her decide to take a break from foster care."

"I can understand that. I'm surprised she didn't kick me out earlier."

"Yes. Well, let's just be glad they didn't have to meet J.R. They came close."

"Too close," I agreed.

"I'll call your Uncle Ron, but this is probably a hard time for him. We'll see. I also need to notify your schools about what's going on and when or if you'll be back."

"No rush on the school part," I said. "I'm fine with a vacation."

The girls agreed. We sat in silence for a moment.

"Whiskers!" Josie exclaimed suddenly. "We need to get the cat! He's all alone."

"I don't think Mrs. Winters will allow a cat," I said. "She's not a pet fan because they aren't clean."

"I'll babysit the cat until Mr. Salsman is released and you're settled," said Mr. Costas. "I'm more a dog person, but I won't mind the company. I get to go back to my house tonight."

"We're so sorry about your dog," said Missy.

"Me, too. But at least now we can all start living again."

CHAPTER 35
FAVORITE COLORS

Later that afternoon, I rang the doorbell by the Winters' front door. Mrs. Winters opened it. "Oh, Jason, or JaDon, I'm glad you're okay. Come on in."

Mr. Costas followed me. "Thank you for agreeing to give them a place to stay for a few nights. These are his sisters, Missy and Josie."

"Nice to meet you." She looked down at the blood spots on our shoes and her eyes widened. "You can all leave your shoes by the door. I'm afraid we don't have enough rooms for so many people, but Mr. Costas said you wanted to stay together anyhow."

The girls nodded. Michael and McKenna came running into the hallway.

"You're safe!" shouted McKenna. "I'm glad you brought your sisters with you this time." She turned to the girls. "If you want to do any *girl* things while you're here, let me know."

They nodded again, but didn't move.

"Thanks, McKenna," I said. "We'll probably just crash for now." I turned to her brother. "Hey, sorry for taking your bike again. That was the last time."

"It's okay. Mr. Costas told us the whole story when he brought it back. I'm glad it kept your father from breaking in. Sounds like he was scary."

"Yeah. Scary."

We trudged upstairs. Josie and Missy talked in quiet voices when we were in my room and were silent when we went downstairs to eat dinner. I couldn't blame them. We were still in shock. Throughout the night, we traded off having nightmares, even with the light left on.

Mr. Costas stopped by after breakfast and sat down with us in the living room.

"I have bad news and possible good news. Which do you want first?"

"Let's get the bad over with," said Missy.

Mr. Costas took off his glasses and wiped the lenses on his shirt. "I'm afraid Mr. Salsman didn't make it. He died during the night. I'm so sorry."

The girls wrapped their arms around each other and tears ran down their cheeks.

"At least he doesn't have to miss Mrs. Salsman now," Josie managed to say.

Missy nodded. "They'll both be in heaven together."

Mr. Costas patted their shoulders. "They were a very kind couple."

"What do we do about Whiskers?" Josie asked. "He'll need a home. I know you said you don't like cats, but…"

"Actually, I decided cats aren't so bad. Whiskers made the empty house bearable last night. We can relate to each other after losing someone we love. I can take care of him, unless you decide you want him back when you're settled."

Josie put her hand on his face. "I think he should stay with you. You need each other."

"Thanks." He swallowed. "I'm afraid there's more bad news. I talked to your Uncle Ron last night. He and the boys are torn up, but are getting by. I mentioned the possibility of you staying with him. He wants you to know he loves you and wants you to visit as often as you can, but he didn't know how he was going to raise three kids by himself, let alone six. He was especially nervous about raising girls, since he has all boys."

My shoulders slumped. "Yeah. I guess that would be a lot."

"That's the extent of your family, as you already know."

"That's what J.R. always told us," I said. "So what now?"

"That's where the good news comes in. At least, I hope you think it's good news. I called each school to give them a brief explanation about your situation. I let them know it would be at least a week before any of you came back…*if* you were coming back."

"Time off from school is good," I said.

"And then I gave the details to Mrs. Garcia and Ms. Jane from Lincoln High. I didn't get a chance to tell you that they were concerned about you when you disappeared and were trying to help find you..."

"I guess that's not too surprising," I said.

"…and Ms. Jane read the private pages in your journal, to see if we could find out where you had gone."

"What?" My anger flared, but then subsided. I thought about it, and realized I had written most of it with her in mind anyhow. But that meant she knew everything. How would I face her in class?

"The detectives had me read some of your home journals too."

"Seriously?"

"I'm sorry. I know that probably feels like betrayal, but we didn't have any more leads, and we were afraid your time could be running out. It seemed like a matter of life and death. I hope you're not too mad, especially with Ms. Jane, because she had a suggestion."

"What?" I asked.

"This morning I told her you didn't have any family that could take you in, and that I would be trying to find another foster family. She said she needed to talk to her husband, but that she would be interested in having you live with her."

Josie sat up. "We're not splitting up again. He can't leave us."

Both of the girls grabbed my arms.

"That's just it. She said she'd like all three of you to move in. She doesn't have any kids of her own and she has the room. Do you guys think that would be a possibility? I mean, I know living with your teacher might seem strange, but she wouldn't be your teacher much longer. We could even move you out of her class now if you wanted."

My mind started whirling. Living with Ms. Jane? I already knew we had books and writing in common. She was easy to talk to. I trusted her, and that was rare. Hope started to fill my chest, and then reality deflated it. "But you said she hadn't talked to her husband. He could say no. Most people would."

Mr. Costas smiled. "Our first conversation was early this morning. She called me back right before I came here. Her husband agreed. They're just waiting to hear what the three of you think."

The girls looked up at me. I felt a slow grin spread across my face. "I think you two would love her. Are you okay with it?"

"As long as we're together," said Missy.

"Josie?" I looked into her pale gray eyes.

"If you trust her, I'm okay with it."

Mr. Costas slapped his knees. "Wonderful! I'll call her right now."

"Won't she be in class?" I asked.

"She said I could interrupt any class she had as long as it was with good news." He dialed a number. "Ms. Jane? It's Mr. Costas. They said yes."

I could hear yelling on the phone. Mr. Costas pulled the phone away from his ear, smiling. He covered the phone. "She's excited."

"We can tell," said Missy. A spark of life entered her ghost eyes.

He put the phone back to his ear. "How about tomorrow evening? Okay, I'll ask." He turned to the girls. "What's your favorite color?"

"Pink," said Missy.

"Green," said Josie.

"Pink and Green. Okay. See you then."

"Why'd she want to know our favorite colors?" asked Missy.

"I have no idea," he said. "But tomorrow evening you can ask her as you settle into your new home. Together."

Mr. Costas took the girls back to the Salsman's house to pack all of their things. During their absence, I stuck everything back into my trash bag and then flopped on the bed. A sense of freedom filled me. I didn't have to push people away. J.R. couldn't hurt anyone ever again. Now I had the choice in how I treated people. I could let them in without fear.

The next night, Mr. Costas drove us to an average-sized house on the edge of town. It was light blue with white trim and had a front porch. Ms. Jane opened the door before Mr. Costas could ring the bell.

"I'm so glad you're safe," she said with a wide smile. She hugged me. It was awkward at first, but then I hugged her back.

"Thanks for taking us in," I said.

"I'm glad to do it." She turned to my youngest sister. "Are you Missy?"

"Yes."

"It's nice to meet you." She looked over Missy's shoulder. "And you must be Josie."

Josie nodded.

"Welcome." She opened the door wider and let us inside. "Let me show you to your rooms." She led us up the stairs. A German shepherd stood at the top, wagging his tail. "Oh, this is Tolkein. He's named after my favorite author. He doesn't bite, I promise. Are any of you afraid of dogs?"

Josie and Missy began petting him and scratching behind his ears. He licked their faces.

Ms. Jane smiled. "I'm guessing that's a no." She pointed to the first room. "This is for the girls."

They wandered inside. Two twin beds lined the walls. One had a dark pink comforter with light pink pillows and a stuffed polar bear. The other bed had a pale green comforter with dark green pillows with a stuffed panda bear. Next to each bed was a nightstand with an alarm clock and a vase of silk flowers. Framed flower pictures covered the walls.

"It's beautiful," whispered Missy.

They both drifted to their beds and dropped their garbage bags to the floor.

"We can change it however you like. You can decide who gets which drawers in the dresser, and then I cleared out the closet for you. And if you're too old for stuffed animals, you don't have to…"

The girls both picked up the bears and hugged them.

Ms. Jane's smile widened. "Your brother will be right next door, and the bathroom is right across from you."

She led me to my room. Framed abstract art was on the walls. A stack of books were on a dresser. The bed had a dark blue comforter with gray pillows. The shoes she tried to give me earlier were on the foot of my bed.

"I never returned them," she said. "I hoped someday you'd accept them."

My throat grew tight. I looked down at my blood spattered, decaying shoes. Even the duct tape was wearing out. "Thanks."

"I'll let you get settled. If you need anything, just let me know." She turned to leave. "I really missed you when you were gone. I'm glad you're home...JaDon."

Home. I knew it was early, but that's what this felt like. After all I'd been through, I should be careful. Take it slow. Not trust anyone. I'm guessing that's how it was going to be for my sisters, and who could blame them? But that wasn't me. I was reckless. And trusting Ms. Jane was a risk I was willing to take.

CHAPTER 36
FAMILY PHOTO

Our life of terror was over. J.R. was gone and we had a safe place to live. My hope was that meant relaxing dreams would replace our disturbing nightmares. But that wasn't so.

My first night in our new home, I crawled under my blue comforter and waited for sleep to come. When it finally did, J.R. was back. He chased me on the bike and when I refused to get in his car, he began beating me. He punched me over and over, until I realized we were back in the old shack, and he was beating me on the floor yet again. I heard the familiar moaning, and pulled myself into the hallway, always searching for the source. This time the ghosts included Mr. and Mrs. Salsman. Their kind, wrinkled faces faded until they were blank. They stepped aside and revealed my gym teacher and Mr. Costas' dog and someone else in the shadows. The moaning grew louder, and the ghosts started reaching for me.

I woke up with a start, breathing hard. I looked frantically around the room. I was awake, but the moaning continued. I cautiously pulled back my covers and drifted towards the hallway. The moaning grew louder. I followed it to the room next door. Josie and Missy were both twitching and moaning in their beds. I woke Josie up first.

"Josie. It's okay. Wake up."

Her eyes fluttered open. She gulped in the air as if she had been drowning. "I was just…and J.R. was…"

Missy startled. She saw us, and whipped off her blankets and jumped into Josie's bed. "I had another bad dream. I'm tired of bad dreams."

I wrapped my arms around both of them and started rocking back and forth like I did when they were little. "I know. Me, too."

Ms. Jane found us the next morning, still huddled together on Josie's bed. I was awake, but the girls were finally sleeping and I didn't want to disturb them.

"I'll come back later," she whispered. "We'll let them rest."

I nodded and soon drifted back to sleep.

Hours later, Ms. Jane called us down for a breakfast of thick Belgian waffles. She set out butter, syrup, and strawberry jam. "I wasn't sure what you liked on waffles, so you can doctor them up however you like."

I drowned my waffle in syrup and took a large bite. The girls smeared a thick layer of butter on their waffles and then tried half with syrup, half with jam. We washed it down with orange juice.

"Don't you have to teach today?" I asked.

"I took a few days off," she said. "I wanted to make sure you got settled in." She started collecting our dishes. "Mr. Costas called while you were sleeping. He wants you to call him back when you're up to it."

"Now's fine," I said.

She got her phone, dialed the number, and handed it to me.

Mr. Costas answered on the second ring. "How was your first night in your new home?"

"Good."

"Did you and your sisters sleep okay?"

"We still had nightmares, but then we finally slept."

"I'm sorry, JaDon. Hopefully those will fade away soon. Hey, I have something I've been wanting to tell you, but thought I should let you get settled in first. Are you in the middle of anything?"

"Now's good. We're just finishin' up breakfast."

"Okay. Here goes. I told you about having to read your journals."

"Yes," I muttered.

"Again—I'm sorry about that. Well, in them, you mentioned your gym teacher getting killed. The police decided to check out the story." He paused. "They found the car in the lake like you said…with human remains inside."

I remained quiet.

"But that's not all. We've been searching for your mother for months. There was no trace of her, even with a possible name change. After reading your story and talking to your Aunt Sophie, we wondered…Well, we wondered if J.R. might have killed her. The police had their trained dogs search in the woods around your house. They found a stick cross miles away and started digging…and we found…someone…and after tests…JaDon, I'm sorry…and maybe I'm still telling you this too soon…but I think you have the right to know so you can heal…"

The waffles in my stomach turned into a brick. I struggled to breathe around it, as what he was trying to say tickled the edge of my mind. "Just tell me."

"I'm so sorry, JaDon. It was your mother."

I felt like I was cracking. Tears began to spout down my face and dripped into the syrup left to congeal on my plate. I couldn't talk. Ms. Jane looked up with concern etched on her face. My sisters clung to me.

"What?" asked Missy. "Tell us."

"Please," begged Josie.

I pulled my sisters closer so I wouldn't have to look into their faces. "They found Mama," I began.

Missy pulled back. "But that's great—"

"No. They found her, but she's dead. J.R. buried her a long time ago."

The girls buried their faces into my shirt and began to sob.

Mr. Costas remained silent on the phone for a moment. "I almost didn't tell you, but closure might be good, and they want to know if you want her buried in the spot where they found her or if you want her near your Aunt Sophie. Your Uncle Ron said he would arrange it if you did."

I thought for a moment, trying to keep it together. "I want her near Aunt Sophie. And then can we…go visit her?"

"Certainly. And I hate to even ask. What about J.R? Where do you want—"

"He can go where she was buried," I spit out. "There's already a hole. That's all he deserves." I struggled to calm down. "He'd want to be in the woods anyhow."

"I'll make sure it's done. Again, I'm so sorry, JaDon."

After I gave Ms. Jane the phone, I just held my sisters as we all cried. Ms. Jane squeezed my shoulder and left the room to give us privacy. We let our tears mingle together, as we released years of pent up sorrow.

I made a point of staying with the girls all day. I held them when they cried, and read books and encouraged them to play with Tolkein when they needed a distraction. I tried to remain steady and calm when they asked more questions. By evening, I was emotionally exhausted. I needed time to sort through my feelings alone before I crumbled apart.

I said good night to the girls and then crashed in my room.

Ms. Jane knocked on my door. I groaned inwardly. I did not feel like being around anyone, even her.

"Come in," I forced myself to say.

She quietly sat on my bed. "I won't stay because I know you need some time alone. I just wanted to thank you for helping your sisters deal with your news. And I wanted to give you this." She pulled out a hardback book with a lock. "It's a new journal. And this one, none of us will read." She hugged me and left.

I sat for a moment, but then opened the journal and let all my emotions spill out onto the pages. My renewed anger at J.R. for murdering Mama. My heartache over knowing she was truly was dead. And eventually, my relief in knowing she hadn't turned her back on us. She had loved us right up until the end. Part of me suspected that all along.

My head eventually dropped on my open journal. Soon I was reliving the night of Mama and J.R.'s last fight. My senses were heightened this time as if I was finally ready to learn the truth. I heard her cries grow weaker and the sound of pounding fists grow stronger. I smelled the beer drip down the walls as J.R. threw bottles in drunken anger and grief. I felt the vibrations in the floor as he dragged her body past our hiding place in the wall. I saw the bloody trail left on the hallway floor. I tasted my salty tears as they rolled down my cheeks and pooled in my mouth. I imagined J.R. digging the grave and dropping my warm mother into the cold ground. I heard him tell us she left us because she was sick of our whining.

This time I yelled back at him. "No! You killed her. She loved us and you killed her. She would never have left us! You killed her!"

Only when Ms. Jane ran into my room did I realize I was yelling out loud. The lights were still on. She wrapped her arms around me and rocked me like I had rocked my sisters. I was almost sixteen. I should have pushed her away. Instead I clung to her and let the dam burst.

Snow began to fall and by morning a white blanket covered the ground. After breakfast, the girls and I found our shabby old coats. Ms. Jane dug out some hats and gloves for us. We spent the morning in the backyard, throwing snowballs and building a dilapidated snow fort. The distraction allowed us to escape our grief for a day.

When we came in, we shed our outer layers. Ms. Jane poured us some hot chocolate. I looked in my mug. White marshmallows floated on top. I looked her in the eyes and smiled, actually glad she had read my journal.

Mr. Arsenault came home from work early due to worsening road conditions. He walked through the garage door dragging three plastic sleds—one pink, one green, one blue.

"Anyone up for some fun in the snow?" he asked.

We didn't have the heart to tell him we had just come inside, so we bundled back up and followed him out the back door. He led us nearly a mile away to a huge hill, and we took turns sliding. He even helped me make a large bump on the slide so we would fly through the air. I needed something a bit more daring, after all.

"I've wanted to sled down this hill for years," he said.

By the time we returned, we were wet and freezing. I started to go upstairs to change clothes, but stopped when I found Ms. Jane standing in the hallway outside our bedroom doors. She had her eyes closed.

"Thank you, Lord, for finally granting my request for children. It wasn't how I planned, but I'm so grateful. Please heal their scars and give them peace…"

Missy came up behind me, "I'm freezin'!"

I put my hand to my lips, but Ms. Jane had already opened her eyes. "You're back! Did you have fun?"

"Yes!" Missy said. "We've never gone down hills on an actual sled before. That works much better than a piece of cardboard. And your husband and JaDon made a ramp. JaDon flew through the air!"

"Imagine that!" said Ms Jane. She smiled at me. "Once you get changed I'll take the soup off the stove. I have biscuits in the oven, too."

We dried off, changed, and warmed our insides with homemade chicken and rice soup. I held the hot bowl in my hands between spoonfuls.

Josie asked, "Do you think school was cancelled today?"

Ms. Jane smiled. "I checked. It was."

"Will it be tomorrow?"

"Tomorrow's Saturday."

"Can we go sledding again?" asked Josie.

Mr. Arsenault smiled. "Sure. As long as I'm not stiff as a board in the morning."

Missy sat thinking for a moment. "When do we go back to school?"

"When do you think you'll be ready?" asked Ms. Jane.

"Maybe in a few days. Is the school far away?"

Ms. Jane shook her head. "It's just a three minute drive. I can show it to you tomorrow. You're both already enrolled."

I started thinking about going back to school. What would the kids say when I started going by JaDon? I had already been gone nearly two weeks. Would Miguel and Parker still eat lunch with me? Would Shania talk to me?

After dinner, we gathered in the living room. Mr. Arsenault propped up two logs in the fireplace. He wadded

273

some newspaper into a ball and lit it on fire. My sisters and I curled up together in front of the fire while Ms. Jane began reading from *The Lion, the Witch and the Wardrobe*. I let the words trickle through my ears, soothing and healing. Mr. Arsenault set the timer on a little camera and let it snap a picture of all five of us.

That night I skipped my nightly session of staring at the walls or ceiling and fell asleep quickly. All of the trips up and down a slippery hill had worn me out. I found myself in my old room yet again with J.R. beating me. He raised a drunken fist above my head, but this time I grabbed his arm. I felt his arm weaken as mine grew stronger.

"Stop," I said.

"Never," he answered, his ice blue eyes locking on mine. Surprisingly, he was the first to look away.

I dropped his arm and got to my feet. "You can't hurt me anymore."

I heard the familiar moaning in the hallway and turned towards it. Mama and Aunt Sophie walked to either side of me, holding my hands.

"I love you and would never walk out on you," Mama said.

"You are strong and brave," said Aunt Sophie.

They walked me to the hallway. The moaning sound changed. I strained my ears trying to hear the difference. I squinted my eyes, trying to see what ghosts lingered.

I sat up. Was I still dreaming? I continued to hear something in the hallway, so I got out of bed and opened the door. My door. Two new pictures were on the wall. The first was of Mama with Aunt Sophie when they were young. A note on the bottom of the frame said, "Love, Uncle Ron, Desmond, DeMarcus, and Darnell." The second was the picture Mr. Arsenault had snapped the night before, already

274

framed and nailed to the wall. A family picture. My family picture.

And the sound. I found the source of the transformed moaning. My sisters were in the hallway with Tolkein. He was on his back and they were scratching his belly while his hind foot beat the ground. A sound I hadn't heard from them since Mama disappeared filled my ears. Laughter. They were laughing. And so was I.